Caroline Hazard

Memoirs of the Rev. J. Lewis Diman, D. D.

Late Professor of History and Political Economy in Brown University

Caroline Hazard

Memoirs of the Rev. J. Lewis Diman, D. D.
Late Professor of History and Political Economy in Brown University

ISBN/EAN: 9783337133740

Printed in Europe, USA, Canada, Australia, Japan

Cover: Foto ©Raphael Reischuk / pixelio.de

More available books at **www.hansebooks.com**

Books by J. Lewis Diman.

THE THEISTIC ARGUMENT AS AFFECTED BY RECENT THE-
ORIES. A Course of Lectures delivered at the Lowell Institute in
Boston. By J. Lewis Diman, D. D., Late Professor of History and
Political Economy in Brown University. Edited by Prof. George P.
Fisher, of Yale College. Crown 8vo, $2.00.

ORATIONS AND ESSAYS, WITH SELECTED PARISH SERMONS.
By J. Lewis Diman, D. D. With a Commemorative Address by
Prof. J. O. Murray, D. D. A Memorial Volume. With etched
Portrait. 8vo, gilt top, $2.50.

Contents: A Commemorative Discourse. J. Lewis Diman. By
the Rev. J. O. Murray. *Literary and Historical Addresses:* The
Alienation of the Educated Class from Politics; The Method of Academic Culture; Address at the Unveiling of the Monument to Roger
Williams in Providence; The Settlement of Mount Hope; Sir Henry
Vane. — *Reviews:* Religion in America, 1776-1876; University Corporations. — *Sermons:* The Son of Man; Christ, the Way, the Truth,
and the Life; Christ, the Bread of Life; Christ in the Power of His
Resurrection; The Holy Spirit, the Guide to Truth; The Baptism of
the Holy Ghost; The Kingdom of Heaven and the Kingdom of Nature.

HOUGHTON, MIFFLIN & COMPANY,

BOSTON AND NEW YORK.

MEMOIRS

OF THE

Rev. J. LEWIS DIMAN, D.D.

LATE PROFESSOR OF HISTORY AND POLITICAL
ECONOMY IN BROWN UNIVERSITY

COMPILED FROM

HIS LETTERS, JOURNALS, AND WRITINGS, AND THE RECOLLECTIONS OF HIS FRIENDS

BY

CAROLINE HAZARD

BOSTON AND NEW YORK
HOUGHTON, MIFFLIN AND COMPANY
The Riverside Press, Cambridge
1887

The Riverside Press, Cambridge:
Electrotyped and Printed by H. O. Houghton & Co.

PREFACE.

In preparing this volume I have been aided by many of Mr. Diman's friends, to whom my thanks are due, not only for the letters and recollections they have sent, but for much kindly encouragement and sympathy. Even where all that I received does not appear, it has still been most valuable in enlarging the field of choice, and in creating an atmosphere of loving remembrance to work in. To President Angell I owe especial thanks; and to that genial Critic, from whose suggestions the volume took final shape.

"What any of us has consciously attempted or achieved is but a small part of his actual work," wrote Mr. Diman. The record of the events of his life can give only a partial and incomplete view of it. The little daily courtesies, the constant overflow of a pure and scholarly spirit, the subtle graces of mind and manner that made the man, these defy analysis, and resent chronicle.

C. H.

Oakwoods, in Peace Dale, R. I.
November 13, 1886.

CONTENTS.

CHAPTER IV.

1854–1855.   AET. 23–24.

CHAPTER V.

1855–1856.   AET. 24–25.

CHAPTER VI.

1856–1860.   AET. 25–29.

CHAPTER X.

1868. AET. 37.

CHAPTER XI.

1869–1871. AET. 38–40.

CHAPTER XII.

1871–1875. AET. 40–44.

CHAPTER XIII.

1872–1876.   AET. 41–45.

CHAPTER XIV.

1877–1879.   AET. 46–48.

CHAPTER XV.

1879–Feb. 3, 1881.   AET. 48–49 AND 9 MONTHS.

MEMOIRS.

CHAPTER I.

On the eastern shore of Narragansett Bay, commanding an inner harbor, looking over the placid waters to Mount Hope, stands the old town of Bristol. Its wide streets, arched with stately trees, its spacious common, set apart at its foundation for public use, its fine public buildings, attest the liberality and love of its inhabitants.

" Here we were born," says Mr. Diman, in his bi-centennial address; " here by the fireside we first heard the accents of affection; here in the school-room we learned our earliest lessons; here in the house of God we were taught the consoling truths that alone compensate for the losses which a day like this brings so vividly to mind. A cloud of witnesses, invisible to mortal eye, look down upon us. There are no ties more sacred than those of which we are now reminded. We have come to the home of our childhood, to the graves of our fathers." Most binding were such ties upon such a man as Mr. Diman, whose life began in this ancient town. His great-great-grandfather, "Jeremiah Diman came to Bristol from Easthampton, Long Island, about the year 1730. The family was of French extraction, and up to the middle of the last century the name was usually spelled Dimont, or Diment. Dimon and Dimond are more modern forms. It would seem that the name was originally Dumont, if it be true, as stated in the 'Patronymica Britannica,' that in the parish register of Brenchley, Kent, it is recorded 'that John Diamond, son of John du Mont, the Frenchman, was baptized in 1612.' The first of the name in this country was Thomas Dimont, who settled in Easthampton about 1656." [1] His grandson Thomas was the father of the first Jeremiah, who came to Bristol in 1730. Deacon Jeremiah Diman was grandson to this

---

[1] *Transactions of the Rhode Island Society for Encouragement of Domestic Industry,* 1865.

first comer and grandfather to Jeremiah Lewis Diman, who was born May 1, 1831, in the town where for four generations his family had lived. This Deacon Jeremiah Diman seems to have been a man of remarkable purity and sweetness of character. He was said to be " peculiarly mild in disposition, gentle in manners, and domestic in his habits. In his religious feelings he was uniformly meditative, peaceful, and abiding ; never excited, never depressed." He was born in 1767, and " carried a vivid recollection to his grave " of the struggle for independence. The burning of the Gaspee and the " wanton attack upon this quiet village, whereby many of its habitations were laid in ashes, and the families driven into the country for protection," made peculiar impression upon him, and we can fancy the tales his grandson must have heard from his lips. He was a great reader, with a good memory, fond of investigation and argument, and was deacon of the Catholic Congregational Church for over twenty years.

Hannah Luther, the wife of this worthy man, has also " left a most enviable record in her neighborhood." She was a grand-niece of Benjamin Franklin, as Frances Franklin, her grandmother, was sister of the philosopher.

" She was a woman of strong character. Though ambitious and of a high spirit, she was contented in a retired life. Tall, with fair complexion, blue eyes, and auburn hair, she was said to look at seventy years more like a woman of thirty. She carried through life a great sorrow, the sudden death of a lovely son, — never mentioning his name to the end of her life. She was a careful reader of good books, and was noted as an excellent housekeeper and for her hospitality to all, particularly to ministers and their families, and for her kindness to the poor and suffering."

Their son Byron Diman, the father of J. Lewis Diman, inherited the strong character of his mother, and the vigorous mental traits of his father. "The most marked feature of his intellectual character," says the writer of his obituary, " was his fondness for antiquarian lore. Possessing a wonderfully retentive memory for dates and persons, he delighted to discuss the days gone by and call back the men of a former generation. With him, it may be safely affirmed, perished one of the largest funds of local history possessed by any man of his time. Nor was his knowledge limited to local traditions. He was well versed in New England history and in the history of the Mother country, especially during the Commonwealth. He was scarcely ever at fault in any statement of fact. A lighter side of his character was shown in his fondness for dramatic literature and the English poets of the last century. In his younger days he had cultivated a talent for amateur acting, and his recitations were uncommonly effective. . . . Of other more purely personal traits we may not here so freely speak,—of the unvarying sweetness of temper, the open hospitality, the benevolence that never turned away from the claims of the destitute, the unwearied good offices that so much endeared him as neighbor and friend. He leaves not an enemy behind, and, to quote the words of one who has often opposed him in the stormy field of politics, ' He leaves behind him not one who in his lifetime has done so many kindly acts.' "

He was for three years lieutenant-governor, and in 1846 was elected governor of Rhode Island. He married Abby Alden Wight, daughter of the minister of the Congregational Church, who " served as surgeon in the Revolutionary war, and practiced both professions in Bristol, trying to save the bodies as well as the souls of his people." The best blood in New England ran in this family.

Mrs. Diman was seventh in descent from John Alden, of Mayflower fame, and also related to the Leonards. Her father's family came originally from the Isle of Wight, where, in Carisbrook, Cowes, and Rye, memorials of them may be found. Mrs. Diman was the beauty of the family, a woman of exquisite taste, and was called one of the handsomest women in Rhode Island. "She was a thoroughly truthful person, — I mean in the sense of never appearing to be what she was not," writes her daughter. "Exceedingly modest and retiring, it was her only ambition to be good and to do good. While looking well to the ways of her own household, she was also most active in relieving personally the wants of the poor and suffering. Her presence seemed to carry a benediction with it. Though extremely delicate in health, with a buoyancy of spirit and cheerfulness of disposition she accomplished a great deal."

Of such parents, with such an ancestry of pure, pious people, was Jeremiah Lewis Diman born. In him all the virtues of the various lines seemed to unite. His noble bearing spoke of the sturdy Puritan; his grace of manner, of his livelier French blood; his phil-

osophic mind was the true descendant of the
first American philosopher ; his tenderness, of
his saintly mother.   He was born in the house
standing on Hope Street, — a pleasant, square
house, with wide hall running through it,
from whose western windows the waters of
the bay can be seen.   "As soon as the little
fellow could walk alone," writes his cousin,
Miss A. F. Alden, "he climbed the garret
stairs each morning to watch the King Philip
enter the harbor, — the first steamboat that
plied between Providence and Bristol.   He
never talked much about his pleasures, and
his mother did not discover this daily pilgrimage for some time."   With what playful and
tender feeling did Mr. Diman write of this
steamer many years after ! —

"The King Philip — shall we scruple to
avow it ? — is linked with the earliest recollections of our childhood.   Well do we remember how, at a time when we were still in frocks,
— for infancy and childhood, gentle reader,
lasted longer in those days than now, — we
used to wait each morning to catch the first
ringing of her silvery bell (the odious steam
whistle had then no existence), and, climbing
to an upper window, used to watch her bowl
along, rolling huge breakers against the shore.

Ruskin tells us that in all the visible creation there is no one object that yields such perpetual and ever fresh delight as the prow of a boat cleaving the glassy flood. Ah, with what raptures would the author of ' Modern Painters ' have gazed at the matchless stem of the King Philip as she used to glide of a calm summer morning into Bristol harbor! Has life, think you, offered the lip any draught more pure and satisfying than that we so innocently tasted? Let thy memory, then, ever be kept green, friend of our childhood, never again, alas, to delight our yearning sight!

" Last summer, by kind invitation of the owners, we were of the large excursion party in one of the new boats that ply between Bristol and New York. Great ado has been made about them, and we do not deny that they are neat affairs, but what are they when compared with the paragon of naval architecture that used to delight our childish gaze? With what awe, on rare occasions, we trod the narrow plank that afforded access to her deck; with what terror we surveyed the lower depths, where unclean spirits fed the roaring furnace with logs of pine; with what wonder we inspected the machinery; with what reverence we contemplated that model of fidelity and promptness, the rough but kind-hearted Captain Thomas Borden, as he stood beside the wheel and guided, with unerring skill, the obedient monster! Somewhat Dutch she was in build, with her broad stern and swelling bow, but a right staunch craft, that did her duty well for many years. But our blessings are on her memory, not for her long and useful career, but for the unforgotten joy that she used to bring us each morning so many years ago."

Miss Alden writes of his childhood, saying he always spoke of it as a singularly happy one. "Yet the young people of to-day, looking for a more vivid life and varied amusements, would call it dull. When trusted to go abroad alone, a frequent pleasure was to visit his Diman grandparents. He would wander about the quiet house, where they were passing a lonely old age, and amuse himself with looking at the miscellaneous contents of an old-fashioned attic, especially a fine model of a sailing vessel. Yet he was not unsocial; he played with other boys, and was always leader in every sport. Not that he claimed preëminence, or that they consciously yielded, but both parties accepted the position as inevitable; it was a matter of course, — 'the natural way of living.'

" Lewis's mother, a woman of rare beauty of person and of character, died when he was twelve years old.   Her sister, Mrs. Alden, was with her during the lingering illness, and often spoke of Lewis's tender thoughtfulness; ' it would have been remarkable,' she said, ' in a girl, much more so in a boy.'   He would sit by her bedside hour after hour, quietly fanning her, or talking with a gentle cheerfulness that never wearied the invalid.

" Lewis always studied faithfully, was punctual, knew his lessons perfectly, yet he was not what is called a precocious boy.   His growth was that of a young oak-tree, vigorous and symmetrical, and ' without observation.'   From his mother, Lewis inherited a certain delicacy of organization, a love of purity, of order, of exactness.   His aunt feared he had inherited a physical delicacy as well. He was not a robust lad; yet he enjoyed out-door sports, skated well, was a good swimmer, took long walks, — in short, was no book-worm.   Yet his happiest hours were spent in his father's library, a well-chosen but somewhat miscellaneous collection.   As he came in from school at noon, he always rushed down cellar to get an apple, then to the library, where the pet cat was awaiting him; with her on his knee, he ate the apple and read the morning paper with equal zest. This beloved cat must have a passing mention. Her name was Minna; her sister Brenda died young, and Lewis and little Henry took great pains with the funeral. He always kept a pet cat; the friends of his manhood remember the quaint names he found for them. This enjoyment of feline companionship is often noted in scholarly men.

"When Lewis was yet a boy, he was walking along a wharf one day, when he saw a little fellow fishing, who lost his balance and fell into the water. Lewis threw off shoes and jacket, and sprang in after him. With much difficulty he managed to swim to shallow water and drag the child up on shore; then he went home, changed his clothes and said nothing. A few days afterwards, a woman rushed out of a house he was passing and overwhelmed him with angry reproaches for having nearly killed her boy. The little rascal had told her that Lewis Diman had pushed him off the wharf, and that he had scrambled out himself! Lewis soon guessed that the boy had been forbidden to fish there, and had told this lie to escape punishment. So he made no explanation, and stood silent until the woman exhausted her wrath. In after years he told the story as an amusing instance of ingratitude.

"One noteworthy work of Lewis's boyhood was writing 'The History of Bristol,' and publishing it in the weekly paper. The undertaking was, in itself, remarkable in a mere boy, but so the careful exactness with which it was carried on. The town records were studied, nothing was set down on hearsay, so that this history may be relied upon as authentic. The style was quiet and simple, — no attempt at fine writing, such as young authors often indulge in. Those were happy years of quiet and yet enthusiastic study. Never was there a more manly, healthy nature, free from all morbid feeling. When he, a mere youth, made a public profession of religion in the Congregational church at Bristol, R. I., the old pastor, who had known him from childhood, asked this strange question before the congregation : ' Do you trust for acceptance to your amiability and your remarkable natural qualities ?' Lewis raised his head in surprise, and simply replied, ' I did not know, sir, that I had any such qualities.' Lewis's aunt, Mrs. Alden, who was at the head of Governor Diman's household for several years, often said that he was the best boy in the world, so nice in the care of his person and clothes, punctual at school, prompt to fulfill every duty, but she did not realize his remarkable intelligence, so gradually had it developed, so modest was his bearing. However, when Mr. Alden returned to Bristol in 1844, he recognized at once the lad's unusual ability. Lewis keenly enjoyed hearing from him of the wonders of Florence and Rome; he eagerly availed himself of his uncle's excellent library, and felt the stimulus of contact with a lover of learning, and an earnest disciple of Christ. In after years he spoke of this as an epoch in his life, a quickening to new intellectual and spiritual growth. Unhappily, this friendship was of short duration; Mr. Alden went to Pensacola, Fla., where he fell a victim to the yellow-fever epidemic of 1846. Lewis said nothing of his sorrow for the dead, or his affection for the living, but he was more tenderly thoughtful than ever of his aunt and cousins.

"His friendship with the late Robert Rogers, of Papoosesquaw, was a part of Lewis's boyhood which must not be omitted. Mr. Rogers lent him books, and many a winter evening was pleasantly spent in discussing their contents. Lewis counted it as one of the felicities of his life, that in after years he could pay a heartfelt tribute of respect to the memory of his friend, at the dedication of the Rogers Free Library, in Bristol.

" This is the simple account of an uneventful and happy boyhood. Of Lewis, as of the Master whom he loved to follow, it may be said, ' he increased in wisdom and stature, and in favor with God and man.' "

To these recollections of his childhood must be added a few details from his sister. " I remember well the first time he was taken to school," she says, " how lustily he cried to be taken home and would not go willingly for some time. A short time after that, I can recall him sitting at a desk in his father's library, most cordially given up to him, poring over his lessons, — a straight, slight boy, of pale complexion, soft dark eyes, and wearing a riband around his head to keep his long light hair out of his eyes while studying. He was a great favorite and of much influence with his playmates ; at one time running a little post-office, editing a newspaper, then a debating club, literary societies of different kinds, etc. The scene of these important transactions was a little bit of a room near his father's back steps.

" Many a homely present did he receive from persons employed about the house, to whom he was always thoughtful and polite. He was very fond of pets, and would incommode himself to any degree to make them comfortable. Very ingenious with tools, he made many a toy for the other children. The rainy days were red-letter days in the old house. Our mother would devote herself to us, and enter into whatever interested us; hemming sails for the boys' boats, dressing dolls, making one of the little audience squeezed into a closet to see a magic lantern, and giving us a better lunch than usual. I know that it was an attractive place, from the number of neighbors' children that came tramping in, much to Polly's disgust, who wished, if folks had homes, that they knew enough to stay in them rainy days."

" He was a bright, healthy, happy boy," writes an old schoolmate, who has now joined him, " better prepared with his lessons than most of us, but always ready for a game of ball, a swim, or a frolic. In all those years I cannot remember seeing him angry. In fact, his good temper was sometimes exasperating to some of us, of more explosive temperaments; and so he was the peacemaker among us."

Some of the letters delivered through the post-office mentioned still remain. The following notice to " W. De Wolf, Esq.," the school friend whose words were last quoted, is reproduced verbatim — the date is early in 1842 : —

Deir Sir — I take this opportunity to inform you and Earl P. Bowin, that L. A. Bishop, and myself have been recently appointed to the office of Post Masters in this town, and shall open the office on the 26 of this month. You may be assured that the office will be punctually attended to by my debuty. Yours   J. Lewis Diman esq.

Mr. Diman used laughingly to recall the beginning of this friendship, which dated from a round fisticuffs and bloody noses on both sides.

Of his recollections of the old meeting-house, since changed to the Normal school, Mr. Diman said in his address on that occasion : —

Many a time, before ever opening the pages of Euclid, had he solved the problem, on that centre-piece, that every point in the circumference was equi-distant from the centre. And often, too often, he had endeavored in vain to determine, by counting the number of panes of glass in one window, and multiplying by the number of windows, how many panes there were in the house. But other, and more sacred and thrilling, associations made this place ever dear and ever venerated.

One story remains to be told, which gives the key to his whole life — his obedience and fearlessness in the performance of any duty. One summer Sunday afternoon, before he was four years old, he was taken to church, and seated near the door. He soon espied the family pew, where the other children were, and tripped quietly up the aisle, the little light head invisible above the tall pews. Just then the minister announced his text in a loud voice: "Jeremiah vii. chapter, 1st and 2d verses: The word that came to Jeremiah from the Lord, saying, Stand in the gate of the Lord's house, and proclaim there this word, and say, Hear the word of the Lord." Thinking he was the Jeremiah addressed, the fearless boy walked on, and mounted the pulpit stairs. There he paused, and turned and faced the congregation, his golden hair making a halo about his head. The older brother, who came to bring him down, whispered, "Where were you going?" "He called me," answered the child. And the people smiled, and remembered it long afterward.

CHAPTER II.

THERE were several schools in Bristol in the days of Mr. Diman's boyhood, one of which he positively refused to attend, reaching home again before his father, who had taken him to it.

"But," says Mrs. DeWolf, "as I look back I realize how much more we learned at home than at school. The children were taught to repeat long pieces of poetry, and the best books were bought for their home reading. Governor Diman's conversation was unusually instructive, and he was never happier than when surrounded by his children, answering their eager questions."

In such a home the intellectual life of the children could not but be fostered. Mr. Diman early committed his thoughts to paper. A little note-book, begun when he was only nine years old, is inscribed with his name, J. Lewis Diman, as he always wrote it, and in a flourishing boyish hand, "Aut Cæsar aut nullus." It contains comments on various home matters such as would interest any boy, and a few jingling rhymes of his own construction, — almost his only efforts in that direction. The pamphlet, of about thirty pages, is filled, the handwriting growing in evenness and nicety as the work proceeds.

In his sixteenth year (1847) he entered Brown University, having been prepared by the Rev. James N. Sykes, and took the first premium for Latin Composition in his entrance examination. His ability as a scholar was immediately recognized, and classmates and professors united in honoring him. In 1848 he began a commonplace book, which he continued throughout his college course, and which furnishes an interesting commentary upon it. These two volumes, filled with closely written pages, each extract numbered, often with cross references, show with what

thoroughness and care he did his reading.
Many of the extracts so completely express
his own opinions and beliefs, that were the
authors' names not given they would pass
for his own utterances. So thoroughly did
he assimilate these books that they became
part of himself, and shaped and influenced
his whole after thinking and life. Those
who have heard his historical lectures will
appreciate how thoroughly he believed this
sentence of Macaulay's, Extract No. 5 : " He
alone reads history aright who, observing how
powerfully circumstances influence the feelings and affections of men, how often vices
pass into virtues and paradoxes into axioms,
learns to distinguish what is accidental and
transitory in human nature from what is essential and immutable." Macaulay and d'Aubigné were read with the greatest attention,
as is proved from the number and length of
the extracts. Most of the well-known sayings
of Luther, — such as " The true well-being of
a town, its security, its strength, is to number within it many learned, serious, kind, and
well - educated citizens," — the saying about
the schoolmaster and music, and many others,
are all written out here. In Luther's character he seems to have been deeply interested,

as the extracts from D'Aubigné relating to
him are arranged to form almost a continuous narrative.

Early in the book occur these lines from
Young, which would well summarize his own
life : —

> " That life is long which answers life's great end,
>   The time that bears no fruit deserves no name ;
>   The man of wisdom is the man of years."

Lord Chesterfield's letters seem to have interested him, and, remembering his own ease
and grace in society, who shall say that this
sentence had no influence : " Manners, though
the last, and it may be the least of real merit,
are, however, far from being useless. . . .
They adorn and give an additional force and
lustre to both virtue and knowledge : they
prepare and smooth the way for the progress
of both, and are, I fear, with the bulk of
mankind, more engaging than either."

For Memoirs Mr. Diman always had great
fondness, and the commonplace book gives
evidence that this branch of reading was not
neglected, but had its place with more didactic
studies. The life of Mrs. Godolphin, " who
amidst all the corruptions of the court of
Charles II. lived a most pure and holy life,"
and of Madame Catherine Andora, he writes

about. This note is the first of his own, giving a résumé in a few words of the lives of these women, and their desire to enter a conventual life, and adding this significant question : "Do these facts rather show, that the general corruption was so great in those times as to prevent a Christian from living with any peace in the world, or do they show that these persons had very obscure notions of their duties to the world as Christians?"

It is impossible to turn over the pages of these books without feeling the stir and life of that rich young mind. Here are quotations, bearing on moral questions, on holiness, on the uses of life, and, side by side with these spiritual matters, discussions of the fine arts, of literature, of famous men and women, and, particularly, of history, to which more than a third of the extracts relate. "The remembrance of the great *past*, the knowledge of its occurrences and spirit, is the only thing which can furnish us with a fair and quiet point of view from which to survey the present." All the variations on this theme are sounded, from essayists and philosophers. He who in later life did so much for the education of women, makes long quotations regarding the achievements of the ladies of the sixteenth century.

Nothing was more noticeable throughout his
life than his friendship with many charming
and clever women. An equal friendship it
was, without frivolity, and his respect for
woman's mind, capacity, and judgment, is
early marked in these extracts.

Toward the middle of the first volume a
change in method is observable. He is not
content with simply copying a passage that
strikes him, but gives the context, or sums up
an argument in his own words. A long note
on Mohammedanism summarizes his reading
on the subject in five separate works. This
note is divided, and subdivided under two
heads, and written in most clear and forcible
style. To his historical reading about this
time, he added poetry, especially Shakespeare,
and Shelley. Hamlet, Two Gentlemen of Ve-
rona, and the Merchant of Venice, were carefully studied. For Shelley he always retained
his early fondness and admiration.

Works of a distinctly religious character
also find large place. Archbishop Whately's
Kingdom of Christ, an essay of D'Aubigné
on Lutheranism and Calvinism, essays from
the Edinburgh Review, and Eclectic Magazine, on the state of the Catholic Church, on
Presbyterianism and kindred subjects, were

carefully read and commented upon. His mind was apparently turning toward the ministry, for after a note on the Rev. Mr. Bowle, who spent fourteen years in preparing a commentary on Don Quixote, occurs this remark : " One might imagine that a clergyman could find other duties to perform besides editing a novel." A complete analysis of the Epistle to the Romans, from Horne's Introduction, was copied in full. Dr. Channing's Memoir was read, and Bushnell admired.

About this time, 1848, there was a deep current of religious feeling in college, fostered and encouraged by President Wayland, to whom so many of the students have acknowledged their debt of gratitude. Mr. Diman, writing years after, of the master he never ceased to venerate, speaks from his own experience : " How the chapel would be hushed with the stillness of death at the Wednesday evening prayer meeting, as in tremulous accents and voice sinking into a whisper, he would dwell on the dread responsibilities of the soul! There was never any cant of stereotyped exhortation, never any attempt to rouse any superficial emotion, but always direct appeal to conscience, and to all the highest instincts of youthful hearts. In this most difficult task of dealing with young men, at the crisis of their spiritual history, Dr. Wayland was unsurpassed. How wise and tender his counsels at such a time! How many, who have timidly stolen to his study door, their souls burdened with strange thoughts, and bewildered with unaccustomed questionings, remember with what instant appreciation of their errand the green shade was lifted from the eye, the volume thrown aside, and with what genuine hearty interest the whole countenance would beam. At such an interview he would often read the parable of the returning prodigal, and who that heard can ever forget the pathos with which he would dwell on the words." [1] There were long talks, and walks with some of his older student friends; and the child who had been taken "into an upper chamber by his mother and there dedicated to God, to be used in his service, as He saw fit," now grown a youth, fulfilled the early promises, and made profession of his faith in the First Church of Bristol.

But to return to the note-books. His year's reading had been Guizot, D'Aubigné, Carlyle, and Macaulay's Essays; three or four volumes of memoirs; Dr. Johnson's Life and Works,

[1] The late President Wayland. *Atlantic Monthly*, January, 1868.

especially the " Vanity of Human Wishes," and " The Adventurer ; " sermons by several clergymen ; Whately's Kingdom of Christ ; and for poetry, Spenser, Shakespeare, and Shelley. On these books there are one hundred and twenty-eight notes, eighty-nine closely-written pages. No wonder a classmate says, " His sophomoric essays were not the crude inflated productions handed in by most of us ; but even then gave evidence of maturity and polish, indicative of the elegant scholarship of after life."

The careful habits of reading formed thus early Mr. Diman always retained. The page and chapter are noted ; if it is poetry the very line is given, as in this note, which embodies his own belief and practice. " If I remember rightly, Mr. Whipple in his remarks upon the nature of philosophical criticism observes, that to judge rightly one must participate somewhat in the feeling of the author. The same idea is advanced by Pope, Essay on Criticism, line 233, etc. :

> ' A perfect judge will read each work of wit
> With the same spirit that its author writ.' "

In after life Mr. Diman used to amaze people with the accuracy of his knowledge of books. Here we see by what careful study that knowledge was acquired, for though the commonplace books were only kept a few years, the methods of reading continued. "A book is of no use," he would say, "unless you can find what you want in it."

The winter of 1849–50 was a fruitful one. His Latin reading, with Professor Lincoln, seems to have been of interest to him. The commonplace book furnishes extracts from Cicero, *De Natura Deorum*, and the analysis of the *Ars Poetica*, by Professor Lincoln, is copied in full. The Homeric Question also interested him. The views of conflicting authorities on the probability of the Iliad and the Odyssey being the work of the same man, are carefully collated. This essay of eight pages seems to be a résumé of several of Professor Boise's lectures.

In English literature there is an analysis of the first book of Spenser's Faerie Queene, the story of each canto told in a short paragraph. "The Defence of Poesy," Burke's Essays, Grote's History of Greece, and Guizot in French, are among the books of the year. But Philosophy now demanded a large place. Cousin's Psychology and Kant began to be studied. It is of this period that Professor George I. Chace wrote, only a few weeks before his death :

"My attention was not especially drawn to him till the middle of his third year. I had previously had charge of his class in only one or two of the physical sciences. Although he made honorable attainments in them, and passed most creditably his examinations, I do not think his tastes and aptitudes lay particularly in that direction.

"In the winter of 1849-50 I was asked by him, with several other members of his class, if I would allow them to meet at my private room one evening every week, to pursue under my guidance certain metaphysical inquiries in which they felt a personal interest. As they were all earnest young men, of ingenious and bright minds, I most willingly, as may be supposed, granted their request. Bishop Butler's 'Analogy of Natural and Revealed Religion to the Constitution and Course of Nature' was chosen by them for reading and study, not so much as an authority, as because it treated of questions of the highest practical moment, which they were desirous of settling for themselves."

"I remember that we sat in the dark. We imagined we could think more abstractedly in the dark," writes Judge Staples.

"It was at the meetings of this voluntary

class," continues Prof. Chace, " that I first became aware of the metaphysical acumen of Mr. Diman, of his power of analyzing complex conceptions, his sagacity in weighing the data yielded by such analysis, and his skill in employing this data whether in building up arguments, or for the purposes of destructive criticism."

The note-book contains an elaborate analysis of the " Philosophy of Immanuel Kant," and also notes on the natural proofs of the immortality of the soul, a condensation, apparently, of the studies of the private class with Professor Chace. The " Phædo " of Plato is reviewed, and Bishop Butler's argument given at length, and commented upon.

" Butler ended in leaving out of his argument the moral nature of man and his capacity for improvement. He also failed to perceive that the real question at issue is not whether the soul be naturally or essentially immortal, but whether He who formed the soul designs to continue it forever in being."

So the last years in college went on. Dr. Arnold's " Lectures on Modern History " were read, more of Carlyle, and various discourses and essays.

Mr. William Gammell, writing of Mr. Diman's college life, says : —

"The room in which he lived was very near my own, and, according to the rules then existing, this fact placed him particularly under my official oversight and care, from the very beginning of his residence. He continued to occupy the same room, I think, so long as he remained a student, so that my official relation to him in this respect continued for four years. My personal interest in him was awakened very early after his residence began, by the fact that he was taken ill of typhoid fever, a malady which is always regarded with anxiety in a college. The case, however, proved not to be serious, but I remember very well that his father and some members of his family came to watch over him.

"It was in the middle of his second year in college that he came under my instruction in studies and exercises pertaining to rhetoric and English literature. This was a part of the college curriculum in which he was specially fitted to excel, for it was in accordance with the tastes and biases of his mind. He gave a ready and studious attention to all the appointed work, and, in addition, he read extensively and carefully the works of such authors as were commended to the study of the class. I remember that he often came to me for special advice as to the books he should read, and as to the sources of information relating to their authors. His literary exercises were always prepared with more than usual care, and he early acquired the rudiments of that direct and lucid English style, of which he afterwards became an acknowledged master. The study of modern history, also had, a few years before, become connected with that of English literature, though it had not then been made a separate department of instruction in any American college. To this new study Mr. Diman devoted himself with an interest, and assiduity, that unquestionably performed their part in preparing him for the pursuits, to which his later years were so usefully and honorably devoted. Much of the work thus done was wholly voluntary on the part of those who were engaged in it, and I well remember that Mr. Diman and many others of the class of 1851 performed this voluntary work in a manner, and with a spirit, which did much to hasten the creation of the separate department of history and political economy, that was very soon afterwards called into existence. He graduated with distinguished rank in his class, and spoke at Commence-

ment the Classical Oration, the subject being
'The Living Principle of Literature.' He
thus closed his college residence, and bore
away with him a manly character, a scholarly
spirit, and an intellectual and spiritual culture
which afforded the best possible presage of
a career of usefulness and honor."

To the recollections of Mr. Gammell, Professor John L. Lincoln adds his remembrance
of Mr. Diman's classical studies.

"He was in my Latin class during the
whole of the Freshman year, and then for
two terms of the Sophomore and two of the
Junior year. He was well prepared for college, especially in Greek, and for excellence
in this study he won the second of the 'President's Premiums.' In Latin he did not reach
very high rank the first term, nor did he early
in the course show signs of remarkable quick-
ness or facility of attainment, or make very
rapid progress. But, from the beginning, he
had a studious, earnest manner, and a way
of settling down to a thing to be done, and
a quiet persistence in doing it well, and in a
well ordered method. I think of him as being
in those days intelligent and thoughtful rather
than brilliant, or ambitious of being thought
brilliant; but he was emulous of excellence,

though not impatient about winning it. I
have looked up his record since I began to
write, and I see that he always went forward,
never backward; his progress was steady and
continuous, and at the end he reached nearly
the maximum mark of attainment. He had
no special aptitude for the philological, or,
as we say now, the scientific side, of classical
studies, but yet he was apt in seeking and
getting the sense of a passage, and the real
meaning of the author, and in apprehending
and feeling the force of his words, and discovering the qualities of his style, and his
merits as a thinker, and a writer. I do not
remember that he showed a preference for
particular writers, or for either poets or prose
writers; but he was sensitive to whatever was
good in all good letters, to whatever was beautiful and noble in sentiment or expression, or
valuable in knowledge, especially in such
knowledge of human nature, and human life,
as belongs to all genuine literature. His style
of recitation was scholarly, such as is the out-
come of a studious spirit and habit; the ap-
prehension of the thought, and the correct-
ness or felicity of expression, in the rendering
of a passage, came quite as much from habitual
effort and practice, as from fortunate natural

endowments. It was by assiduous application that he made his daily studies means of his culture, and of these studies the Greek and the Latin doubtless contributed an important share of educating influence. Probably my conversations with him in later years suggest this last remark, quite as much as my remembrances of him as an under-graduate student. In one of the latest of these conversations, he spoke of the peculiarities of Juvenal as a satirist, and, much to my surprise, quoted a passage from a college lecture on that poet, which I might have naturally supposed he had long forgotten. In what I have now said I have spoken of those college studies of Professor Diman of which I had more direct knowledge; there was, however, so far as I remember, no indication that they might ever become with him professional studies, or directly determine the profession which he would choose. The same may be said, indeed, of other studies, as intellectual and moral philosophy, in which he excelled in college, and even of historical studies, in which he afterwards rose to such marked distinction. But it may be said with certainty, that while he attained high rank in all departments of the college course, yet his prevailing tastes and tendencies, as well as his best work, showed themselves in literary rather than in scientific studies; and at his graduation, when upon the Commencement stage he delivered the Classical Oration on 'The Living Principle of Literature,' it was clear enough that, whatever might be his professional pursuits, he would be distinguished as a literary man."

A few letters of this period complete the story of those college days, so far as it is possible to tell it. "He was not a very good correspondent," writes President J. B. Angell, to whom he wrote more letters than to any of his friends, "that is, he did not write often, and his letters were brief. He seldom opened, in letters, into those rich veins to which confidential conversation led him. There was often a bright touch of his quaint humor, but he rarely *discussed* questions."

The first letter bears the date of Bristol, December 14, 1849, a simple note accepting a Christmas invitation to Narragansett.

"Over a turkey fattened upon grasshoppers alone, we shall possess peculiar advantages for discussing the long-vexed question, relative to the real existence of matter. You remember I used to be more than half a convert to your views; I must confess however that an unlucky blow which my nasal prominence received last summer, nearly put my skepticism to flight."

To the same friend, Rowland Hazard, he writes : —

Bristol, *February* 27, 1851.

Now that there is so much agitation here on the subject of slavery, I should like exceedingly to see the practical workings of it for myself. Are your own impressions made any more favorable by your Southern tour? It seems to me that the feeling at the North must grow stronger, and stronger, every day. All sensible men, of course, repudiate any resistance to the laws, but whenever any new fugitive is arrested to be carried back to bondage, they feel more and more disgusted with a system which requires such measures for its support. An effort was made in our legislature a few days ago, to pass a resolution directing the attorney-general to defend at the cost of the State, any person who might be arrested on charge of being a fugitive slave, but it did not succeed.

I often think, my dear R., of the times when we used to meet together in our college prayer meetings, and they seem to me doubly dear, now that I am about to be deprived of them. I can hardly realize that after one more term is passed, my college days will be ended. Like yourself I constantly experience the sorrowful reflection, that I have done but little in the cause of my Redeemer. It is now just three years, since I arrived at my determination to give up all for Christ, and I feel as I look back upon them, that I have miserably failed in accomplishing what I proposed to myself at that time. The bitterest reflection of all is, too, that I continue on in the same course, in spite of perpetual vows to do better. I have been trying of late, more and more to realize that I can do nothing of myself, but only in humble dependence upon the Holy Spirit. I think that I have felt more enduring satisfaction, since I formed the reso-. lution to fit myself for the ministry, and I earnestly hope that the thought that I am so soon to enter upon this sacred calling, may constantly work in me a stronger desire to conform more perfectly to the will of God.

TO JAMES O. MURRAY.

PROVIDENCE, *March* 23, 1851.

I have hastened this evening to get, or rather glance at, my German, and am resolved to devote what remains of it to you.

I have really been so much occupied for the past two weeks, that the calls of friendship have all been unheeded. When you hear what I have been about, you will excuse me, I know. You see (to let you into something which you have no business to know anything about), we have been having a little bit of sport in the Brothers Society. For some time past, the interest of the members has been sensibly on the decrease, and many were dilatory about responding to the treasurer's calls, and we thought that, on the whole, it was best to have a little stirring up. So at the meeting held a fortnight ago last Saturday a committee was appointed, of which your humble servant was the chairman, to inquire into the condition of the society, and report on the same. Well, last Saturday we brought in a report commenting very severely on the recent debates, ridiculing the questions submitted for discussion, complaining of the non-attendance of members, and urgently calling for more vigorous enforcement of the laws. After a spirited debate, a resolution was carried, that all who owed anything to the society, who should not pay before the next regular meeting, should on that day be expelled, and an amendment to the constitution was also introduced, which provided that hereafter all who should suffer the debts incurred during one term, to remain unpaid till the close of the succeeding term, should also be expelled. We confidently anticipate that in the course of the coming fortnight the money bags of the United Brothers Society will wonderfully enlarge. Now, when I inform you, my dear fellow, that the aforesaid report occupied some twenty-three closely written pages of letter-paper, whereof your friend wrote almost the whole, you will see how it happened that I was too much occupied to be able to answer your letter. . . .

I am getting on in the most agreeable manner with my last term. It is not quite as easy as the last term used to be, when the ancients of your day were in college. I dare say your eyes will open when you hear what studies I have selected. German, Moral Philosophy, and Astronomy! Do not, however, let me entreat of you, conjure up any fond recollections of Norton, at least as you had him, bound in sheep. Happier than you, instead of the cold and lifeless volume, we have the living and speaking man. But the best thing of all is, that we have no co-sines and co-tangents, but the lectures are almost

purely descriptive. Occasionally the old
Adam will show itself, but not often. Under
the Doctor we have been rather trenching
upon the studies of the middle year, *i. e.*, discovering depravity, and the origin of sin.
We both recite from the text-book and take
down lectures. As the latter not unfrequently
conflict with, and demolish the former, it is
sometimes difficult to keep the two apart. I
think that the Doctor is rather ambiguous in
expressing his views relative to depravity, indeed most of us could make nothing very
definite out of what he said. Enough was
said however, it seemed to me, to indicate
that his opinions are very different from the
old-fashioned New England views on the subject, yet, so far as I could see, correct. Indeed I have often thought that there is no
man whose system of theology I could more
readily undertake to swallow, than Dr. Wayland's. He seems, least of all men, run in the
mould of any particular school.

Talking of theology reminds me that I have
something that I wish very much to speak to
you about. After I wrote you last, I went
down to Newport to see Mr. Thayer. He
was very urgent in the request that I should
come and stay with him a year, before going

to Andover.   He proposed that I should give
my attention to Philosophy and German, in
both of which he is abundantly qualified to
teach me.   I confess the plan was sufficiently
inviting to stagger my previous arrangements.
After going home I consulted father, and
found that he would much prefer that I
should devote some additional time to study
before going to Andover.   However, nothing
has been decided upon yet.   When you are
here we will discuss the whole matter.

CHAPTER III.

1851–1853.   AET. 20–22.

At Commencement, 1851, Mr. Diman was graduated from Brown University, pronouncing the Classical Oration. He then went to Newport to continue his studies according to the plan mentioned to Mr. Murray. His letters give a full account of his work and experiences.

TO JAMES B. ANGELL.

NEWPORT, October 15, 1851.

It was quite refreshing to hear another speak of being lonely and homesick, as that had been the burden of my own song for some days after I came here. I had not a single companion here of my own sex, with the exception of B., and for a little while the time dragged heavily. But the Dominie soon gave me a specific, which effectually relieved me of all such indisposition. I came here Saturday, September 13, and before six o'clock on the ensuing Monday morning, as I was cosily looking at the sun from beneath the bedclothes, I was startled by a deep voice calling out in three or four different languages in rapid succession something which, even with my slight philological acquirements, I had little difficulty in translating into a somewhat summary invitation to get up. I found myself pitched in *medias res* immediately.

You ask what I am doing. Well, to begin. The study I give most attention to on the whole is German. Besides writing exercises, I am reading a theological treatise on the "Christian Doctrine of Sin," by Dr. Julius Müller of Halle. It is exceedingly difficult, and I am very much afraid I do not grasp the whole of it. It requires rather a more extensive knowledge of theological opinions than I yet possess. However, I hope by careful reviews to make it out. With how much more zeal one can take hold of a thing when not wearied by the insufferable tedium of a recitation-room! The object of the Dominie in selecting such a book was the sooner to make me acquainted with the theological dialect, so

that when I go to the Seminary my knowledge
of the language can be made immediately
available. On other accounts it would have
been pleasanter, perhaps, to have read works
of a different character.

The rest of my time is devoted to Philosophy. I am reading Ritter's History of Ancient Philosophy, and have nearly completed
the first volume. The account of the early
Grecian sects is rather dry in itself, but is of
course essential in order to obtain a complete
view of the whole progress of development.
It is curious to notice how in the earliest ages
the human mind commenced busying itself
about the same problems which perplex it even
yet. The most specious phase of modern skepticism, Pantheism, was taught years ago on the
banks of the Indus, and I have just been reading this evening an account of the speculations
of one of the early Greek philosophers on the
origin of the human race, which seem almost
identical with those advanced by the author
of the "Vestiges of Creation." How the
human mind treads round an eternal circle of
skepticism and error, when unillumined by the
light of revelation ! I do not see how we can
compare with a candid mind the ancient my-
thologies and philosophies with the Bible, and

have a doubt as to its divine origin. The relation of philosophy to theology, is so close that I expect my present studies will be of essential service to me hereafter. I look forward with especial interest to an examination of the influence exerted by the later Grecian sects, in the formation and development of Christian doctrine.

One day in the week I give exclusively to Greek. I am reading the "Birds" of Aristophanes, and enjoy it highly. If I could have had the drilling four years ago that I have now, I might have made a tolerable Greek scholar. As it is, I feel at times half inclined to disavow any acquaintance with the language whatever.

But perhaps of more importance than all these is the practical knowledge I hope to gain, during my residence here, of those duties which will hereafter devolve upon me. I have a fair chance here to study the discouragements and supports of the Christian minister, and you will readily believe me when I tell you, that though there are many trials, both around and within one, yet the life of a faithful pastor never seemed to me so inviting as it does at this moment. But I have seen enough to show me how true is the saying of old Andrew Fuller, that "preaching is glorious as a profession, but most wretched as a trade." The consecration to the service of God must be entire. I trust that my retired life here will have the effect to withdraw my mind more entirely from secular things. I was glad to hear that you were so pleasantly situated in this respect, that you had such favorable opportunities for the exercise of your Christian activity. Do you not sadly miss the spiritual advantages which college life used to afford? I find nowhere here that ready sympathy, and that frank interchange of sentiment and feeling. I can never forget, my dear J——, your faithfulness to me in the hour of my deepest need; for to you, more than to any other human being, I trace those influences which have made me what I am.

NEWPORT, November 16, 1851.

. . . . A prominent reason which led me to pass this year with Mr. Thayer was that I might become acquainted a little with the practical, as well as the theoretical, or rather the scholastic side of my profession. I must confess that the slight acquaintance I had formed with theological students, and the little I saw of their life when I visited Murray

(at Andover) last winter, did not entirely satisfy me with the cast of character that a Seminary develops. Preaching seemed too much
with many of them a profession, and too little
a life. But experience has taught me that it
is a very different thing to study Christianity
as a beautiful system of morality, and to feel
it in the heart. I begin to set less and less
value on the intellectual element, when compared with the spiritual. A humble, prayer-
ful spirit is a better preparation for the pulpit than a whole army of commentators. But
the intellectual ferment of a Seminary, and
the almost total absence of practical duties,
seemed to foster one of these elements to the
almost entire exclusion of the other. Accordingly, when I came here, it was with the understanding that I was to be brought in
contact with practical duties, and be made
somewhat acquainted with the every-day trials
and labors of a pastor's life. So far as the
latter indeed are concerned, my knowledge
has been in the main derived from intercourse
of the most familiar kind with Mr. Thayer,
but I trust I have learned some good lessons.
I have learned, at least, that he who would
enter the gospel ministry, with the hope of
deriving any comfort from the performance of

its duties, must do so with the most entire
consecration of all his motives and impulses
to Christ, and with the most utter forgetful-
ness of self. It may seem hardly necessary
for one about to enter so humble a calling, so
far as all outward appearances are concerned,
as the ministry, to guard himself against ambition, but I have been taught that the failing
is more common than is generally supposed.
The very tendency of Congregationalism so
strongly to develop the individual is in many
respects a most unhappy one, so far as the
ministry is concerned; it is so apt to result in
lionizing, in producing the pestiferous race of
what are termed "popular preachers."

But some of the best influences that I have
been brought in contact with, have arisen from
the little practical duties that have at times de-
volved upon me. Of these not the least is taking part in family worship. Often, when the
Dominie and Mr. Ried happen to be away or
engaged, it devolves upon me to officiate, and
I need not tell you that it is a very delightful
exercise. It takes the place, more than anything else, of our old college prayer-meetings.
To be sure there is the weekly prayer-meeting
of the church, but it is apt to be a little cold
and formal, and besides, I am so slightly

acquainted with most of those present that I naturally do not feel so much interested. Besides this, I have a fine Bible-class of boys. We are at present engaged upon Hebrews. I have felt somewhat discouraged for two or three Sundays back, as it has been very stormy and the attendance was rather small, but to-day I had a capital time, and begin to feel quite encouraged again. But the thing after all most novel to me, and perhaps the most beneficial of anything I have undertaken, has been conducting religious services on Sundays at the Asylum on Coaster's Island. There are about seventy-five inmates, and usually one of the clergy of the town officiates, but sometimes it happens that none of them can go, and then they call upon the lay brethren. I have been twice. The services are similar to those in ordinary congregations. I wish I had space to describe to you the motley audience. There are every age, sex, and color — the lunatic, the vagrant, the strumpet, and the drunkard; yet among them there are some sad and serious countenances, men to whom it is a pleasure to talk, because they make it an earnest business to listen. How wonderfully the Gospel adapts itself to their condition ! The poor broken-hearted, despised

inmates of a poor-house can see in it a richness
and depth that the rich and happy have never
felt.   Is it not pleasanter to preach to paupers
than to a fashionable congregation ?

Bristol, R. I., *September* 7, 1852.

. . . I was much interested in your estimate of the advantages and disadvantages of
European travel, and I shall wish to converse
with you at length upon the subject after
your return, for I have not yet relinquished
all the day-dreams that you and I used to
build so pleasantly together.   I am especially
anxious to ascertain as nearly as possible how
much benefit may be derived from a year or
two's residence abroad for the purpose of
study, after one has gone through with a
course at home.   I finished my studies at
Newport about a month ago, and on the
whole think I have reason to be satisfied with
the results of my year's labor.   Mr. Thayer
was very desirous that I should remain with
him another year, but for several reasons I
thought it best to proceed to the Seminary
this fall.   Though I was very pleasantly situated in Newport in every respect, yet I felt
exceedingly the need of some associates of
my own age and of congenial tastes.   On this

account I look forward with much pleasure to meeting Murray and other friends at Andover next month. I used formerly to have many visions of the advantages of solitary retreats, and secluded "cloistered halls," for the purposes of study, but after a year's experience I have come to the conclusion that man is a decidedly social animal.

You can readily conjecture, my dear J——, that much can be learned during a year's residence in a pastor's family, besides that to be obtained from books. Indeed, as I review the past year, I am far from ascribing the highest importance to my mere literary acquisitions. I trust that I have learned that a minister needs, for the successful prosecution of his work, far other and higher preparation. To me the hardest thing about a minister's life is, that in consequence of the high and sacred nature of the duties he is called to perform, a sanctity and holiness is attached to his character which he is always conscious that he does not possess; and while his convictions of right force him at all times to denounce all Pharisaical affectations of superior piety, he feels condemned in his own heart of seeming better than he is. How little the world estimates the real trials and difficulties of a min-

ister's life ! How mean and paltry would
seem the worldly sacrifices and privations,
were he only buoyed up by the conviction
that he was worthy to be a guide to others,
and to tread in the footsteps of the Apostles !
I have never had such conviction of my own
unworthiness to be a minister as during the
past winter, and sometimes I have almost felt
like giving it up. I have been so discouraged
by my slow progress in holiness, by my repeated relapses into coldness and indifference
to the truth. But such feelings I know are
wrong, and I ought to struggle against them.
If I did my duty every day, I should not be
troubled with them. This makes me feel
impatient to be in a position where I shall be
engaged in direct personal Christian labors.

ANDOVER, *November* 2, 1852.

. . . When I wrote to you, if I remember,
I spoke somewhat about coming to Andover,
and my feelings in regard to it. Well, here
I am at last, and from an experience of a
couple of weeks feel prepared to say something about it. You remember that I had
some doubts and fears. I rejoice to say that
they are being rapidly dissipated. Thus far
all my impressions of Seminary life have been

of the most delightful and, I trust, profitable character, and I only regret that you are not here to enjoy them with me. How happy could we be could we but renew that familiar intercourse which, to me at least, was fraught with unnumbered blessings! . . .

I have found in the Seminary a much greater degree of spirituality than I had been prepared to expect. Perhaps my last year's life of solitude, and exclusion from the social communion to which I was so much accustomed in college, leads me to estimate it differently from what I otherwise should have done, but I cannot help feeling myself better every day by being brought in contact with such an atmosphere. I feel more encouragement in view of what will devolve upon me hereafter, and above all I have felt myself in closer communion with my Saviour than for many months. And I hope and pray that my life here may be a continuation of the same glad experiences.

We are now fairly embarked upon the studies of the term. In Hebrew we are under the instruction of Prof. Barrows, who is said as a teacher to be inferior to none in the United States. In the Greek we are committed to Prof. Stowe, husband of the world-renowned authoress of " Uncle Tom's Cabin." Hebrew is a terribly uncouth language at first acquaintance, but I cannot help thinking that when we become tolerably familiar with it, it must prove extremely interesting. It is so fresh and new, and so unlike all our Occidental tongues, and withal it is so rich in magnificent imagery that it cannot fail to reward a good deal of labor. And then, too, a knowledge of it will disclose so many new beauties in the sacred writings.

So far as personal matters are concerned I am very pleasantly situated indeed. I room with Bancroft,[1] whom, upon closer acquaintance, I have learned to esteem very highly. Our room is a very nice one, and is very neatly furnished, and besides is just opposite to Anthony[2] and Durfee,[3] and in the same entry with Murray[4] and Allen.[5] So you see that, so far as worldly comforts are concerned, I could not be better off. Indeed, if you could peep in upon us at the present moment, and see us sitting by an open fire, with a bright solar lamp shedding its rays around the room, you would say that we were the very picture of comfort.

[1] Dr. Lucius Bancroft. [2] Rev. George N. Anthony.
[3] Rev. Simeon B. Durfee. [4] Rev. James O. Murray.
[5] Rev. George E. Allen.

ANDOVER, *April* 4, 1853.

. . . I came very near crossing the water a little while ago, though I fear I should not have been able to make you a visit. A party of friends sailed three weeks ago for a six months' tour, and I was strongly tempted to join them. It would have caused such a serious interruption, however, to my studies, and, moreover, have defeated my plans of studying abroad, that I was compelled to give up the plan. . . . I did not go with them mainly because I have been thinking more and more seriously of late of leaving the Seminary at the end of the second year, and going abroad for a year and a half, and then coming back and graduating with the next class below. I shall be governed very much by your opinion, and that of a friend who will be back here in about a month. I cannot help viewing the question with a good deal of anxiety, as it will affect so much, for good or bad, my future usefulness. We will talk it all over next fall.

In two weeks the present term will close, and my first year of Seminary life will be nearly at an end. With some drawbacks it has been a happy one. I have enjoyed myself of late in the renewal of scenes which have carried my mind back to five years ago. There has been a revival among the students of the academy, where I have a large Sunday-school class. I have derived much benefit from the few earnest conversations I have had with those whose souls were yearning for the truth. It was a kind of food that I had been in need of for a long time. I hear on every side conversations among those who are soon to leave the Seminary, which remind me constantly that my time will come before long. As the time approaches my heart almost draws back from such manifold and mighty responsibilities. Indeed, when years ago you and I used to talk the subject over, could I have seen all the difficulties which have now presented themselves, I almost fear that I should not have made the decision that I did. I should like it much better if you were to be with me. Would n't it be nice if we could only have adjoining parishes? I have just been reading a little book called "Shady Side," a story which gives the darker phases of pastoral life, and it may be that that has affected my views a little. One of the students here told me that if he had read it while in the academy, he would have given up all thoughts of the ministry. But I know this is a wrong view to take of it. There must be much self-denial, and silent uncomplaining toil, in any post where one faithfully and resolutely carries into practice the doctrines of his faith, and I doubt not that the reward is only sweeter for having been earned by such costly sacrifices.

I envy you the study of Goethe. I was quite enraptured with what little knowledge I obtained of Schiller last winter. This winter I have had little to relieve the dry, dull monotony of my class studies. One could hardly fly off in raptures over Hebrew Grammar and Exegesis.

The author I have learned most from the past winter is Coleridge, whose writings and views generally I am beginning to fancy hugely. I have been reading of late Henry More, a divine of the age of Charles Second, who resembles Coleridge in many respects. Let me whisper in your ear that I greatly prefer the old English divines to the hair-splitting theologians of New England. But more of this one of these days. . . .

The Rev. James Gardiner Vose adds these recollections of Seminary life : —

"At Andover I found the graduates of Brown University taking a very high rank.

In fact I had known very little of the college
before, and was somewhat surprised at what I
there learned.   Professor Park was then in
the freshness and brilliancy of his lecturing
career, and his Alma Mater, of course, acquired a lustre in our eyes from the fascination of his eloquence.   But the students
whom I learned most to admire were nearly
all of them Brown University men : Professor
Fisher, who was then a resident graduate at
the Seminary, Professor Murray of Princeton,
Dr. Lucius Bancroft of Brooklyn, whom I
associate with Diman in his rooming with him
a little while, and others, such as Dr. Atwood
of Salem, and two who are not living, — Professor Clarendon Waite and Rev. G. N. Anthony.   The best of the Seminary seemed to
be from Brown University, and I have always
regarded it as one of the greatest blessings of
my life that I knew these men and was admitted to their friendship.   Many were the
discussions, serious and otherwise, in which
we took part, and if it be true, as I believe,
that a man learns more from his companions
than from his teachers, certainly I owe a
great and never-to-be-forgotten debt to the
friends of my youth.   The Rhode Island
boys were not only proud of their college,

but quite disposed to take up the cudgels in lively contests as to its merits, and those of the little State they came from. Diman was especially loyal, and I can bring before me his look and manner, as he gave thrusts and parried them in her defense. But my first impressions of Diman, which never wholly wore off, even in the most familiar intercourse, were those of a very reserved and serious-minded man. As a student he was unusually quiet and thoughtful. He carried with him, even in those early days, a certain loftiness of manner, a self-poise and dignity, that were beyond his years. His features were finely cut, and more than one person has remarked his striking likeness to the well-known bust of the young Augustus, especially in profile. In our student days, both at home and abroad, when we all lived in the plainest and most inexpensive way, there was something about Diman that befitted a man of rank and distinction, and never failed to command respect."

"It was before Andover had been discovered by the architects," writes Dr. Leonard W. Bacon. "The school of the prophets was a dismal broadside of brick barracks, and the broad horizon about the Seminary hill was only a partial compensation for the bleakness of the exposure. It cannot be denied that there was something in the tone of the theological discussion (notwithstanding the great ability of some of the faculty) that was congruous with the surroundings. New England theology was at that time only beginning to emerge from its mediæval scholastic period, and in the lecture-rooms they were still threshing away at the chaff of the old pettifogging debates about fate and free-will. I shudder to think what my two years at Andover would have been, but for my happy association with a knot of fellow-students whose 'society was an education' as well as a delight. The heart of this little coterie was from Brown University, and the heart of the heart was Lewis Diman. Beside much high discourse on theological and philosophical themes, there was amongst us a certain amount of ' giggling and making giggle,' in which I must have had my share, for I remember Diman's saying to me long years afterwards, ' I believe you saved my life that year we were at Andover together; I should have died of dreariness if you had n't been there to make me laugh.'

" Diman was always hunting through unexplored alcoves of the noble library at Andover.

For a while the 'Lettres curieuses et édifiantes' of the Jesuit missionaries had a great fascination for him. It was very characteristic of his historical genius, that while reading in these old journals of missionary zeal and devotion, of the discovery of the ancient monument of Singan-fu, he should collate the record with the ancient history of the Nestorian church on the one hand, and with the daily newspaper on the other, then teeming with strange stories of the rebellion in China. The result of this little by-play of his studies was the striking article on 'Early Christianity in China,' which he gave me to send to the 'New Englander,' and which appeared in November, 1853. His previous article in the same Review, on 'Dr. Grant and the Mountain Nestorians,' showed how little his keen critical and satirical insight availed to check the glow of a generous enthusiasm.

"I saw very little of Diman after I left the Seminary; but I have questioned sometimes whether those who knew him in the fullness of his learning, and the ripeness of his powers, were so very much to be envied by those who remember the grace and beauty, and splendid promise of his youth."

CHAPTER IV.

In accordance with the plan mentioned in the previous letters, Mr. Diman sailed for Europe August 12, 1854, when the first entry in the foreign journal occurs.

"At 12 o'clock sailed in the Herman, Father and Henry on the wharf. At three passed Sandy Hook, dropped the pilot, and stood off to sea. Ate a good dinner, feeling some uncertainty whether I should soon have that happiness again.

"*Aug.* 13. Woke with a composed mind, but had much disagreeable reflection while dressing. In consequence felt some reluctance to go to the breakfast-table, so took my coffee on deck. Had a controversy about Christianity with Mr. D., a disciple of Feuerbach. Was supported by an unknown ally of good appearance, and apparently highly educated.

"*Aug.* 23. A beautiful day ; wrote, read, and talked. Heartily tired of the monotony of sea life. No romance at all. The ocean has disappointed me. Think that to enjoy the ocean one must look at it from the land. The narrow range of vision makes it seem quite small."

On August 24th the monotony of the voyage was broken by a collision with a large bark, the Raindeer. The steamer lay by her all night. "Remained on deck two hours; in consequence took cold.

"*Aug.* 25. After a sleepless night got a little nap in the morning. Woke with a severe pain in right side. Rose, but was compelled to lie down again. Doctor came and pronounced it pleurisy. Compelled to lie on my back all day, and consequently did not see the Scilly Isles and Land's End. We had the bark in tow all day. T. (his companion and fellow-student) was very kind and attentive, and was worth a ship-load of doctors. Heard that they had an exciting day with the bark. We left her next morning at Falmouth. By night I felt much relieved. Under ordinary circumstances I should have regarded my accommodations as rather limited, but as I could not move without pain, I found my domain quite large enough. Rather odd that my only sick day was one of the most agreeable to me that I passed on board."

So the voyage continued. The 27th they lay off the Isle of Wight, and heard the chimes from shore.

"*Aug.* 28. All day in the North Sea. No land in sight. The dullest and most disagreeable day of the voyage. In the evening played my last game of bagatelle with P., and retired to my berth, thankful that it was the last time I should have to clamber to that elevated resting-place."

They landed at Bremen August 29.

"My ocean voyage is ended. It was a long cherished and bright dream, the romance of many years. The reality was a disappointment. On a retrospect I can recall no hour of hearty enjoyment upon the passage. I formed many acquaintances, but not one friendship, and I left those with whom I had lived for sixteen days without a single regret."

From Bremen the students went to Hanover, and September 1st arrived in Brunswick.

"Called at the Sack's. Struck with the outside of the house built in 1590. Stands

in a quiet square, close by the Domkirche.
Found that they only expected me, but agreed
to take us both. Pleased with our rooms, and
especially with our kind reception. Heartily
rejoiced to have a place once more that I can
call home. After tea the engravings of Providence, which Angell had sent, were brought
out, and I explained all the localities. Found
that we could speak German enough to understand and make ourselves understood, though
it was very fatiguing work. Agnes is to be
our teacher. The rest of the family consist
of Mr. and Mrs. Sack, and Therese."

In this pleasant German home, in the
quaint old city, the two students remained five
weeks, sharing in the family life, seeing all
there was to be seen, and improving daily in
their German. The Rathhaus, and Palace, the
Cathedral, and the courts were visited. A
German christening is described.

" *Sunday, Sept.* 10. In the afternoon Wilhelm Sack's child was baptized in the Domkirche. Very curious spectacle. We all assembled first up-stairs, and had many greet-
ings, etc. Went to the church, and in a
room at the south transept found a minister
standing before a table on which were two
large candles. Before him a small table and

basin of *warm* water. The service was long, and to me unimpressive. At the conclusion many congratulations again, as if it were a wedding. I was introduced to the minister. Afterwards saw in the church the celebrated biblical critic Tischendorf. We came back to the house and had a merry time in the evening. The baby's health was proposed by the god-father and drunk with hearty good-will.

"*Sept.* 22. This evening attended an examination in the school where Agnes is teacher, and was exceedingly interested. The pupils were all girls, from eight to fourteen. The exercises commenced with singing, after which followed a short prayer. The children were then examined in the fundamental doctrines of religion by a pastor, in a very familiar, fatherly way. The answers were prompt, and evinced a thorough acquaintance with the subject. They were then examined by different gentlemen in geography, history, and arithmetic. Essays were read, and short pieces of poetry were recited in French and English, the latter very creditable indeed. There were also some recitations in German. With some songs, well sung of course, the exercises closed. I was especially impressed with the happy, good-natured faces of the children."

The stay in Brunswick was broken by a walking excursion up the Brocken, making the ascent in seven hours. " I carried two carpet bags and an umbrella, and most of the way had Therese on my arm. The rain set in soon after our arrival, so of course nothing was to be seen of the fine prospect from the top." The walk back the next day was very beautiful, and they returned, heartily pleased with the excursion.

"*Oct.* 7. To-day we bid good-by to Brunswick, after a stay of five very pleasant weeks. The family seemed very much to regret our departure, and exhibited evident signs of grief when we presented them with our little parting gifts. Before dinner we went with Wilhelm to an out-of-the-way place and drank, or tried to drink, *Mumme*, the famous beverage of Brunswick. We left at four in the afternoon, Mr. Sack and Wilhelm going with us to the station and giving us a very cordial good-by. The weather was stormy, and our ride to Magdeburg presented nothing of interest.

"*Oct.* 9. Left Magdeburg at eleven, and after a ride of two hours through an uninteresting but very rich country, reached Halle, and having been subjected to an examination at the custom-house, got to our new home, and met with a cordial reception from Madame Müller.

"*Oct.* 10. Well pleased with our new home. Walked this morning, and saw the Waisenhaus, a high but ugly pile of buildings, where three thousand children receive instruction, the Dom, if possible, still more ugly, the post-office and university. Dined with Young and Simon at a restaurant, which is the universal practice here. Called in the afternoon on Professor Tholuck, who received us with great kindness, and arranged a walk for the next day.

"*Oct.* 11. Had a very pleasant walk of two hours. The conversation turned mainly on the movements of the extreme Lutheran party, which seemed to grieve him exceedingly. 'When they say to me,' he exclaimed, '*nur Einheit, nur Einheit,* I reply, *nur Wahrheit, nur Wahrheit.*'

"*Oct.* 13. Commenced the tedious process of matriculation by going to the University, surrendering our passports, going before the rector, and then to the secretary, where we wrote all the particulars respecting our birth-places, names, and manner of life upwards, in a huge book. About thirty other students were present, many in uniform, serving their time in the army.

"*Oct.* 15. At eleven o'clock went to the University and heard Erdmann deliver an eloquent address in commemoration of the king's birthday. In the evening the city was illuminated. Took tea with Tholuck. Mrs. Tholuck, a very pleasing woman, who speaks English with great fluency. Met there Professor Hursy, and talked about Professor Stowe and Jonathan Edwards. He was surprised to hear that the latter was dead. The other day I called on Professor Ulrici and presented a copy of 'Edwards on the Will' from Mr. Thayer, which he mistook for a work by Professor Edwards, and proposed to notice in his Review, among the new books of the day.

"*Oct.* 17. Went to the University according to order and received my *Anmeldebuch* from the curator, after having been sent back to the secretary to change R. I. to Rhode Island in the entry I had made. Called on Professor Witte, but he was not in. In the afternoon we called with Young on Julius Müller and were much pleased with him.

"*Oct.* 19. In the morning at nine o'clock had the first lecture from Müller on Dogmatics. Understood it pretty well, though his enunciation is very indistinct.

"*Oct.* 20. At last completed our matriculation. Introduced into a large room, heard a short speech from the rector, Professor Leo, —a Latin oath was read, to which we all gave assent, then went one by one to the rector, were taken by the hand, and each received a large document attesting his matriculation and admitting him to all the privileges of the University. Called on Tholuck, and received his signature to my *Anmeldebuch.*

"*Oct.* 23. The lectures have begun in good earnest, after waiting here two weeks. Müller every day at nine, on Dogmatics, and Wednesdays and Saturdays, at six P. M., on Introduction to Dogmatics. Erdmann every evening at five, on History of Philosophy. Tholuck four times a week at three P. M., on the Life of Christ, and on Saturday at ten A. M., on the Doctrine of Paul. Schwarz on the same subject at eleven A. M. on Wednesday.

"*Oct.* 24. Called to-day on Professor Leo, and had a pleasant conversation running on German and Anglo-Saxon languages. Besides our lectures we study in private Kant's 'Critic of Pure Reason.'

"*Oct.* 28. In the afternoon we dined with Professor Erdmann. Much pleased with Mme. Erdmann. Very elegant dinner. Had a fine view from the balcony of a procession of students. First a marshal on horseback, with cocked hat, feathers, velvet coat, long sword, white trousers, and long boots. Then a band, mounted, and in uniform. Then a cavalcade of horsemen, dressed like the first. Then the dignitaries of the University in open carriages drawn by six horses with postilions. Then a fellow on horseback representing a fox, or freshman. Then a venerable-looking fellow, in a carriage with a huge dog. Then the inferior members in carriages. The whole was the most characteristic feature that I have yet seen of the German student life.

"*Oct.* 29. Heard Tholuck preach at the academic service in the Domkirche. Was much pleased with the Liturgy, especially with the chanting of the choir-boys. Tholuck is interesting as a preacher, and his sermons have more in them than those I have heard.

"*Nov.* 6. Called this morning on Professor Roediger. Was received with great kindness, and had a most agreeable conversation of an hour, chiefly about oriental subjects.

"*Sunday, Nov.* 19. Heard Erdmann preach in the Domkirche. Seemed odd enough to see him in gown and bands. We have all been exceedingly interested for some time past in Müller's theory of the Personality of God, and the Trinity. As a lecturer he satisfies my utmost desires. I feel an interest in Theology that has never animated me before.

"*Dec.* 3. We went to-day at eleven to Tholuck's, and spent a couple of hours with him walking up and down in an arbor in the garden, discussing some points which had arisen in his lectures on the Life of Christ, principally relating to the Logos, and to Genealogies. As to the first he was not very clear, his idea seemed in many respects akin to Plato's. He borrowed from Aristotle an illustration of the Trinity: $\acute{o}$ νοῶν, το νουμενον χ $\acute{o}$ νοῦς. The last being the unity of the other two.

"*Dec.* 10. In the morning read Strauss's 'Leben Jesu.' Begin to feel a great interest in the historical criticism of the origin of Christianity.

"*Dec.* 11. Took tea at Professor Witte's. T. and I read aloud from Longfellow's 'Kavanagh.'

"*Dec.* 13. Took tea this evening at Professor Erdmann's. Müller has not lectured in consequence of sickness, so I have given more time to the 'Critic of Pure Reason,' which I have about two thirds read."

December 18th, there was a disputation in the University, which is described with interest. Christmas Eve was spent at Professor Roediger's, and much enjoyed: the tree was admired, and the following day a party of students gathered to "make way with some nice cake and sausages" from the good friends in Brunswick.

"*Dec.* 31. Took tea this evening with Tholuck, in company with some of our Scotch and English friends. While waiting for tea Mrs. Tholuck read a beautiful German hymn for Christmas. At tea had a very pleasant conversation on serious topics. Professor Tholuck spoke of his visit to Oxford, where he met Pusey, Newman, etc. When tea was over he read a chapter from the Bible, made some remarks appropriate to the close of the year, and a short prayer. The whole was very impressive, and seemed more like a Christian family scene than anything we had seen in Germany. When we reached home quite another scene presented itself; the New Year's feast was going on in the common style. In Mme. Müller's parlor was a big tureen of punch, up-stairs another, where the students were drinking. In another room the piano was going, and the students were dancing with the servant-girls. Got away to bed, but could not get asleep on account of the noise in the house. The instant the clock had ceased to strike twelve a tremendous shouting commenced in the streets to welcome the new year."

A couple of days in Leipsic finished the vacation, and January 4th "the lectures, which have been suspended for two weeks during the vacation, recommenced to-day."

About this time Mr. Diman wrote home:

"I met this evening a young Russian student, in whom I was exceedingly interested. It is a little singular that here in Germany I have been most pleased with Hungarians, Swiss, and Russians. Of course he talked mostly of Russia and the war. He said that it was very popular with the Russian people, and that though Russia might be disconcerted at the outset, in the end she was sure to conquer; that Russia was yet a child, her history ran back but a century and a half; that her exhaustless resources were yet undeveloped; that an illimitable future was hers; while France and England had passed their grand climacteric. He said that the common idea of Russia was entirely false, that the emperor was much belied, and that during his entire reign he had labored

to improve the condition of the serfs, which
had greatly changed for the better; that it
would be folly to give them at once political
freedom, as they would only abuse it, but that
to all efforts to prepare them for it the emperor gave a most generous aid. He said that
the serfs, though not generally educated, were
almost always intelligent, and being attached
to the soil, families could never be separated,
that every one could have his freedom at a
price fixed upon by law, but that most preferred to remain serfs, as they were then entitled to maintenance at the hands of their
masters. In short, from his account I concluded that our idea of the Russians was about
as accurate as the popular notion of an American here, where he is always represented as a
man with a wide straw hat and striped trousers, a revolver and bowie-knife, and a whip
in his hand to use over the slaves. I was glad
to hear this side of the case clearly presented
by one who spoke with an entire absence of
all bitterness, and in a calm, philosophic
spirit. Of course the greatest interest is felt
by all here, relative to the progress of the
war. I think that as a general thing the
middle and lower classes are on the side of
England, but Erdmann, Leo, Witte, and men

of this stamp, of absolutist tendencies, sympathize with Russia. The professors, however, are by no means unanimous. There are two or three Republicans among them, who were delegates to the famous Frankfort Parliament in 1848. Of course they are now all down, but no professor is ever removed here on account of his opinions, unless they are directly subversive of all order and decency. They have the liberty of teaching what they choose, which gives rise to a most agreeable variety; at Bonn, for example, where the professors are both Catholic and Protestant."

So the life at Halle went on to the middle of March. Almost every evening was spent with the professors.

"In the evening with Professor Leo. Enjoyed ourselves, as usual, very much. Mrs. Leo, by her kindness of manner, has quite won my heart." Such entries occur constantly. His own enjoyment proves the pleasure he must have given.

"*March* 16. This morning sent all our books to the Waisenhaus, where they are to remain till we return to America. Called on Mrs. Tholuck, but she was sick and unable to see us. Had a pleasant call on Mrs. Erdmann, and left her little tokens of our regard. Spent

the time in packing till five, when we called
on Tholuck, and received notes of introduction
to professors in Heidelberg. In the evening
gave a farewell supper to Young and Simon,
all who remain of our pleasant circle in Halle.
The evening till eleven was passed in pleasant
conversation and reminiscences of the happy
hours we have passed together here during the
last winter. We shall never forget them.

" And so ends my life in Halle."

The Rev. Charles C. Tiffany, so often al-
luded to in the previous pages, sends the following sketch of these days of travel, and
enthusiastic study : —

" I am to write of my sojourn abroad with
my friend Diman, when we were students together at several German universities.

" How shall I fittingly recall to others what
lives so vividly in my own recollection ! The
facts and incidents become indistinct and
misty as one looks back to the experiences of
thirty years ago ; but the feeling of exhilara-
tion as we walked the steamer together in an-
ticipation ; the sense of quiet and freedom as
we studied together under the inspiring Professors of Halle, Heidelberg, and Berlin ; the
enlarged view of life and the high purpose to

live well in it, as we returned, — these are unfading memories, because they were impressions which, once taken, live on forever.

"It was in August, on the twelfth day of the month, I think, in 1854, that Diman and I sailed on the steamship Herman for Bremen. We had been fellow-students two years at Andover, and were both looking forward to the ministry. We shared a common longing to know more of German thought and to gain riper acquaintance with the German tongue; and so we started with that eagerness of enthusiasm which young men have when looking out upon a wider horizon than that which has heretofore limited their vision. It was a voyage of discovery before us. Though the old world, it had to us all the freshness of a new. And the most delightful element in the new prospect to both of us was the fact that we were going to taste the old. The historical associations of the centuries were to be the dear environment in which we were to pursue our investigations into the most recent modern thought.

"This, in fact, was the especial key-note to my friend Diman's character. There lay in him great reverence and longing for the past. There abode in him also an eager intellectual desire to know and test the latest fruits of criticism and speculative research. But the latter had little or no value in his eyes unless it were the evident growth out of old knowledge and remoter thought; and the old found its potent fascination as the obscure, but still real root, of the strange tangle of growth in modern thought and institutions; through which labyrinth we need imperatively the knowledge of the older threads of thought to guide us safely, not into shallow indeterminate speculation, but into rational progress.

"How ardent we were when we set out! Each day on the steamer, notwithstanding qualms of sea-sickness, and the temptations to listlessness, a certain task of German grammar and phrases was gone through regularly. Diman, by his fine, manly beauty, his undeviating courtesy, his thoughtful conversation, won from the few passengers we had as companions a very hearty appreciation and respectful recognition. In some difficulty which occurred between the captain, a fiery Southerner, and the passengers, he was requested by the elder men to draw up the protest and give expression to the sentiments of the aggrieved. I remember well, too, the fine scorn he showed for two harmless and heedless young fellows, who, rich and careless, seemed to look upon their first visit to Europe as the opportunity for an unbounded spree. When we anchored off Cowes at night, and had our first view of England on the Sunday morning following, and were delighted by the beauty of the ivy-clad towers of Hurst Castle, and charmed by the sound of the church-bells, and were basking in this first realization of our dreams of England, our entrance through the enchanted gate of historical Europe was rudely shocked by the urgent invitation of these two young men to hurry off to land and make use of a half hour's delay to 'eat a real English beefsteak and drink genuine English ale on the spot, you know.' Diman could hardly get over that. He would have liked to enter one of the pretty churches, and have heard an English service, or would have climbed with ardor and scaled the height crowned by the castle turrets ; but to go, as the first visit in Europe, the Europe of boyish dreams and manhood's meditations, — to a restaurant to eat and drink, albeit English beef and ale, this was a little too much. He could hardly be civil all day. Bremen is a quaint but rather stupid town now, I find, but then it was all poetry and glamour both for Diman and myself.   After a day in Bremen we went down through Hanover to Braunschweig, where we were to study till the semester in Halle began.   How we revelled in Hanover! Here we saw our first palace and marveled at its historical pictures.   I cannot forget our intense amusement at a London cockney, who accompanied us through the palace.   Diman remarked, 'They have here all Napoleon's defeats, but none of his victories.'   'That's because he never had any,' exclaimed the English snob.   The fine statue of Leibnitz, in the square, called out his admiration as he repeated the fine sentence concerning him, — 'One who drove all the Sciences abreast.'

"And now we were in Braunschweig, that quaint, lovely town with gallery and cathedral and old churches, and a palace and the beautiful *Anlage*, the park made out of the old ramparts.   We studied hard to learn to understand spoken German; and such German as we spoke together as we walked there! Our host, Herr Sack, who lived just opposite the old Domkirche, where Heinrich der Löwe and Queen Caroline, 'the murdered queen of England,' lie buried, was an antiquarian, and Diman reveled in his old manuscripts and coins and autographs.   Here we gained a genuine smack of the old flavor which pervades the atmosphere of the old historic towns. We visited Wolfenbüttel, hard by where Lessing had been librarian, and had written ‘Nathan der Weise.’ We made an excursion into the Hartz Mountains, and climbed through the Elsethal to the Brocken, and mounted the Devil’s Pulpit, where is laid the scene of Goethe’s Walpurgis Nacht, in Faust. Every day unfolded something new of the old, and work found its potent stimulus in all our surroundings. Six weeks soon fled, and we were at Halle, the great centre of theological interest at that time. Though reticent, Diman made much impression on his distinguished teachers, and his fellow - American students soon looked upon him as their chief. He enjoyed his studies; he also enjoyed greatly the social life in the Professors’ families where he was welcomed, and the *Kneipen* and *Verbindungen* of the students which he visited. It was a winter of earnest and arduous study, and we were ready for the spring vacation when we left Halle and went to Munich for our holiday.”

CHAPTER V.

1855–1856.   AET. 24–25.

THE two students left Halle March 17th, going to Leipsic for a day, thence to Dresden, where a week was spent, chiefly in the gallery. The pictures of interest were noted, and art studied with the same thoroughness and care that was lately bestowed on theology. The first day in the gallery is always confusing, particularly as it was " raw and uncomfortable, especially to me, suffering with a cold. Found nothing in the early German school that pleased me. A little disappointed with the Italian masters, though there were some that answered all my desires. I was hardly in a state to judge them. Paul Veronese and Titian disappointed me, except the Tribute Money of the latter." Other pictures that pleased him were mentioned, but he says, "far above all these, the divine Madonna, in which all my ideal of art is realized.

"*March* 20. At the gallery again with unceasing admiration of its treasures. Found much to admire that I had passed over yesterday, and admired more what I had before noticed." The week was spent in sight-seeing, and everything of interest noted. Two days followed in Nuremberg, which were greatly enjoyed.

"*March* 26. After breakfast made the complete circuit of the city, examining its ancient defenses, and numbering its quaint and massive towers. Then visited again the St. Lawrence church, and went on a pilgrimage to the house of Hans Sachs. Had previously seen that of Albert Dürer. Derived the greatest enjoyment from the quaint and beautiful architecture of the city, its high roofs, its numerous little turrets, and its elaborately carved windows. The Middle Ages were all about us."

A fortnight was spent in Munich, chiefly in the Pinacothek, and in visiting the artists' studios. Furness was then in Munich, and several visits to his studio are mentioned. Almost every day a visit to the gallery was made and some fresh impression recorded.

"*March* 28. Got as far as the Rubens Hall in the centre, and was more impressed with his paintings than ever before.

"*April* 2. Delighted with the beggars and children of Murillo. Pleased with Domenichino, but not with the Italians in general.

"*April* 4. All the morning at the Pinacothek, looking at Italian paintings. More pleased with the Holy Family of Raphael. Saw many of his earliest paintings in the style of Perugino. Several by Perugino, and fine ones by Andrea del Sarto. The Italian paintings please me more and more.

"*April* 7. Not well satisfied with the Destruction of Jerusalem by Kaulbach. Exquisite in detail, but seems to lack unity as a whole. Too many ideas are crowded on the canvas. The mind hesitates between them. The supernatural element, too, is too palpably introduced. Not enough is left to the imagination. There is something incongruous in a Roman general being preceded by a band of angels with white wings."

At the end of the entries for Munich the

journal contains a list of the paintings in the Pinacothek which were particular favorites. They embrace works by forty-one masters, each with a few descriptive words so that they may easily be recalled. The careful study given the subject afterward bore fruit in some of Mr. Diman's most charming lectures and essays.

Augsburg and Ulm had a passing visit, and April 12th they arrived in Heidelberg. "Took a stroll up to the old castle, where we had a magnificent view. The old ruins enchanted me.

"*April* 17. Feel well pleased with Heidelberg in every respect, and look forward to a delightful summer. Am struck with the cleanness of the streets, the meanness of the University buildings, the solidity of the gates, the peculiar situation of the town, the smallness of the steamboats, the ugliness of the river craft, and in general with the exceedingly deliberate manner in which the arts of navigation seem to be practiced by the men.

"*April* 24. Heard a lecture from Schöferlein on Theological Ethics. The matter was interesting, but the manner dull.

"*April* 28. We went to the University at twelve o'clock to-day and were matriculated.

Process by no means so long and complicated as at Halle. Got through it in an hour.

"*April* 30. This afternoon heard Mittermaier, the great lecturer on Criminal Law. The room was crowded. His personal appearance is very striking, as his hair and beard are perfectly white. He lectured with great animation, and with a profusion of illustration. His mode of address was very simple, almost undignified, and his profanity was enormous, even according to a German standard.

"Am very much interested now in Rothe's lectures on the Logical Process of Development of the Deity. Chevalier Bunsen says that it is the greatest course of lectures now read in Germany. Feel German speculation is every day becoming less and less misty. Love this deep view, and this constant struggle after unity. Had a talk with Simon to-day on the subject. His interest is concentrated on the objective nature of the Atonement, mine on the Person of Christ. Feel more and more every day, that the common prevailing notions with us on the subject are grossly erroneous. Feel that while Christ was the ideal man, so it is ever to be the aim of every one in the same manner to realize the ideal man, and thus be also a manifestation of the Logos in the flesh. Each believer should be the living word of God.

" *May* 13. *Sunday.* Have amused myself in translating two verses from Paul Gerhardt, whom I greatly love.

O GOTT, MEIN SCHÖPFER, EDLER FÜRST.

O Lord, Creator, King of Heaven,
  Thou Father of my life,
If not to Thee that life is given,
  I wage an empty strife.
Living — my spirit dwells in Death,
  Wedded to sin alone ;
Who, wallowing in the mire of sin,
Forgets the nobler Life within,
  True Life has never known.

O happy he, who constant feeds
  From food and drink of Heaven,
Who nothing sees. nor tastes, nor needs
  Beyond what Thou hast given ;
Gift of that mystic life. the Spring,
  That man with God shall spend,
That Life where angels joyous sing,
Where songs of praise forever ring,
  Forever, without end.

May 28th to June 2d was occupied by a walking trip on the Rhine, which was greatly enjoyed.

"*June* 18. Loomis and I called on Bunsen.[1]

---

[1] " Bunsen was greatly impressed by Diman's fine eye and forehead, and by his scholarly deference and intelligent questionings," writes Rev. C. C. Tiffany.

Found him in the garden. A fat, cordial man, with noble forehead, and most benevolent-looking face. We had a long conversation, chiefly on the principles of editing the text of the New Testament. He praised Lachmann, but spoke very disparagingly of Tischendorf, whom he termed a coxcomb. When I was first introduced he paid a compliment to Rhode Island, saying that it had a proud history.

"*June* 29. In the afternoon we called on Bunsen. Saw him, as usual, in the garden. He asked about American politics, the relation of the Know-nothings to slavery, etc. Said he agreed with Sumner.

"*July* 20. Called upon Bunsen. He gave us his grounds for the antiquity of language, and explained quite fully the work on which he is now engaged on the Bible. Asked about the Catholic schools in America. A sudden storm detained us awhile, and we had a pleasant conversation with Mrs. Bunsen.

"*July* 23. Heard Umbreit this morning, on the 118th Psalm; a remarkable man, with white locks and pleasing countenance. His style of lecturing was clear and pleased me.

"*August* 3. T. and I took tea at Bunsen's. Met there Mr. and Mrs. Hill, the missionaries

at Athens, and the daughter of the Archbishop of Canterbury.

"*August* 10. Called this afternoon to take
leave of Chevalier Bunsen. Had a long conversation. He once more expressed his desire
that the Baptists and Congregationalists in
America might become one. Spoke earnestly
of the defects in the Unitarian system, but
approvingly of Channing. He took leave of
us with great kindness."

So ended the four months' stay in Heidelberg. The lectures seem to have made less
impression than those at Halle. Mr. Diman
and his friend Loomis "concluded that we
had derived but little from Rothe." But
the intercourse with Chevalier Bunsen was
something that left an indelible impression,
and to which he often referred in his after-
life. The beautiful walks about the city, and
into the country, which were of almost daily
occurrence, were also a source of delight and
pleasant memory. The last week of his stay
was made bright by the arrival of his brother
Henry. "I was glad enough to see him.
We passed nearly the whole day in conversation about home, his travels, etc." At the
death of Bunsen, in 1860, Mr. Diman wrote of
him : —

"Those who have wandered amid the ruins of the old castle of Heidelberg may remember on the opposite bank of the river a capacious but unpretending house, its yellow walls almost washed by the water, its terraced and well-shaded garden enough raised above the road to secure privacy, without hiding any feature of the surrounding scenery. In this garden, of a pleasant summer afternoon, Bunsen was almost always to be found seated in an easy-chair, sipping his cup of coffee, and conversing with some visitor. Few men of mark came to Heidelberg without wending their way across the old bridge to that hospitable mansion.

"The young Americans, who were at that time students of the neighboring University, were welcomed with especial kindness. Partly from a generous interest that seemed never weary of rendering assistance, and partly, without doubt, from that disposition so often shown by men of original ideas to surround themselves with impressible spirits, Bunsen seemed to take a peculiar pleasure in conversing with young men. His eye would sparkle, his voice would become tremulous, his whole being would seem alive when expatiating on his favorite topics to them, who, if they felt disposed to question his conclusions, had little opportunity to do so.

"Those who know Bunsen only through his books, where unaccustomed ideas are often clothed in involved and scholastic style, can form no conception of the surpassing charm of his conversation. In person he was below the middle height, inclined to corpulence, and with nothing in his external appearance that attested his wonderful industry. His head was finely formed, and his face, with its regular outline and delicately chiselled features, was handsome. His knowledge of English was only too exact, robbing his sentences of that careless grace that marks the perfect master of discourse. His command of words seemed unlimited, and the fire and eloquence with which he would enter at once on some chance topic suggested by a visitor, some question, perhaps, of biblical interpretation or ecclesiastical antiquities, the boundless erudition with which he would illustrate his arguments, the facility with which he would quote the various readings of some disputed text, the earnestness with which he would controvert any opposing views, rendered intercourse with him as delightful as it was instructive."

Then follow two crowded and delightful

months of travel. A walking trip in Switzerland was taken, and all the usual ascents in Chamouny were made and recorded with enthusiasm. From August 21st in Geneva, till September 13th in Zurich, a merry party of six students spent most of the time walking. Then a few days of sharp illness overtook Mr. Diman. "High fever, and throat badly swollen. Dr. came, young but good. Felt very sick and uncomfortable."

"*Aug.* 16. In bed all day, but better, though throat still very sore. Began to feel restive at the delay. Savage and Tiffany very kind." The next day they pushed on, crossing the lake by boat. The party separated, and Mr. Diman and Mr. Tiffany continued their journey for ten days in the Tyrol. A week was given to Vienna, a couple of days to Prague, and October 15th "reached Dresden. Found Vose and Williston."

"*Oct.* 16. All the morning at the gallery; again after dinner.

"*Oct.* 17. Morning at the gallery. Studied especially the Spanish pictures, the landscapes, Titian's Christ, and the Madonna. Left at three for Berlin. And so ended our pleasant vacation wanderings.

"*Berlin, Oct.* 20. At noon at the University, but could not be matriculated, as we had no dismission from Heidelberg.

"*Oct.* 25. Had our first lecture from Trendelenburg. Pleased with matter and manner.

"*Oct.* 27. Heard Vatke on recent History of Theology.

"*Oct.* 29. This morning heard Ranke on the Middle Ages, but found it quite impossible to understand him, his style of lecturing is so peculiar. Lays his finger on his nose, looks up to the ceiling, speaks very rapidly and indistinctly, often lowering his voice to a whisper, wriggles himself out of his chair, to all appearance quite lost in his train of ideas.

"*Oct.* 31. To-day T. and I were matriculated, with a crowd of others. The little dump of a rector made an eloquent address on the importance of observing the laws, and gave us the usual right hand of fellowship.

"*Nov.* 1. In afternoon heard Lepsius on History of Egypt. Much pleased with matter and manner. No flourish, but a practical way of urging without pretense what he felt was worth being said. A younger man than I expected.

"*Nov.* 3. Heard Althaus on Hegel.

"*Nov.* 5. In the evening went with Vose

across the bridge to Nitzsch's house. In the courtyard students were assembled with torches and a band of music, which played as they sung. The Professor made a short speech from the window. The students again sang, the music played, the torches were thrown in a heap. *Gaudeamus igitur* was sung, and we dispersed.

" *Nov.* 18, *Sunday.* Attended the prayer-meeting in Tiffany's room.

" *Dec.* 1. In the evening, while reading, a poor girl came and begged for food, as one did a week since. It makes the heart sick to witness the poverty and suffering here. Hardly a day passes that I do not have some call at my room for relief.

" *Dec.* 2. In the afternoon went to hunt up two girls who had been here begging and whose address I had taken. Found no trace of one. The other lived in a little dark court ; a man, woman, and five children. Mother and two children at home. The mother told me that her husband was a tailor, that he could not always find work, and that when he did, got but twenty cents a day. But the family below did not give him a good character, and I could not exactly satisfy myself that they were fit objects of charity.

" *Dec.* 6. This evening, instead of hearing Nitzsch, heard Ritter, the great geographer. Splendid-looking old man; white hair, lofty forehead, large and most liberal collar. Spoke of the knowledge the Romans had of Germany, their excursions for amber to the North Sea. Not highly of the geographical and historical value of Tacitus' *Germania.*

" *Jan.* 5. This afternoon T. and I called on Trendelenburg. He received us with great kindness, and entered into a long conversation. Said that he did not hold with Erdmann to German philosophy as most perfect, and thought that true philosophy would be a mingling of the thought of all nations, and peculiar to none.

" *Jan.* 7. This evening attended with Tiffany the first lecture before the *Evangelische Verein*, by Professor Hegel of Rostock, on the Missions to the Germans. Merely a historical epitome, with a single reference to Bunsen's attack upon Boniface.

" *Jan.* 13. Finished my first sermon, which I have been busy over all the week. This evening Tiffany, Davis, and I took tea with Professor Trendelenburg. Quite a large party of students assembled. Saw his wife and sister. Sat by his side at table, and had a

long conversation about the discovery of the
new Greek book, which is now exciting so
much interest among literary men.

"*Jan.* 20.   At the meeting this evening
we had a long conversation on the need of a
deep religious experience as a preparation for
preaching.   Afterwards Loomis and Tiffany
took tea with me, and we passed the evening
in discussing our theological opinions in view
of our approaching examinations.

"*Jan.* 22.   This afternoon heard Von
Raumer on the reign and character and mis-
tresses of Louis XIV.   Only ten present.
Nothing striking in his appearance or manner,
or much in handling the subject.

"*Jan.* 30.   This afternoon went with
Tiffany and passed an hour with Privat-doc.
Strauss.   Met his father the preacher, and a
certain major, all very pious and orthodox.
Over coffee and cigars we discussed the condition and prospects of religion.   Conversation
turned first on their mission in Jerusalem,
then to the Baptists.   They all agreed with
Stahl that no proselyting should be permitted.   Spoke of a great revival of religion that
took place here thirty years ago, since which
time, they said, the condition of the Prussian
churches had been constantly improving.

"*Feb.* 12. Been all day writing an account of the Bunsen and state controversy for the *Bib. Sacra.*"

This review of Bunsen's book on the "Signs of the Times," covering five closely printed pages, appeared in the *Bibliotheca Sacra* for April, 1856. To it is added an account of forged manuscript of Simonides, the " new Greek book " referred to, which a committee of the Royal Academy of Berlin had pronounced genuine, but which the learning of Lepsius detected as spurious.

"*Feb.* 17. In the evening we were at Professor Trendelenburg's. At the table sat by the side of Mrs. T., and had a most pleasant conversation about the Germans in America, church music, Luther's hymns, etc. The Professor showed us a late *Bib. Sacra,* which had an article from Angell on Geibel, over which Mrs. Trendelenburg made herself quite merry on account of blunders in the printing of German words. At the close of the evening, when the conversation had turned on political theories, I astonished them all by an assertion of the necessity of parties to a free government, *weil gerade deswegen ist es natürlich und gesund.* The Professor at first denied, but when I had explained, acknowledged that there was something in it.

"*Feb.* 22. This evening heard with great delight the beautiful opera of Orpheus and Eurydice, by Gluck. All the parts were by females, that of Orpheus by Wagner. She appeared to great advantage in classical dress, and sung beautifully.

"*Feb.* 24. In the morning enjoyed very much a sermon from Nitzsch on the temptation of Peter. In the evening at our meeting we had a long discussion about the Christian year, and Liturgies.

"*March* 5. In the afternoon with Davis and Tiffany to coffee with Dr. Strauss. Met there a number of gentlemen. We had a warm discussion about the Evangelical Alliance. Strauss could not join it because it was too strong against the Catholics, and too much in favor of religious freedom. He wished to see the alliance a confederacy of churches, and not of individuals. The Moravian minister exposed the sins of state churches, especially in reference to the sacraments, and strongly urged the rights of personality, urging that Heaven would consist of individuals not of churches.

"*March* 9. Had our usual prayer meeting at six. All felt deep regret that it was the last. Called on the Trendelenburgs to bid good-bye. Had a pleasant chat as usual with Mrs. Trendelenburg."

And so ends Berlin, and with it student life in Germany.

"There was much in Berlin," writes Rev. C. C. Tiffany, "to develop the æsthetic as well as the philosophical side of Diman's mind, and traces of it may be found in the elegance which characterized every sentence he wrote. We saw less student life, but in company we studied Kugler's hand-book of art, and then on Saturdays walked up and down the admirable museum of pictures to illustrate our reading. We often went to the Beethoven concerts, and the finer operas, and learned to know what true musical interpretation meant. We were often at the embassy, where Gov. Vroom, our minister, dispensed frequent hospitality, and where we met members of the diplomatic corps. Indeed, this winter at Berlin had a cosmopolitan influence. It ended the purely student life of Lewis Diman, but was a fitting capstone to the culture which it crowned."

March 10, Mr. Diman and Mr. Tiffany took their way toward Paris. Wittenberg and Weimar were visited, and a day spent with the friends in Halle. At Eisenach they " climbed the Wartburg; saw first in the castle the rooms which are being piously restored to the old Byzantine style. Among them the hall in which the famous contest of the Minnesingers took place, which we had seen represented in the Tannhäuser. Then saw the room which Luther used, which is in its original condition, and is very uncomfortable-looking. From the windows of the castle a beautiful prospect in all directions. Fine hills covered with woods." Thence they pursued their way to Brussels, stopping at the places of interest on the way.

"*March* 18. Spent the day at Waterloo. Greatly interested in fighting the battle over again."

Three busy weeks were spent in Paris.

"*March* 23. This morning we went to Notre Dame, to hear grand mass performed by the archbishop. The church was crowded. We made an unsuccessful attempt to obtain places for the Te Deum which followed, for the birth of the imperial prince, who to-day completes his first week.

"*March* 24. After a day of sight-seeing for an hour or two before dinner, I strolled about in the garden of the Tuileries, watching the boys sailing their boats in the basins of the fountains; the gold fish that put their noses out of the water to nibble crumbs, and the swans. In the evening we went to the Italian opera to hear Grisi and Mario, in Lucretia Borgia. Disappointed in Grisi, but much pleased with Mario. The house itself seemed very small and mean in comparison with the opera-house at Berlin.

"*April* 1. We went to-day at twelve over to the Champs de Mars to see a grand review in honor of the peace. The streets all the way crowded with troops, and citizens hastening to the scene. We found the vast enclosure densely crowded with people. Had a pressing experience of a Paris crowd; found them very good-natured and jovial. Intensely hot, and obliged to wait an hour and a half before the Emperor came on the ground. He arrived at half past one, accompanied by a numerous and brilliant staff, including the plenipotentiaries of the Peace Congress. After riding along the vast lines of troops he took his stand in front of the military school, and the troops marched before him. The scene was splendid and impressive. There seemed no end to the long ranks of infantry, the rattling artillery, and the glittering cavalry. More than 50,000 in all. In the even-

ing walked the boulevards with Wilcox to see
the illuminations, like our 4th of July."

Numerous visits to the Louvre are recorded,
and special mention made of the pictures admired ; but " on the whole," he writes, " I have
not found in the gallery of the Louvre so
much enjoyment as in the other large galleries
I have visited."

" *April* 7. Went to the Sorbonne, and
attended a lecture on astronomy. Found students and lecture were much the same as in
Germany."

April 9, the two students left Paris for
London, where a busy fortnight was spent.

" *April* 12. Walked through St. James
and Hyde Park, and as we were coming back
met the Queen and received a bow from her.
Noticed that her Majesty had a very red nose.
Found cards from the Lord Mayor to dinner
on Thursday to meet the American minister.

" *April* 13. In the afternoon went to Lincoln's Inn and heard Maurice. He preached
on John v. 1–20. Sermon was very simple
but not very clear, especially with reference to
what was meant by the angel. His tone was
earnest and sincere, and on the whole I was
much delighted. His appearance is pleasing,
and corresponds to the idea that I had formed

from his writings. The psalms were beautifully chanted by a double choir of men and
boys standing on opposite sides of the chapel
and responding to each other. The responses
and amens of the clerk here, as at the morning service, were a jar. The chapel is interesting, the main window being made of the arms
of old officers of the society. Beneath we
noticed a crypt with finely ribbed vaulting.
Lincoln's Inn Fields looked very pleasant in
their dress of early spring."

Of Maurice, Mr. Diman wrote later: " No
one could forget, who had ever heard those
sad sonorous tones that used to fill the chapel
of Lincoln's Inn, tones at once charged with
humility and with conviction, as if almost
shrinking from giving audible expression to
verities which the heart accepted and loved."

" *April* 14.   Attended a meeting at Willis'
rooms in behalf of Christian missions in Turkey, the Earl of Shaftesbury in the chair.
Heard speeches from Sir Robert Grosvenor
and others, all warmly eulogizing the labors
of the American Board, and expressing the
most cordial feelings toward America.

"*April* 16.   Met by appointment Rev. Mr.
Malone, and with him went to the worst parts
of Westminster, visiting the industrial school

for boys, the ragged schools, the washing and bathing house, the reformatory, and the asylum for destitute girls. Examined with especial care the reformatory, which will hold about 100, but now has only 16. Only voluntary inmates are admitted, who must undergo a fortnight's probation, and after a year's residence are generally sent abroad."

The Lord Mayor's dinner is described, and many expeditions in and about London.

"*April* 25. Went to the House of Commons, where we heard a great many amusing complaints growing out of the late naval review. Heard Lord Palmerston, Sir Charles Ward, and others. Saw Lord John Russell, Disraeli, etc.

"*May* 1. My 25th birthday. A dark rainy day. We went this morning into the city and made arrangements to ship our trunks to Liverpool. Afterwards to J. B. Ford's Old Bond St., where I secured a berth in the steamer Niagara to sail on the 24th for Boston. Then to the London bridge, where we took steamer for Greenwich. At home all the evening packing my trunk, rejoiced to think that it was the last time. And so ends life in London."

The remaining twenty-four days of the stay

were spent in rapid travel in England and Scotland.

"*May* 2. To Royston near Cambridge, to visit our old Halle friend, Simon.

"*May* 4. Royston. Preached in morning my first sermon."

Warwick, Stratford, Kenilworth, Rugby, and Chatsworth follow, and May 10th "arrived at York. Saw the minster and chapter house, castle, and ruins of St. Mary's Abbey."

Thence by way of Newcastle, Berwick, Melrose and Abbotsford, to Edinburgh, where a couple of days were spent. A little trip in the Highlands followed.

"*May* 16. After a day of travel, had time to walk down to Loch Katrine and see a fine sunset." Three days were spent in walking and rowing on the lochs, and the short stay among the English lakes.

"*May* 20. After dinner had a fine row on Derwentwater.

"*May* 21. Had a pull on Lake Windermere.

"*May* 22. Foggy and rainy. Rode to Windermere and took train to Liverpool.

"*May* 24. Bade Tiffany farewell, my companion for nearly two years, and sailed for home in Cunard steamer Niagara.

"*June* 5. Reached Boston at sunrise. Met father at the Tremont House; at half past ten went with him by train to Providence. So ended the long dream of my student life abroad."

CHAPTER VI.

1856–1860.   AET. 25–29.

AT Salem, Massachusetts, on the 1st of July, 1856, there was a meeting of the Essex South Association of Ministers, " whose views of evangelical truth accord substantially with those of the Westminster Assembly of Divines." By this association Mr. Diman was licensed to preach, " having been carefully examined in regard to his Christian character, the soundness of his faith, his acquaintance with theology and literature, and his ability to teach."

The Old South Church in Boston, and the

First Congregational Church in Fall River sought to secure him. It was at this time that a great sorrow came to him, in the sudden death of Miss Maria R. Stimson, to whom he was engaged to be married. This grief, for the time, darkened his life, till, as he himself said, God led him "by paths he had not known" into the serene happiness of after years.

In deference to Mr. Diman's bereavement, the church at Fall River withheld their call for several weeks, "but when at length it was made," Mr. Diman writes at the end of September, "I did not feel justified in subjecting them to any further delay. I have accordingly accepted their invitation." He entered upon his new duties at once, and on the 9th of December was ordained as pastor.

The following letters show the spirit in which he began his labors : —

TO MISS EMILY G. STIMSON.

FALL RIVER, *December* 21, 1856.

. . . Another Sabbath day is passed, to me a season of high enjoyment, so that I begin already to look forward with impatience to the next, when I shall again be permitted to preach the Word of Life. My sermon this morning was especially addressed to the church, from John xv. 5. I have had a pretty busy day, and have preached twice, conducted a third service this evening, making some extemporaneous remarks, been into the Sabbath school, and have made, besides, five pastoral visits among my sick. But I am not tired. It is labor that carries with it every moment its own exceeding great reward, and every day I bless more and more that Providence which has made me a minister of Jesus Christ. . . . I feel very often my own great deficiencies, and pray for a deeper experience in my own heart, and for a more entire consecration. If I am to expect the blessing of God upon my labors, my meat and my drink must be to do his will. . . . Hopeless, indeed, would the task seem if the conversion of men rested on our efforts alone. There is another and mightier power which alone can render the truth effectual.

TO THE REV. JAMES O. MURRAY.

FALL RIVER, *February* 16, 1857.

. . . The first months of pastoral life come laden with many cares; in my own case, perhaps, with an unusual number, as there has been a great amount of sickness in the parish.

It was work, however, full of the highest consolations, for my own sadness was soothed by the thought that I was doing what I could to lessen that of others. You can imagine what a new chapter it opened in life, to assume the solemn duties of the ministry, and in the first week to stand at three dying bedsides.

The course which everything has taken has been in the highest degree gratifying, and I am not aware of a single circumstance that should cause me to regret my decision in coming here. In the church everything is harmonious, and in the congregation there has been a decided increase. There are indications of a deeper seriousness than usual.

My first Sunday was signalized by the inauguration of a new order of morning service, which has given great satisfaction, and adds to the interest of public worship. I shall eventually make still further modifications.

Parish duties break in necessarily to some extent upon the hours of study, but the long winter evenings have given me opportunity to prosecute a plan, which I entered upon while abroad, to perfect my acquaintance with the spirit and thought of the apostolic age. To this end I have read Barnabas and Clemens, and design going through with the Apostolic

Fathers in course. They yield nothing **be**yond a more vivid conception of the early Christianity, and how different **in its** whole mode of thought and doctrine from our own. Genesis, too, has claimed more of my attention in connection with Ewald's History. I congratulate myself that on many of these questions I was not subjected **to** the strict examination which would have awaited me in Boston.

The baptismal font, to which the following letter refers, still stands in the Congregational church at Bristol.

TO REV. THOMAS SHEPARD, D. D.

FALL RIVER, *January* 18, 1857.

REVEREND AND DEAR **SIR,—As a token** of my undiminished interest in the church to which for nearly two centuries my ancestors have belonged, and of which for fifty years my grandfather was pastor, I ask leave to present to **it** this baptismal font. May it do something to connect the past with the future, and to keep alive with those who shall come after us the remembrance of **those who have** gone before.

TO MISS EMILY G. STIMSON.

FALL RIVER, *April* 14, 1857.

If it were only as easy to write as to talk, then what a famous correspondent I should be, — but, alas, the pen is not the tongue — which scribbles away merrily on the ear, without the preliminary ceremony of being dipped into an inkstand. These sober reflections have been suggested to me by the contemplation of some dozen letters in my drawer, now waiting patiently to be answered.

I have thought a good deal about the subject of our conversation one morning last week, the use, or rather the necessity of meditating upon truth, or to me a word which you did not seem to relish, doctrine. . . . These questions are not empty speculations, like many of the questions of philosophy, but spring by an immediate and irresistible necessity from the practical demands of our moral nature. Augustin, Pascal, Edwards, John Foster, were not led to ponder these subjects by mere curiosity, they were absolutely driven to them by an inward experience of sublime energy. Just in proportion as the moral faculties are developed will these questions force themselves upon the mind for solution. It avails nothing to say they can never be solved. We are not so much led to them by the expectation of definite and practical results, as driven to them by an inward impulse of our nature. It is not so much the truth itself as the search after it, the exciting and vigorous exercise of all our faculties that does us good.

Then the emotions, though they are the basis of religion, can never furnish the highest development of religious life. The soul needs also to breathe the bracing atmosphere of thought. It needs for its own healthful growth to meditate upon these great questions, which, though they lie out of the circle of immediate practical usefulness, yet exercise a mighty influence over the whole development of thought and character.

TO REV. JAMES O. MURRAY.

Fall River, *February* 18, 1858.

. . . With changes all about us so sudden, and so overwhelming, who can look with any confidence to the future. For my own part I have renounced all day-dreams and castle-building. I think often of the striking anecdote of the old monk at Madrid, pointing to the picture on the altar, from which the forms stood out with the freshness of life, and saying

" that as he thought how all his companions
one by one had been taken away, it seemed as
if *they* were the shadows and these figures the
realities." . . . To tell the truth, I am more
sober for having recently been reading the
" Life and Letters of Byron," which, by the
way, have given me a far deeper sympathy
with him than his poetry ever awakened.

My own work goes on as usual. Respecting
the matter which we discussed together I am
no nearer a conclusion. That by changing
my church relations I should be more useful
or happy, is by no means clear. At times I
think we make most progress when dissatisfied
and yearning. Content in this life is often
but another name for spiritual torpor. . . .

The matter under discussion was the advisa-
bility of Mr. Diman's entering the Episcopal
Church. Toward it he had strong inclination,
and for several years the question occupied his
mind. The beauty of the liturgy attracted
him, the " decency and order " of the service
was grateful to his reverent mind. Throughout his life he held that the communion service
of the Church expressed his own views more
fully than any treatise on the Atonement.
This service, and the chapter on Justification,
in Barclay's Apology, he once recommended

as being the most complete and spiritual expositions of the great truths of Christianity.

While in Fall River several churches tried to obtain Mr. Diman's services. The Huguenot Church of Charleston, S. C., approached him on the subject, in the autumn of 1857. The next year he was desired to confer with certain gentlemen who visited him on behalf of the Mercer Street Presbyterian Church of New York. The following year the Shawmut Street Church of Boston sought him. All these offers were promptly refused on the ground that Mr. Diman did not feel at liberty to take any step toward severing his connection with his parish, having been in it so short a time.

A call which made more impression upon him was from Hartford in 1858. In the spring of that year Dr. Horace Bushnell visited Fall River. Dr. Bushnell's failing health made it necessary that he should have a colleague. He admired Mr. Diman greatly, and desired him to take the office.

FROM DR. BUSHNELL.

HARTFORD, *May* 31, 1858.

I know not how it is, but I have taken to you with a feeling I never expected to

have toward any one who might come into
such a peculiar relation, and finally take my
place. I think I am drawn to you thus by a
higher than merely human affinity, by the private impulse of God. So that if only I had a
mantle, I should be quite ready to put it on
you. . . . The proposition is that while I re-
tain the name of *pastor*, in accordance with
the wish of my people, and you take the place
of associate pastor, it be understood, as between us, for nobody else can settle any such
arrangement, that you are to be the real responsible active pastor, only consulting me
when you choose, and using me to preach if
I am able, in such ways as will best serve
your convenience. Everything is from the
first to be in your hand. . . . I only add here
that my symptoms are looking all the time to
my speedy removal. I do not really expect
to live for a year.

I pass to the matters of duty, for I am quite
willing with you to throw out of the question
all considerations of position, ambition, taste
and the like, and rest the question wholly on
the matter of duty. God grant that you may
have grace to hold the question away and
apart from every other test. . . .

Then follow eight pages of argument on the question, ending with an invitation to come to Hartford to preach.

TO DR. HORACE BUSHNELL.

FALL RIVER, *June* 5, 1858.

You will not, I am sure, suspect me of any want of courtesy, when I decline wholly to accede to your proposition to preach in Hartford. Under ordinary circumstances nothing could afford me greater pleasure, but while I remain the pastor of this church, I cannot consistently with my own views of honorable dealing, either directly or indirectly, present myself as a candidate to any other. The same consideration forces me to decline your kind invitation to visit you.

Let me add, too, that further consideration has not disposed me to recognize more than at first the conclusions of your arguments, and therefore if your church chooses to proceed any further in this matter, it must be wholly on their own responsibility.

FROM DR. BUSHNELL.

HARTFORD, *June* 7, 1858.

Your note of Saturday is just received, and I must say that I heartily respect your answers to my requests. . . . As I just now read your note to my wife she said, as her conclusion, "I like him!" The only thing *I* do not like is that you make so little of my arguments.

Dr. Bushnell was too deeply interested in the plan to think of relinquishing it, and the church proceeded to appoint a committee to recommend a colleague. This committee after visiting Fall River, reported on the 6th of July, and the church formally invited Mr. Diman to become associate pastor, "as a man eminently endowed and qualified for that office."

FROM DR. BUSHNELL.

HARTFORD, *July* 8, 1858.

This will introduce to your acquaintance my very dear friends Messrs. Dunham and Owen, who visit Fall River as delegates from the church and society to communicate the call which has just been proffered you. I can hardly tell you how great satisfaction I have in this call, and the perfect unanimity of it. . . . I hope you will assume whatever time is necessary to a wise and right decision on your part. Meantime, I will invite you to come to Hartford, and be my guest for as long

time as you please. I should like mightily
to show you into my pulpit Sunday of next
week, but you will soon use your own liberty
in that matter. . . . With many prayers that
God will guide you into a right decision, I
am yours with great esteem and affection,

HORACE BUSHNELL.

About the middle of July Mr. Diman accepted Dr. Bushnell's invitation, and went to
Hartford. Among the incidents of the visit
were the attentions of Dr. Bushnell's white
cat. Mr. Diman encouraged her advances in
the evening twilight, saying he liked cats,
and allowed her to climb over his knees and
shoulders. The next morning he was late at
family prayers. After half an hour's waiting
the family proceeded to breakfast. At length
Mr. Diman appeared, explaining, as he smil-
ingly pointed to the still scattered white hairs
on his black suit, that the cat had cost him
an hour's work with the brush, and adding
that he should never forget her! In later
years he often told the story, and laughed
over his embarrassment, which was, indeed,
serious for a young minister who was to appear before an expectant congregation.

TO DR. BUSHNELL.

FALL RIVER, *August* 2, 1858.

If I saw any reason to suppose that longer delay would modify my decision, I would gladly withhold for the present my answer to the invitation of your church, but my convictions since I left Hartford have tended so persistently in one direction that I feel persuaded a longer consideration on my part would only be doing injustice to you. I have, therefore, to-day, through Mr. Owen, declined the call.

In announcing to you this step, it is hardly necessary to recapitulate arguments which have been already fully discussed. I have endeavored throughout to keep my mind perfectly open to arguments on either side, but I have been at no time able to resist the firm conviction that the claims of a field where experience had demonstrated my acceptance, and which held out the promise of increasing usefulness, were too imperative to be set aside.

A further study of the present condition of my church convinces me that it would be largely detrimental to its interests to dissolve so speedily the connection between us, and believing that the interests of a connection already existing should take precedence of any other, I have no alternative but the décision I have made.

FALL RIVER, *October* 6, 1858.

. . . I was much interested in what you wrote of your sermons. You have a capital plan marked out, and a rich vein to work in. Oddly enough, something of the same sort has been running for some time in my own brain, only the idea that I had was to present the cardinal features of the old dispensation in the form of biographic studies of Moses, etc.

For a long time my thoughts have been more or less directed to the study of the relation of the old dispensation to the new, of the Law and Grace, and I am looking forward some day to an extended examination of the Mosaic system in all its scope and significance. There is an element in that old Hebrew culture that we need to emphasize if we would escape the shallow inanities of the present day.

I have been preaching with great interest to myself, indeed I never felt more in the mood for work than now, satisfied that I did a wise thing in remaining here. . . . About the *De Civitate* I think with you. The fact is, the folios of the Fathers, with much that is deep and true, are nevertheless cart-loads of rubbish.

Mr. Diman's deep love and reverence for the office of preacher powerfully affected his congregation. His manner in the pulpit was most grave and reverent. No hasty gestures, no unseemly vehemence marred his chaste, severe delivery. The hand, so beautifully formed, moved with deliberation, and almost solemnly emphasized his words. His utterance was somewhat rapid, though very clear, with a certain urgency which carried his hearers with him. His voice was well pitched and resonant, easily filling large spaces. There was something peculiar about it. It seemed to flow on, a continuous stream of sound, from which the words came perfectly uttered. This effect was due largely to the cadence of his sentences. They were rhythmic, and though his preaching was the farthest remove from intoning, the rise and fall of the voice was plainly noticeable. In his sermons, he had a few habits, which marked the deep reserve which underlay his open and frank manner. His congregations were not addressed as " my friends," but simply as " my hearers."

On rare occasions, warmed by the power and tenderness of his theme, he said " Beloved," using the word as St. Paul does, " beloved in the Lord." He usually spoke of Christ as " Our Lord," but of His titles none were more dear to him than the " Son of Man."

TO MISS EMILY G. STIMSON,

Mr. Diman writes : —

" When preaching gushes forth readily and spontaneously, and when all outward nature seems in such perfect sympathy with it, it becomes a delightful service. Some one has said that preaching ought to be lyrical and musical, a flowing song; the inner life pouring forth its full tide of emotion. To realize this fully doubtless belongs only to the very highest order of spirits, and yet I have at times felt moments in my extemporaneous preaching when my subject seemed suddenly to seize me and carry me beyond myself. One such gush will redeem a whole sermon, and if we led the lives we should, with our sensibilities ever attuned, and our hearts ever flowing over with the divine love, such states would be our natural states, a perpetual seraphic ecstasy; so that life itself would flow on like a joyous psalm of praise."

The following passages from letters to Miss Emily G. Stimson, written in 1859 and 1860, give some idea of the extent and variety of Mr. Diman's reading, and of his state of mind, which he calls one of transition. Of these " deeper questions of the soul," which perplexed him about this period of his life, he afterward wrote, " I imagine it is an experience through which all young persons pass, whose spiritual nature is roused to much activity."

The passage on human destiny is of special interest, in connection with the last course of lectures Mr. Diman delivered. " Is there progress in history ? " he asked. " The question must be limited. There is not progress in all directions ; not progress at all times ; yet progress on the whole." He then confidently went on to show that this progress is moral.

Critical studies of belief and opinion had always a great fascination for Mr. Diman. His candid mind saw the truth that underlay error, and at this period of his life he was still laying the foundations of the full and deep convictions of maturer years.

" You doubtless wonder what I mean by a disturbance of my ideas. The phrase is not a very definite one, but it expresses better than anything else the state of mind that I seem to be in. The Germans have a phrase that hits it exactly, *im Werden,* that is, a transitional state. Most of the opinions with which I began life I have either greatly modified or wholly given up, and not yet attained to peace and comfort in any other. I used to have great faith in human progress and the capacity of the race for ultimate perfectibility, but of late my mind has been a good deal exercised by the totally opposite views of the millenarians, who hold to no solution of the problem of human destiny under the present dispensation, but look for another. They come to a similar conclusion to that of the Swedenborgians, though they reach it in a very different way. . . .

"I am intensely interested in Dr. Bellows' sermons. For a long time I have not seen a book that so reflects the phases of my own experience. I perfectly sympathize with his craving for an established historic faith, for a worship expressive of our refined religious sentiment, and not less with his inability to sympathize with any prevailing forms. The sermons are written with great power."

Speaking of "Jacqueline Pascal," "Though

disfigured to some extent with the superstition and false views of Romanism, yet it records the struggles of a noble soul in a dark and unpropitious age, and has in it that sublimity of self-consecration, that perfect yielding up of self to God, of which the Catholic Church presents us so many examples. One feels exalted to a loftier state of being when brought into contact with such a spirit."

After reading Robertson : —

" What greater satisfaction can one have than in dying thus to leave behind a book that will continue to minister to other lands and ages. What monument of brass or marble can compare with this? I have often thought that of all things I should prefer to write some little work connected with man's highest interests, that should live in his love and memory. How, for example, a single hymn of Heber has gone singing round the world ! "

" So you like Robertson ? " Mr. Diman wrote to a friend some years later. " He has always been a favorite of mine. Indeed, among recent preachers I do not know of any one I would put beside him."

" Most of the morning I have spent in reading, in the stately pages of Clarendon, how a great and prosperous people were drawn step by step into a bloody civil war. The deep interest I take in passing events, which almost in fact withdraws me from my proper studies, gives to his sombre narrative an irresistible charm. . . . Clarendon is the Vandyke of historians. I cannot resist the feeling that our own nation may be entering on a history as tragic. . . .

" The heavy rain this morning kept me closely housed, and before a bright fire I read Theodore Parker's sermons, attractive from the freshness and vigor of the style, and the frank, outspoken tone that pervades them, but after all unsatisfactory, as they do not meet our higher instincts, and leave untouched the great mysteries of life. I turn from them to read the New Testament with a new relish. . . .

" I have been writing a sermon this morning from Pilate's words to Jesus, ' What is truth ? ' and am trying to show that the great obstacle to truth is not honest doubt but worldliness and indifference. . . . This week have devoted my evenings to Pascal's Provincial Letters. I do it chiefly as an exercise in French, but the wit, eloquence, and satire afford me endless enjoyment. I think I shall read next the famous treatise of De Maistre, ' Du Pape,' the best argument for an infallible authority ever made. . . .

" So we go — who shall teach us the way, the truth, and the life. I find myself turning more and more from controversy to a struggle after personal holiness. The pure in heart see God."

Fall River, January 10, 1860.

The die is cast . . . the Rubicon crossed. Sunday morning at the close of service I requested the church to stop, and after the congregation had gone out, coming down from the pulpit and standing by the communion-table, where we had so often celebrated together the Sacrament of our Lord's death, I resigned back the charge which they had entrusted to me. It was a solemn scene. I was perfectly calm when I began to speak, but as one face after another was bowed in tears, I was warned not to test my self-control too far.

In January came a severe blow in the sudden death of Mr. John J. Stimson of Providence.

TO REV. J. O. MURRAY.

Fall River, *January* 27, 1860.

. . . I could not feel the loss more deeply were it my own father. Indeed, for nearly ten years Mr. Stimson, has been a father to me. It is a great comfort to me to think that my relations to E. had all been definitely fixed, and had received his cordial approbation and blessing. How his death will affect my plans for the future does not yet appear. . . . But I feel willing to leave all in the hands of God, who so strangely leads us by paths we have not known.

CHAPTER VII.

On May 15, 1860, Mr. Diman was married to Miss Emily G. Stimson, daughter of Mr. John J. Stimson, of Providence, and the home was begun which Mr. Diman counted " next to that faith without which all earthly blessings are but curses in disguise," the chief cause of thankfulness.

He had lately accepted a call to the Harvard Congregational Church in Brookline, Mass., and it was there that he took his bride. We have seen that he congratulated himself " that on many of these questions " — Genesis and the doctrines of early Christianity — " I was not subjected to the strict examination which would have awaited me in Boston."

That strict examination came before his ordination as pastor in Brookline. The man who did not hesitate to declare that the "folios of the Fathers, with much that is deep and true, are nevertheless cart-loads of rubbish," could not be expected to be bound by the conventions of orthodoxy, as held by "the hair-splitting theologians of New England." In the "deep view," which he says he loved, and "the constant struggle after unity," he refused to recognize Congregationalism as the one church indicated by the Apostles, answering, to the confusion of his questioners, when asked what church then was indicated, "Without doubt Episcopacy." But the main trouble was with what was at that time considered his unorthodox view of the Atonement. Five years before this time he wrote in the foreign journal the confession to which he adhered to the end of his life. He had been talking with a friend on the subject. "His interest is concentrated on the objective nature of the Atonement; mine on the Person of Christ." It was the Life of Christ, and the Life never more manifest than in the Death, that Mr. Diman clung to as the great fact of Revelation. His philosophic mind refused to see in the crucifixion an isolated event, or even an event of vital moment, *un-connected* with the previous life of obedience. When he quoted "the blood of Christ cleanseth from all sin," he meant the life-blood of Christ, and the life as assimilated by the believing soul. "Through the mysterious alchemy of a daily communion, must He be made our life, and we be transformed into His image. His spiritual nature must be assimilated, even as our physical frames assimilate the nutritious principle of food, till by degrees He becomes so completely inwrought into the believing soul, that it can say, 'It is no longer I that live, but Christ that liveth in me.'" [1]

Mr. Diman's latest utterances, as well as the earliest, are in accord with the deep and spiritual view of the nature and office of Christ he so loved to contemplate. Writing only three years before his death, he says: "In our Lord's discourse on the night before he was betrayed, He had distinctly taught that the great work which he had assumed would not be completed by His death. That was not the last result towards which all things had tended, but was itself the transition step to a greater result, the necessary condition of

[1] *Orations and Essays:* Christ the Bread of Life.

another and more glorious stage of spiritual development, the door of a nearer approach to the invisible world." [1] . . .

And again : " What theologians have called the plan of redemption has been dissected with all the confidence with which science investigates the phenomena of matter. The most signal, pathetic, persuasive exhibition of yearning love for men, ever compassed within the limits of a human life, has been analyzed into dry, repulsive syllogisms, and summed up in the metaphysical dialect of creeds, and made the shibboleths of contending sects. For even the story of redemption could be easily perverted into an abstract theory of the divine administration. But when we study the doctrine of the Spirit, we pass from the theology of the intellect to the theology of the feelings. We are in a region of insight, of experience, of inner recognition, where intellectual conclusions no longer satisfy." [2]

At this time, and later, it was said of Mr. Diman, that he inclined towards Unitarian views. Notwithstanding his sympathy with Unitarians, which arose from his thorough appreciation of their standpoint, he never

[1] *Orations and Essays :* The Baptism of the Holy Ghost.
[2] *Ibid.*

thought of acting with them, as his letters prove. The belief that he might do so probably had its foundation in the fact that he loved to dwell upon the humanity of Christ. Throughout his life his writings on this subject are in perfect accord. As a theological student he wrote : " While Christ was the ideal man, so it is ever to be the aim of every one, in the same manner, to realize the ideal man, and thus be also a manifestation of the Logos in the flesh. Each believer should be the Living Word of God." The Brookline pastor wrote : " Theology in part must be held responsible for this (*i. e.*, the separation of ethics from Christianity) by exalting the Son of Man above the race whose nature He expressed, and creating an impassable gulf between Redeemer and redeemed. In her zeal to enthrone the Lord of Life above all principality and power, and all that may be named in heaven and on earth, faith has been at times forgetful that it was the Son of *Man*, whom the dying Stephen saw standing at the right hand of God, and whom John beheld in Apocalyptic glory. . . . Let us not forget that man's normal nature is seen in Christ, and not in us. . . . It is this sense of a common nature, of a nature whose essential qualities and capabilities no sin, degradation, nor long centuries of alienation have rooted out, that establishes the sympathy between us and the Son of Man. Without this there is no redemption. *Because* He is Son of Man, is He Saviour of the world." [1] Six years later the University professor wrote : " Are men weary of the story of the cross? Are they weary of sunrise and of spring? It is ever old, yet ever new. Only a pitiful failure to comprehend these various and profound aspects in which the Son of Man stands related to the spiritual constitution of the race, these aspects which Himself intimated when He declared, ' I am the Way, and the Truth, and the Life; no man cometh unto the Father but by me,' — only a pitiful failure to comprehend these could have betrayed any into the terrible delusion of thinking that they could climb up some other way." [2]

And writing in the last year of his life Mr. Diman says: " The highest, and at the same time the simplest, aspect in which Christianity is revealed is that of a spiritual force revealing itself in human souls.

" That stupendous fact which we term the

---

[1] *Orations and Essays :* The Son of Man.
[2] *Ibid. :* Christ the Way, the Truth, the Life.

Incarnation meant no more than this. It was the dwelling in human nature of a divine life and power, the lifting of the human race to a higher level of spiritual experience and action. When Jesus chose for his most habitual designation of himself the title of " Son of Man," He hinted this great analogy between the natural and the spiritual. For as Son of Man He expressed and illustrated the crowning result of a human development, since in Him humanity was first conscious of divine affinities. Even when asserting his most intimate relations with the Father He ever described himself as Son of Man. And what he claimed for himself He accorded to his followers." [1]

The deep mysticism and lofty purity of Mr. Diman's views, the spiritual heights on which he walked, might well cause less elevated souls to fall back in confusion. And it was hard for him, except in the pulpit, where all personality was laid aside, to express his truest thoughts and convictions. In any argument he was apt to be, if possible, too fair. He saw the other side so clearly, he generally knew the history and growth of the opposite

---

[1] *Orations and Essays :* The Kingdoms of Heaven and of Nature.

opinion so well, that he was often believed to incline toward it. He also, in his later years, used the satiric method with the effect of entirely confusing his antagonist.

"I do not mean," he writes, "that it is a matter of little moment how truth is stated. On the contrary, because it is a matter of so much moment, must we hesitate before accepting any statement as final. Nor are differences of statement on the part of theologians to be sneered at as mere slight and verbal differences; on the contrary, they often express broad divergencies of understanding and belief, and precisely because these divergencies are so broad does it seem likely that the best men 'knew in part, and prophesied in part.'"

·　　·　　·　　·　　·　　·　　·

"Our faith is in the Father, and the Son, and the Holy Ghost; not in either one as separate from the rest, but in the three together, as forming one truth, one object of belief, one method of salvation. The problem for each regenerate soul is to recognize in the unity of one experience this threefold revelation. If we believe in the Father it must be as manifest in the Son; if we believe in the Son, it must be as revealed by the Spirit; if we believe in the Spirit, it must be as bringing us through the Son unto the Father. The divine vestment cannot be rent asunder. If we dwell exclusively on either one of these correlated truths, if we suffer either one to exert undue influence in shaping our belief, we sacrifice the proportion of faith. This doctrine formulates the threefold adjustment to human wants, and according as we symmetrically grasp it are we made partakers of the divine nature. It was not designed for theologians, but for believing men. Of nice dogmatic statements we have had enough. What we need is a deeper intuition of the interior meaning; an anointing of the spirit that shall bring us to such open vision of the Lord of life, that we, being transformed into his image, may have our lives hid with him in God. Thus will it be felt that the doctrine, which through so many ages has lain imbedded in the richest fruition and understanding of the love of God in Christ which passeth knowledge, is no dead abstraction; thus will the deep things which so long have baffled the intellect, interpret themselves to the heart, as the believer —

'From Hope, and firmer Faith, to perfect Love
Attracted, and absorbed '—

sees at last no longer through a glass, but
face to face." [1]

After a prolonged discussion and a heated
controversy, the council decided to proceed
with Mr. Diman's installation as pastor of the
Harvard Congregational Church. Here he
remained four years, years which were filled
with work in which he delighted. Two children were born here, to complete the happiness
of his home life.

His preaching attracted marked attention,
so that he was sought for other fields. Dr.
Roswell D. Hitchcock again wrote to him
about the Mercer Street Church, in New York;
the First Congregational Society of Hartford
approached him; and in 1863 churches in
Philadelphia and Springfield desired his services.

" He was before all the Congregational
ministers who are known as 'orthodox,'"
wrote Dr. Rufus Ellis, " certainly in this
neighborhood, in the offer of an exchange of
pulpits to a Unitarian clergyman. At his invitation we took each other's place on Sunday,
May 10, 1863, he officiating in First Church,
and I in his house of worship in Brookline." [2]

---

[1] *The Monthly Religious Magazine*, September, 1863.
Sermon : Father, Son, and Holy Ghost.

[2] *First Church in Boston : 250th Anniversary*, p. **191**.

To this exchange of pulpits the following letters refer : —

TO THE REV. RUFUS ELLIS.

BROOKLINE, *April* 24, 1863.

I reciprocate most heartily your fraternal sentiments, and will gladly exchange with you on any Sunday that you will indicate. It has long seemed to me that the issues, on which the Congregational body divided, are dead. The deeper religious consciousness of the present day is independent of either extreme. I have never assented to the so-called New England divinity, and have held myself studiously aloof from all denominational connections. If anything can be done, not to heal the breach simply, but to build again on a more catholic and apostolic foundation, I shall heartily rejoice.

BROOKLINE, *May* 15, 1863.

I make haste to thank you for your kind note, and to express my gratification at the reception given me by your people. When I selected the sermon it was with the conviction that it presented no " strange doctrine."

It is with shame and regret that I am forced to confess that my own people have shown a less liberal feeling than I had hoped for. This has not, however, shaken in the least my own conviction that I acted as became a minister of Christ. In justice to yourself I ought to add, that no exception whatever was taken to your sermon, but only to your ecclesiastical position. Perhaps, however, these things are no more than we ought to expect. The leaven must be allowed a little time to work.

Mr. Diman on several occasions delivered the so-called " Thursday lecture " in Mr. Ellis's church. This was an old custom, which Mr. Ellis had revived shortly before Mr. Diman came to Brookline.

A pleasant feature of the Brookline life was a club of six young ministers of different denominations, from the various churches in the neighborhood. They met at each other's houses, and read the Agamemnon of Æschylus in the forenoon, and after dinner took up matters of mutual interest. " We were all nearly the same age," writes Mr. Young, " and though we occupied different theological positions, yet we had much in common."

The word heretical, having once been mentioned, is apt to cling to a minister, and Mr.

Diman was no exception. Before long some of the congregation began to think his sermons unorthodox. A strong and influential party in the church delighted in them, and heard with hearing ears. All united, however, in praising his blameless life, his admirable performance of all parish duties, and his personal charm of manner. Such was the condition of affairs in 1864. The very sermons which he preached in later years to delighted congregations in Boston and Providence, and which no one called unorthodox, were found fault with. His upholders and followers were devoted, and the church was on the brink of disruption. At this juncture came the offer of a professorship in Brown University, made at the suggestion of Professor William Gammel, who was about to retire from the chair of History and Political Economy.

TO HENRY W. DIMAN.

Brookline, *February* 24, 1864.

Dr. Sears came down in person to see me, and urged the matter in most pressing and flattering terms. Soon as my church got wind of the matter they began to stir, and presented a request in writing, signed by almost everybody in the congregation, that I should remain. Many beside remonstrated in person, so I was driven to think seriously whether it would be right for me to leave. If I decide to go it will be mainly on account of my disagreeable relations with the denomination. I am heartily disgusted with the incessant twaddle about soundness and unsoundness.

On many accounts I should be sorry to leave Brookline. All my social relations are exceedingly pleasant, and the advantages of various sorts are unsurpassed. My four years here have been very pleasant.

Professor George P. Fisher adds the following paragraphs, on

THE THEOLOGICAL POSITION OF PROFESSOR DIMAN.

A stranger conversing with Professor Diman might have received the impression that he was highly conservative in his religious tastes and opinions; or, on the other hand, he might have carried away the impression that, besides being a fearless advocate of progress, he was not in the least indisposed to bold innovations in theology. Such a "chance acquaintance" might have heard from him expressions favorable to characteristic features of the Protestant Episcopal, or even of the Roman Catholic Church, — expressions that would have struck him with some surprise, as falling from the lips of a Congregational minister. On the contrary, remarks appreciative of certain traits of the Unitarians might have been equally unexpected from an " orthodox " scholar and preacher. Yet there was not a particle of insincerity, and no real inconsistency in all these comments. In the freedom of conversation, to break up somebody's " dogmatic slumber," and perhaps in a partly humorous spirit, novel opinions might be thrown out, and that in a paradoxical form, which were likely to provoke astonishment, if not dissent, especially if the listener were deficient in breadth and discernment. But underlying all these diverse expressions, there was a consistent mode of thought; and there was a like consistency in the course of conduct which Professor Diman pursued in ecclesiastical affairs and relations. To be sure, we must take into account the ingrained personal independence, and the outspoken habit, which characterized him. He did not hesitate, although always with courtesy, to say just what he thought, unawed by the disagreement of others, and not tempted to cloak his opinions from a desire to please. In order to do justice to Professor Diman, one had need to bear in mind the fact that while he was free and fresh in his intellectual activity, not afraid to think for himself, having a certain delight in the higher fields of speculation, he was imbued, if I may use the expression, with a profound historical sense. The present he saw in the light of all the past. Whatever could fairly be said to have a historic justification, engaged, at least to a qualified extent, his sympathy. The more ancient ecclesiastical bodies, with their stable forms of polity and their impressive liturgies, he looked upon with an appreciative regard. For the old Puritanism of New England, and the simple dignity of its ecclesiastical system, he cherished a like reverent feeling. It was something to be highly honored and respected, — something which had a legitimate origin and had performed a worthy and noble work. From his Rhode Island birth and early education, from his training in college under Dr. Wayland, from his wide opportunities for culture both in New England and in Germany, and from the instinctive tendencies of his own nature, Diman was lifted above everything narrow, one-sided, exclusive. Merely providential tests of doctrine, demands made on the intellect by local opinion, creeds manufactured yesterday, did not attract from him any deference. He respected the leaders of New England theology, from Edwards to Taylor and Park, but he could not be counted among the followers of any of them. The masterly way in which he could deal critically, and in a broad, impartial spirit, with the history and special peculiarities of the different religious bodies, is finely exemplified in his article on "Religion in America." Nothing has been written on the subject, certainly not in so brief a compass, which is equally discriminating and learned.

Now add to the peculiar natural qualities, and to the rich, varied culture of Professor Diman, the circumstance that he attained to manhood late enough to be able to contemplate great religious controversies in a dispassionate way,— somewhat as an on-looker from abroad might have regarded them. His position set him free from partisan bias, such as even one like him, at an earlier date, might not have been able to escape. The controversy of Churchman and Puritan, the controversy of Orthodox and Unitarian Congregationalist, were not, indeed, wholly things of the past;

yet Diman was so placed that he could scan the contending parties from a higher plane of observation. To neither of them could he surrender himself with an undivided sympathy. As regards Congregationalism, he deplored the great division which placed the children of the Puritans in two antagonistic camps. He would probably have gone with the most pacific in the endurance of differences of belief, had it been possible in that way to avoid the separation. The Unitarian churches and ministers, in particular such as held fast to the supernatural origin of the Gospel, he regarded not only with no antipathy, but was disposed to go decidedly farther than his brethren generally in friendly approaches toward them, and in the exchange of ministerial courtesies. He looked upon the ministers and churches of this description as members of a broken household to which he was fond of looking back as it existed in its earlier day of conscious strength and unity. When questioned by an installing council respecting his doctrinal tenets, in the midst of an atmosphere engendered by a long theological conflict, he would show no anxiety to satisfy scruples or to allay suspicions. He would take no pains to express himself in conventional phraseology.

To those who could not recognize evangelical
truth except in the traditional dress, to all who
listened to catch the sound of their shibboleth,
there was a savor of heresy in the young
preacher's definitions of doctrine. A more
conciliatory bearing on his part would certainly
have been politic. Possibly, it might have
been judicious and advisable. Individuals not
wanting in catholic and kindly feeling might
have thus been delivered from needless suspi-
cion and alarm. The result, strange to say,
was that he was looked on as a latitudinarian
by not a few, at the same time that some of
the most conservative of the " Old School "
ministers found in him much that was congenial with their ways of thinking, and sometimes defended him as " sound in the faith "
against aspersions from the " New School "
side. I believe that certain views which he
happened to avow respecting the observance
of the Lord's day — views more akin to those of
Luther and the Reformers than to the stricter
Puritan idea — drew upon him at one time
considerable censure. The particular point in
discussion related to the running of horse-cars
on Sunday. The virulence with which he was
denounced by one or more of the Congregationalist ministers near him, was among the

causes that led him to attend, for a while at least, an Episcopal church, situated in the neighborhood of his dwelling.

To speak a little more in particular of Diman's theological opinions, I think that he would have given his full assent to the Nicene Creed, the great symbol in which the divinity of Christ is asserted and defined. I have no reason to think that he had any doubts respecting the doctrine of the Incarnation, as generally held in the Church. On the subject of the Atonement, while he did not consider particular theories — the governmental theory, for example — an adequate explication of the subject, he believed that the work of the Redeemer goes beyond any mere teaching or legislative function, and includes a relation to God and to a righteous moral order. He attached most weight to the moral and spiritual elements of the Atonement, and was specially desirous to explore and ascertain their precise significance. His view of the Inspiration of the Scriptures was not in accord with the traditional formularies. While he had a sincere and deep reverence for the Bible as the authority in matters of faith, he did not consider its records to be free from historical discrepancies, and from other blemishes belonging to compositions in which human agency has a part of its own to fulfill. On one subject he came at last, I think, to differ from the convictions commonly entertained in the Christian body to which he belonged. In a sermon preached at King's Chapel, February 10th, 1878, in a course of sermons by different divines on Future Punishment, he took his text in the first Epistle of John : " He that hath the Son hath life ; and he that hath not the Son of God hath not life." He concludes that "there is no warrant whatever for erecting the bold, naked, literal dogma of everlasting punishment into an article of Christian faith ; that a grievous wrong is done when any who shrink from accepting it are excluded from the communion of Christian people ; and that a religious body which insists on this as an essential test will bar from its ministry many of the most thoughtful and most earnest of the present generation. The early records are silent on this point ; the Church of England omits it from her articles ; those who venture to affirm it, affirm what Jesus himself made no part of his direct, explicit teaching. Where he was silent, we well may pause."

I am aware that the foregoing remarks will give those who did not know Diman, a very inadequate conception of his peculiarities as a theologian. To gain a true idea of that rare mingling of spiritual perception with logical clearness and accuracy, which belonged to him, and of the felicity of the language in which he spoke and wrote on the topics of the Gospel, the reader must resort to the sermons printed in the volume of his " Orations and Essays."

CHAPTER VIII.

THE offer of a chair in Brown University
was accepted after some deliberation, and in
September, 1864, Mr. Diman began his college work.

From Providence, October 1st, Mr. Diman
writes to a friend: " The pressure of many
new duties has caused me to neglect my correspondence. We wanted to send for you to
pass Commencement with us, but have been
delayed much longer than we expected in getting into our house. Next week we expect to
move into it, and as soon as we are fairly settled we shall claim your promised visit."

The house referred to is the one on Angell
Street, in which all of Mr. Diman's life in

Providence was passed, and which had for many years been a centre of activity and usefulness. "Rose Farm" was the old name of the pleasant orchard-clad acres that surrounded it. Its hospitable doors were always open, and with the coming of Mr. and Mrs. Diman the place renewed its youth. How many distinguished guests were welcomed here from a distance! while the best and cleverest the city afforded were constant visitors. A chance guest, detained over night, writes long after:

"I obtained a glimpse of your home life, that has followed me as a heavenly vision to this hour."

The first winter in Providence, 1864–65, was apparently entirely devoted to college work. It was entirely new work, and the letters remaining are few. To his brother he writes that he is well pleased with it, and should he decide to take a parish again, the time would not be lost.

But the next winter he engaged in some of the outside work, which was, perhaps, even more effective and useful than the college instruction. A course of evening lectures on Political Economy was given at Bryant and Stratton's Business College. The opening lecture was largely attended, and the whole course received with attention.

TO REV. J. O. MURRAY.

PROVIDENCE, *November* 10, 1865.

. . . Truly there is no trial that so sorely afflicts us as the sickness and death of our little ones. We have had a long season of anxiety this fall with our little boy, and at one time were fain compelled to relinquish almost all hope, but he has been mercifully preserved, and is now nearly recovered.

What are the difficulties of faith that men make such ado about, compared with these real and most appalling facts that touch our every-day life?

Every thing goes on pleasantly with me, so far as duties are concerned. As I am less driven I feel much more satisfied with my work. This term I have been giving most of my attention to early French history, a subject most obscurely treated by English masters.

I endeavor to economize in book-buying, but yesterday I gladly gave twenty dollars for an English copy of Edward Irving's works. One of the sermons that I read last evening almost repaid me. I wish you might read the one " On the Death of Children," written after the loss of his little boy. . . .

With his new work Mr. Diman did not relinquish preaching. He was ever ready to respond to the calls made upon him, and at various times supplied pulpits for many consecutive weeks. The Beneficent Congregational Church had been without a pastor, and during the winter of 1865–6 Mr. Diman supplied its pulpit, filling it with great acceptance to the people.

On the fourth of July, 1866, Mr. Diman delivered an oration before the city authorities and citizens of Providence, on "The Nation and the Constitution," in which he eloquently sets forth the doctrine, that "the nation holds not from the law, but the law holds from the nation."

"No nation ever existed that depends so little as does ours upon its mere form of government. To my mind, the crowning moment of our great conflict was not when the first gun fired on Sumter was followed by the magnificent uprising of a great people ; when the whole North burned with an enthusiasm that has had nothing like it since the days of the crusades ; but rather, that dark, that dreadful hour, when, with the nation reeling beneath the blow that smote its beloved Chief, the great duties of the state passed without a

break or a jar to the hands of his successor.
That was the real triumph of our institutions." [1]

TO PRESIDENT ANGELL.

PROVIDENCE, *November* 27, 1866.

. . . For the past week I have been very
busy writing new lectures for my class, and
preparing for the press an edition of "John
Cotton's Reply to Roger Williams," which will
be printed by the Narragansett Club. I have
been much interested to study in the *original*
authorities the question of his banishment,
and my opinions have been somewhat modified.

This week is the usual recess. The term
has gone very pleasantly thus far. I have
used the book on "Feudalism" which I showed
to you, and derived many new ideas from it.

My wife and children are in Boston. I
go down to-morrow to pass Thanksgiving. I
propose to do the eating, and let others do
the preaching.

PROVIDENCE, *January* 27, 1867.

We got through (the term) last week. My
examination was, on the whole, the best I have
yet had. It was both oral and written for
the whole class, and was regarded as pretty

---

[1] *The Nation and the Constitution*, p. 22. Providence Press
Company, 1866.

severe. I was gratified with the result because I have taught Guizot for the last term by a new method, giving up the daily recitations, and having a written analysis of a whole chapter presented at once. It saves much weariness, and by grasping a subject as a whole, the class get a better idea of it. Besides, it already does away with the old parrot style of exact recitation.

With regard to the first two chapters of Guizot I have always taught them. They are far behind the present discussion of the subject, but are useful to hang remarks upon.

With regard to Political Economy, I doubt if you will find the preparation of a daily lecture (of course I mean the heads) any more laborious than getting a long lesson out of a text-book. . . .

In the summer of 1867 a vacation excursion was taken, and thus described : —

CHICAGO, *July* 24.

Which of all the lost treasures of ancient literature one would care most to have recovered, has been a favorite question for the leisure moments of literary men. Respecting an answer, there has been as little agreement

as with the scarcely less important questions,
What song the Syrens sang, and What dress
Achilles assumed when he hid himself among
the women. The historian of the " Decline
and Fall of the Roman Empire " did not hesitate to declare that for himself he would prefer the " Lost Decades " of Livy to the accu-
mulated stores of the Alexandrian library.
The judgment of your correspondent may
have received an unconscious bias from the
circumstance that his early days were passed
in a seaport town, where the whale-fishery still
flourished in a glory undimmed by kerosene ;
but it has always seemed to him that beyond
comparison the most curious production of antiquity that could be recovered from the de-
stroyer, Time, would be the diary, or, in more
exact nautical phrase, the log-book, kept by
the prophet Jonah, during the three days and
nights of his experimental cruise along the
eastern shores of the Mediterranean. In the
absence of the original record, the emotions of
the distinguished navigator can only be matter of conjecture ; it seems, however, not un-
reasonable to infer, in view of all the circumstances, that the remorse caused by a willful
attempt to evade duty was not the sole source
of discomfort. Be this, however, as it may,

and without pausing to quote on both sides of
the question the learned and voluminous opinions of the leading German and Dutch commentators, I risk nothing in asserting that had
the whale been fitted, in respect to his interior
accommodations, according to the patent of
a namesake of the prophet, Mr. Jonah Wood-
ruff, the trip to Tarshish might have been
accomplished without, at least, any physical
inconvenience.   The fact deserves to be noted
by all those who hold to a kind of divine
significance in proper names.

     .   .   .   .

Time flies apace, and my fuller impressions
of Chicago must be reserved for another letter.   The city whose daily price-current de-
termines the price of grain throughout the
world, can hardly be dispatched at the end of
a sheet.   I will only add, that, although the
skill of the Garden City has succeeded in tap-
ping the bottom of Lake Michigan to obtain
an abundance of pure water, some misgiving
as to the extent of the supply seems, as yet, to
have prevented any extensive adoption of it
as a beverage.   It may be that the apprehen-
sion has arisen, that should the water of the
lake be used too freely, not enough would be
left to keep up the " solemn bass " of Niagara.

TO PRESIDENT ANGELL.

PROVIDENCE, *August* 14, 1867.

I was delighted with your address. It gave me a feeling of deep regret, as I recognized your high ideal of academic training, that we were not working in the same institution. The state of things here is discouraging. Much is said of the importance of having a "consistent Baptist" at the head of the institution, but not a word about elevating the standard of scholarship, or extending the means of instruction. We have a set of men in the corporation who are not enough interested in the inner working of the college even to attend the examinations.

You have made a good move in changing the mode of electing your trustees. We ought to do the same thing. Gammell and I are doing what we can to bring it about by seminal articles in the paper.

By the first opportunity I shall send you a copy of "Cotton." The view which I advance, so far as I have been able to find, is new. It naturally has not met with much favor here, but has been very warmly commended by some of the Boston men. . . .

This reprint of "Master John Cotton's An-

swer to Master Roger Williams " is the second
volume of the publications of the Narragansett Club. The editor's preface is dated
March, 1867. It makes a volume of over
two hundred pages, with an appendix, and a
hundred and eight notes on the text, the results of Mr. Diman's researches, and study in
the original authorities, to which he refers in
a previous letter.

" After this most able analysis by a Rhode
Island scholar and professor in her University,
of the statements of both Cotton and Williams,
there should no longer be any want of agreement among the historians of Massachusetts
and Rhode Island, as to the opinions which
Williams held, and the relation which he sustained to the churches and to the civil authorities of Massachusetts during his residence
there, or as to the true reasons for his banishment from that colony." [1]

Dr. George E. Ellis, of the Massachusetts
Historical Society, writes of this volume:
" Professor Diman's view and presentment of
the character and course of Roger Williams
seemed to me to be the most thoroughly adequate, impartial, and judicial treatment of his
subject that has ever been given."

[1] *North American Review*, April, 1868.

A learned discussion in relation to Roger Williams, between " Clericus," Mr. Samuel L. Caldwell, and " Historicus," Mr. Diman, was printed shortly after this, in the columns of the " Journal." The discussion covered a period of some months, and for several years Mr. Diman occasionally wrote on the subject. " What Williams taught," he asserted, " was not the duty of the civil ruler to tolerate religious opinions, but the far more fruitful doctrine, that religion did not need to ask for toleration, and was in its nature separate from all civil power."

Many will remember the memorial address on the life of Professor Robinson Potter Dunn, and have special interest in the following letters.

TO PRESIDENT ANGELL.

PROVIDENCE, *September* 24, 1867.

In accordance with a very generally expressed desire it has been decided that a discourse in commemoration of Dunn should be given before the college, and as it is designed to be an academic matter, the choice has fallen upon me. I feel a good deal of hesitation about it, although no one appreciated Dunn more highly, or is more sensible of the loss the college has sustained; but my relations with him were never quite as intimate as yours, or perhaps Caldwell's. Had you been here, the choice would not have fallen upon me. Having accepted the task, however, I am very anxious that it should be adequately performed, and it would be a very great favor if you would make any suggestions that may occur to you. I want especially to present him in his relations to the college. You were intimately acquainted with him several years, and of course must have received a marked impression of some sort. If you have time to give me a hint or two it will greatly oblige.

We have had serious trouble in College. Chace has taken the Senior Class, giving up the Juniors to an inexperienced tutor. The death of Dunn required that a similar arrangement should be made with Rhetoric. The latter was a necessity, but in the former case the class felt, and I think justly, that their rights had been disregarded. To be deprived of two professors at the same time was too much. Several have left, and serious dissatisfaction still exists, although there will probably be no open resistance. When will the Corporation learn that the success of a college depends upon accomplished teachers? Unless they wake up, Brown will sink to the rank of an academy. In this respect, how irreparable the loss of Dunn !

And now let me tell you a good story. Who should make his appearance in the "Journal" office yesterday, in a towering rage, but the Rev. Dr. ———. He demanded his bill, and said that the "Providence Journal" should never enter his doors again. And pray what do you think was the cause of all this ? A brief article, giving an outline of a recent opinion of Judge Read of Philadelphia, on Sunday cars, and indorsing the opinion. Now the joke of the whole matter is that the article in question was written by your humble servant.

This article on Sunday Cars is the one to which Professor Fisher refers, and which at the time excited much comment. It concludes : —

" We have given at some length an abstract of the opinion of Judge Read, because in its wide and complete discussion of the subject it touches upon points which will interest every thoughtful reader. Already, as it seems, the opinion has provoked violent assaults, but we do not doubt that in the end these views will commend themselves to the good sense of the community, sustained, as they are, by the judgment of the most eminent Biblical students, not less than by the instincts of humanity. As Judge Read truly calls it, the passenger car is the poor man's carriage."

The busy Berlin student, we have seen, took time to hunt up and relieve some poor neighbors, and to the end of his life, however busy he might be, Mr. Diman was a regular visitor of the sick in the hospitals, an errand of mercy in which, in later years, his daughter accompanied him. Her sweet voice was often heard among the children, following the lessons she had been taught both by precept and example.

The following brief article, entitled "Sermons in Storms," appeared in the "Journal" in December, 1867, and well did Mr. Diman practice what he so persuasively preached.

"The injunction to remember the poor, a willing compliance with which is always a leading characteristic of pure and undefiled religion, has come to us during the past few days, charged with peculiar emphasis. Who of us has not heard it in those wild northern blasts

that so mercilessly have swept our streets; who
of us, when seated by our cheerful firesides,
has not thought of the homeless and the destitute? The season has set in with unusual
severity, and finds a larger number than usual
unprepared to meet it. The continued de-
pression of business is already telling upon the
laboring classes. But in the most favorable
seasons there must always be many, in a community as large as this, who need a helping
hand to enable them to struggle through the
long winter. There are always some whom
sickness has kept from their usual employment, and some whom death has deprived of
the one to whom they looked for support.
These are the persons most deserving of help,
for their poverty is not the result of idleness
or vice, but of circumstances over which they
have no control.

" We have in our city ample provision for
public charity. The care of the poor is entrusted to capable officers, and we have no
doubt that the trust is faithfully and wisely
executed. We have, also, several excellent
private organizations, all of which are doing a
good work. But none of them should be allowed to take the place of personal effort in
this direction. That charity is thrice blessed

which we administer ourselves. A kindly word will sometimes do more to cheer a desponding heart than a gift of clothing or food; and the bread given to the starving is sweeter if a genuine sympathy goes with it. We entreat our readers, whenever a case of destitution and suffering shall come under their notice, to give it at once their personal attention, and not relinquish to any organization the most blessed of all privileges, the privilege of making those around us happy. We may rest assured that we shall never hereafter look back with repining upon the time that has been spent in thus personally administering to the wants of the poor."

Mr. Diman himself bids farewell to the year : —

" The days which are declared, in the most ancient and impressive of books, to be swifter than a weaver's shuttle, have again finished their appointed round, and we greet our readers for the last time in eighteen hundred and sixty-seven. It is only repeating a commonplace remark, yet one that to-day suggests itself to every mind, when we add that each year seems shorter than the year before. True, the external measurements of time remain unaltered. The planets pursue the same even course which they pursued when the wondering eye of the patriarch noted the stately steppings of Arcturus and the Pleiades. But the inner and spiritual milestones of life's journey crowd closer and closer together as we draw nigh to the end, so that many, we doubt not, among our older readers, will repeat with emphasis, to-day, the solemn burden of the Psalmist, " We spend our years as a tale that is told ;" and however trite and familiar the reflections which the dying year awakens, it can hardly fail to be of some benefit to every one of us to give a few sober thoughts to the unreturning Past. What have we done for it, and what has it done for us ?

" It has been ordered, by the unerring wisdom that shapes all events, that we should weave the mystic tapestry of Life, like the Gobelin workmen, from behind, seeing the rough shreds and confused colors, but not the complete and perfect work. It is a thought full of comfort and hope, amid the jars and wrecks of earthly things, that these pictures of time, that to human gaze seem so unlovely and confused, seen from the divine side, blend into perfect harmony. Whether for good or for evil, the largest results lie hid from our

inspection.   What any of us has consciously
attempted or achieved, is but a small part of
his actual work.   And what is true of the individual life, is not less true of the larger life
of society.   So that, curiously as we may reflect upon the events of the past year, and dili-
gently as we may ponder what seem to us the
chief aspects in its ever shifting scenes, yet it
must be with the humbling acknowledgment
that the long results of time are hid from
human view, and that no mortal is worthy to
take the Book which discloses the future, and
to unloose the seals thereof."

CHAPTER IX.

Connection with the Providence Daily Journal. — Editorials.
— English Politics. — German Politics. — Franco-Prussian
War. — Reviews. — Religious and Educational Topics. —
Fourth-of-July, Thanksgiving, and New Year's Articles. —
Christmas.

AT the time of Mr. Diman's coming to Providence his friend Mr. James Burrill Angell was editor of the Providence Journal. For this paper Mr. Diman began to write foreign articles, reviews of books, or comments on the events of the day.   It must be remembered, to make any fair estimate of his life and character, that he was a preacher and critic, first and foremost.   The two, he would have said, were not only compatible, but could hardly exist without each other.   A preacher proclaims truth ; a critic, in the best sense, leads men to see it in what exists.   The reticence in expressing his deepest convictions, and the reserve that underlay his open and frank manner, have been already noticed.   Behind the veil of the editorial, he was able to express himself as freely as in the pulpit, and from this time an important part of his life's work appeared in the columns of a daily paper. Those who read with delight the liberal discussions of European affairs, the stimulating and pertinent articles on Rhode Island topics, or listened to the solemn voice that set forth the mercies of God at Thanksgiving time, or bade farewell to the dying year, may well agree that his life made a part of their own.

Mr. Angell left the "Journal," and Providence, in 1866, but Mr. Diman continued to write for the paper throughout his life.

The bulk of his work was done in the years immediately following Mr. Angell's departure, and covered a wide range of subjects. His views as to the function of a newspaper he thus sets forth : — " The successful conduct of a daily paper aiming to take high rank as a guide of public opinion is attended with peculiar difficulties, difficulties which our readers cannot fully appreciate. If we conceived that our only function was to wait on public sentiment, and echo the prevailing opinion around us, the labor would be greatly simplified. But believing that our readers look to us for an honest and straightforward expression of our own sentiments, we cannot avoid the peril at times of offending some for whom we cherish the utmost respect, and of being misunderstood by others upon whose good opinion we place the highest value. The articles that appear in a daily paper cannot be prepared with the care that is devoted to the articles in a quarterly review. The good old days have long since departed when editors went home to tea, leaving the paper ready for the press. We have often to write with a swift pen, and no one can be more conscious than we ourselves are, that much that is written might be improved, and that sometimes a word is said which were better left unsaid. But we have in all cases submitted to fair and manly criticisms, and have freely opened our columns, in every instance, to those whose opinions differed widely from our own, whenever such opinions were expressed in courteous and temperate language."

In English politics Mr. Diman always had special interest. Mr. Gladstone has been the central figure there for years, and what Mr. Diman wrote of him in 1868 is still true.

" Hailed at the beginning of his career as the rising hope of the High Church party, and as such severely handled by Macaulay, in one of those brilliant articles which promised for a time to restore the Edinburgh Review to its old position at the head of the English quarterlies; afterwards a most devoted follower of Sir Robert Peel, in his secession from the Conservative party on the memorable question of the Corn Laws; then entering the Cabinet as member of a liberal administration, although until quite recently the favorite representative of the University of Oxford; always a distinguished proficient in that fine classical scholarship which Oxford so loves and cultivates; Mr. Gladstone has proved himself altogether too brilliant and versatile a man to keep, for a long time, on good terms with any party. Always fond of nice discrimination; not unfrequently balancing the opposite bearings of a question with such appreciative justice as to leave his own final conclusion enveloped in no little doubt; at times leaping forward to theoretical results with such rapidity as to leave his followers in dismay, and again showing evident irresolution in dealing with direct practical issues; Mr. Gladstone is not the kind of leader to carry with him always, such a peculiarly constituted body as the House of Commons.

" The opponents of Mr. Gladstone have not

been slow to reproach him with inconsistency, but we cannot so interpret his political career. It seems to us that all his changes are capable of being easily explained as the logical transitions of an active, inquiring, progressive mind. He is not ashamed to confess that thirty years have modified his opinions. He has been called mediæval by one party, and revolutionary by another. This means simply that he is many-sided, and, like all men of large and varied culture, he is liable to be misunderstood by mere party-men. 'No man,' was once said in the hearing of Goethe, 'is a hero to his valet.' 'Not,' replied the poet, 'because the hero is not a hero, but because the valet is a valet.' " . . .

There were editorials on " The Premier's Perplexity," " The Irish Church Question," " The House of Lords," tracing the decline of its influence, and on " The Queen," giving an outline of her inherited tendencies and prejudices. Mr. Diman's power of presenting persons, as the embodiment of institutions, was never better shown than in such articles as these. Of the leaders in England, Disraeli and Gladstone, he wrote with the keenest insight. His faith in Mr. Gladstone's capacity of leadership wavered a little. Years have only proved the truth of what he wrote in 1868. " There is apt to be something mediæval, academic, pedantic, in his way of putting things, indicating after all a lack of large practical grasp. . . . It may be questioned whether if the time spent by Mr. Gladstone in investigating the Homeric page, had been devoted to matters directly before his eyes, he would not have made a far more successful minister.

" The present aspect of affairs in England is full of interest to the thoughtful observer. Few people in this country, we imagine, are aware of the extent of the revolution which is there taking place. Vast as was the change effected in 1832, it was, as the ' Times ' truly remarks, insignificant by the side of the change effected in 1867. A complete transference of power has been silently effected, the results of which the wisest cannot venture to predict. With a sovereign whose power is reduced to a constitutional fiction, and whose sceptre has been rendered more shadowy by years of seclusion; with a Church powerless to define and vindicate its own faith, and confessedly unable to allure to its service the leading young men in either University; and with a House of Lords that

has virtually abdicated its functions as a legislative body, England seems to be on the
threshold of some momentous transformation.
Obsolete institutions are maintained in existence for a time by the respect which men in-
stinctively feel for what has long continued,
but the most firmly rooted sentiment is in
danger of being vanquished when it is found
that repairs have come to be more troublesome
and costly than building from new foundations." . . .

Mr. Diman's gift at describing a man in a
few words which bring him vividly before the
mind, is well exemplified in the following : —

"The personal traits of Lord Brougham
were most happily represented by his nose, a
feature which ' Punch ' always delighted to
draw, and which has been most aptly described as ' protuberant, aggressive, inquiring,
and defiant; unlovely, but intellectual.' His
caustic temper and close invective, an exception to parliamentary usage, involved him in
frequent personal collisions, and when on one
occasion he so far forgot himself as to insult,
from the woolsack, a far more eminent lawyer
than himself, it drew forth the just retort that,
if Brougham only had a little decency, he
would have a smattering of almost everything."

His years of study in Germany gave Mr. Diman special interest in German affairs, and he watched the successive stages in the growth of the German empire with the greatest attention. " Those of our readers," he wrote in July, 1866, " who were familiar with Berlin ten years ago, when the present king was crown-prince, will remember his well-known habit of standing by a window of his palace that faced the statue of Frederic, chatting with his aides-de-camp. Perhaps even then, with the prospect of succeeding his childless brother, he may have caught some inspiration from the gaunt bronze figure that he could not fail to see whenever he raised his eye ; but his wildest and most ambitious dreams, if he indulged in them, could hardly have compassed the reality he has lived to see. On one day the dignified assembly, which embodied the majesty, and claimed to direct the military force of fifteen dynasties, was issuing at Frankfort those Federal decrees, to which twenty-six millions of the German race had been accustomed to accord a willing, and twenty-five millions of other races a forced obedience ; and four days later twelve of these dynasties had ceased to possess any independent political existence. Saxony and

Hanover were seized without a struggle ; the Elbe duchies, the innocent occasion of the strife, incorporated with Prussia by the simple omission of a word ; the despised and hated elector of Hesse driven from his dominions ; Oldenburg and Anhalt compelled to renounce the confederation ; the lesser dukes forced to accept commands in the Prussian army, or at least to abdicate their separate military power ; the fine city of Hamburg held by a Prussian general of division ; surely, could the bronze lips of Frederic speak, they would utter grim satisfaction at such results as these."

Mr. Diman gathered his information from the foreign papers, and constantly wrote editorials setting forth the latest views of German affairs as presented in them, adding his own comments, and making the most complicated series of events perfectly intelligible to his readers.

Throughout the Franco-Prussian war his pen was busy. Editorials on " The Proceedings of the French Emperor," " The Tender Mercies of War," " Chalons-sur-Marne," and " The Tuileries," are among the most important. " No revolution," he writes, " would be complete in France that lacked a dramatic element, and the spectacle of the white flag marked with the red cross that now floats over the palace of the Tuileries gratifies a sentiment in the national heart hardly less strong than the love of glory itself. The palace is a monument to the wonderful vicissitudes of French history; and its walls, had they tongues to speak, could tell a story stranger and sadder than was ever embodied in any fiction." Then follows a brief history of the palace from the time when Catherine de Medicis " conceived the design of converting the desolate tile yard, that stretched westward from the Louvre, into the site of a fair royal residence," tracing its fortunes through the days of Henry IV. and Louis XIV., and the Reign of Terror. " No royal residence has ever been the scene of more memorable revolutions, but among them all, none has awakened such hearty acquiescence as that which has substituted for the frivolities of a corrupt court, the sweet ministrations of the Sisters of Charity."

The closing events of the war were set forth in an editorial on the Downfall of Napoleon III. . . .

" For the most conspicuous actor in this strange, eventful history, we confess to feeling little sympathy. Those who sow the wind have no reason to complain if they reap the whirlwind, and the public sentiment of mankind recognizes the just retribution which has so swiftly overtaken him, whose supreme, miscalculating selfishness was willing to threaten Europe with the horrors of universal war. . . .

" The surrender at Sedan will be memorable in history, not so much for marking the overthrow of a war as the overthrow of a system. It is devoutly to be hoped that Cæsarism has received its death-blow. When our civil war broke out, the announcement was somewhat prematurely made that republican institutions had proved a failure. The first European sovereign to be convinced of this, the one who urged most pertinaciously the recognition of the Southern States, was Napoleon III. He may now profitably ask himself the question whether the system of personal government has proved a complete success. For wellnigh twenty years he has held the reins in his own hands ; his absolute will has controlled the internal administration not less than the foreign policy of France, yet in the hour of trial he has seen his army of ill-disciplined conscripts shattered by the citizen-soldiery of Prussia, while he has not dared to trust himself within the walls of his own capital. He has been weighed in the balances and found wanting. With an opportunity of making himself the organ of an enlightened public sentiment seldom vouchsafed to a man in any age, he has initiated no useful policy and created no permanent institutions. He has done nothing to fit France for self-government; he has interfered with foreign states only in behalf of arbitrary power. His occupation of Rome was as clear an index of his political sympathies as the disastrous experiment in Mexico, which proved the prelude to his fall."

Beside the foreign articles, some idea of which can be obtained from the foregoing extracts, Mr. Diman wrote reviews of books, and articles of a more local character. Tuckerman's "Book of the Artists" had a long notice, tracing especially the influence of Rhode Island artists upon the growth of American art. "The continuous historical development of American art did not begin until Bishop Berkeley induced the Scotch painter Smybert to join with him in his benevolent scheme of carrying arts and letters to the new world." Thus Rhode Island became the birthplace of American art.

Some years later Mr. Diman wrote reviews for the "Nation" and for some of the monthlies, which were brilliant and suggestive. But for the " Journal," while his reviews were not so extended and elaborate, there were articles on new books which much more than set forth their merits or defects. He called attention to any important essays in the current magazines, and in examining the views of opponents, had to an eminent degree the spirit he commends in the Duke of Argyle.

" How rare and beautiful," he writes, " is the spirit that breathes in the following sentence : —

" ' Then as regards opponents, who has ever tried to follow their arguments with candor, without finding how much more they have to say for their opinions, than we had conceived possible before? How strong is their hold of some important truths to which we perhaps had been comparatively insensible, and how much there is really good and true at the bottom even of their very errors.'

" For expressing these sentiments we doubt not that the Duke himself will be denounced by all such as believe that misrepresentation and abuse are legitimate weapons of religious controversy, but they are views which will commend themselves to the increasing number who hold that charity has a place among Christian virtues."

The following review of " The Day of Doom " is so characteristic that it is given entire.

" The curious little poem which bears the above title, and which has just been reprinted by the American News Company of New York, may be best described as the *Dies Irae* of New England. We do not mean by this that it has the solemn grandeur and majestic rhythm of the masterpiece of mediæval song, some of the verses of which Dr. Johnson could never repeat without tears, but simply that as the *Dies Irae* set to music the fundamental religious conceptions of the Middle Ages, so the Day of Doom sets forth in a very striking manner the popular religious notions prevailing in New England at the close of the seventeenth century. In one respect the Day of Doom has a great advantage over the *Dies Irae*. The author of the latter poem has never been clearly ascertained. While it has been commonly ascribed to Thomas of Celano, there have not been wanting writers to urge the claims of Gregory the Great, and even of Felix Hammerlin, a church dignitary of Zurich, whose name was latinized into *Malleolus*, or, as we should say in English, Little Hammer. But respecting the authorship of the Day of

Doom, we are not aware that the most audacious critic has ever raised a question. We may question whether any such man as Homer ever existed ; we may give up the Epistles of Phalaris ; we may reduce Ossian to a Scotch mist ; but there seems no good reason to doubt that the Day of Doom was actually composed, as the title-page declares, ' by Michael Wigglesworth, A. M., teacher of the church at Malden, in New England.' Our young readers perhaps need to be informed that in those good old days, when Quakers were whipped, and witches were hung, the duties of the ministry were considered too arduous for any single individual, and accordingly most churches rejoiced in two spiritual heads, a pastor and a teacher. That the Rev. Michael Wigglesworth is not, after all, a myth, but did actually, and in the flesh, hold this office, is proved beyond any reasonable doubt from the fact that there still exists in print a funeral sermon, setting forth his virtues, which was preached at Malden, June 24, 1705, by that most modest and veracious of Massachusetts divines, the Reverend Cotton Mather, D.D., F.R.S.

" No poetry was more popular in New England a century ago than the Day of Doom.

It was first published in 1662, and the first edition, consisting of eighteen hundred copies, was sold within a year, a popularity which, when we take into account the extent of the reading public of that age, is not surpassed by the most famed productions of Scott, or Dickens, in our own time. The poem at once took its place by the side of the Catechism ; at the beginning of the present century many an aged person was alive who could repeat almost the whole from memory. In his funeral sermon, Cotton Mather speaks of it as having 'been often reprinted in both *Englands* and may find our children till the *Day* itself arrive.'

" As the title indicates, the poem is a description of the Day of Judgment. The various conditions of men, who will make their appearance on that dread occasion, are represented as coming before the Final Arbiter and urging their several pleas. After the saints have been justified, the several sorts of reprobates are described. Among these are hypocrites, 'civil honest men,' and heathen. But altogether the most remarkable and interesting of this class are the reprobate infants, who in their turn come forward, and urge the injustice of being made to suffer eternal torments for a sin which they had never committed, and for which Adam alone, they claim, should be held responsible. Say the infants : —

> ' Not we, but he ate of the tree,
>   whose fruit was interdicted ;
> Yet on us all of his sad Fall
>   the punishment's inflicted.
> How could we sin, that had not been,
>   or how is his sin, our,
> Without consent, which to prevent
>   we never had the power.'

" To this shocking theological heresy the Final Judge, or we should rather say, the Rev. Michael Wigglesworth, teacher of the church at Malden, replies. His words deserve to be quoted as a most curious illustration of the popular theology of the time. We assure our readers that the whole was not introduced as a grim burlesque, but expressing the serious convictions of that age. After reading these lines no one will cavil at the remark of the editor of the volume, that ' Mr. Wigglesworth borrowed little from other poets.' This is the answer to the plea of the infants respecting their relation to Adam : —

> ' He was designed of all Mankind
>   to be a public Head ;
> A common Root, whence all should shoot,
>   and stand in all their stead.
> He stood and fell, did ill or well,
>   not for himself alone,
> But for you all, who now his Fall
>   and trespass would disown.

> 'Would you have griev'd to have received
>   through Adam so much good,
> As had been your forevermore,
>   if he at first had stood ?
> Would you have said, ' We ne'er obey'd
>   nor did thy laws regard ;
> It ill befits with benefits,
>   us, Lord, to so reward ' ?

> ' Since then to share in his welfare,
>   you would have been content,
> You may with reason share in his treason,
>   and in the punishment.'

"But while the relation of infants to Adam is a crime, still a distinction is drawn : —

> ' A crime it is, therefore in bliss
>   you may not hope to dwell ;
> But unto you I shall allow
>   the easiest room in Hell.' "

Questions of the day could not fail to interest Mr. Diman. In an editorial on "Sectarian Religion in Public Schools," he maintained that the children of the Baptist, the Quaker, the Methodist, and the Catholic, must meet at school upon exact terms of equality. He also wrote on "Our Roman Catholic Brethren," and a "New View of Ritualism." "It is always easier to ridicule the external badges of a party than to appreciate their honest motives," he wrote; and in these articles he extended "the fair play to our Rit-

ualistic friends," which he was of the opinion
they had not received.

In a long article on a Free Church, he set
forth his convictions of the importance of the
subject : —

" There is no practical problem now pressing with more urgency upon the consideration
of Protestant Christians, of every name, than
that which relates to the most efficient methods of placing the Gospel within the easy
reach of every class in the community. On
the solution of this problem depends the further question whether the whole voluntary system shall be regarded as a success. For few
will hesitate to confess, that, if the voluntary
system simply means that those who can afford it shall enjoy the privilege of listening,
for a brief portion of one day in seven, to the
polished discourses of favorite pulpit orators,
and the strains of well-paid tenors and so-
pranos, the sooner the general religious instruction of the people is undertaken by the
State the better. The crying fault of the
voluntary system is its exclusiveness, and no
one can tread the nave of a great European
minster, where the rich light, streaming
through the painted window, bathes king

and beggar alike as they kneel together before a common Maker, without feeling that American Christians have much to learn respecting the right method of worshiping that Being, who is no respecter of persons." . . .

All educational problems were of interest to Mr. Diman, especially were his sympathies called out for the deaf. A lengthy article is devoted to an historical review of the Methods of Deaf-Mute Education. The public schools also received his attention. For six years he was on the school board, and had a personal interest in their conduct. He called attention through the " Journal" to their needs, or to the annual reports, and pleaded for the establishment of a summer school where something of the Kindergarten system could be introduced.

The Rhode Island Historical Society also felt the stimulus of his interest, and he wrote the " seminal articles " [1] on Brown University affairs to which his letters refer.

The love for his birthplace found expression in articles on " the first Church in Bristol," on " the late Robert Rogers," one of the famous merchants of the old seaport, and on

[1] See page 161.

" Crowne the Poet," who was singularly connected with the town.   The fair peninsula,

> " Whose girdled charms
> Were Philips' ancient sway — "

" narrowly escaped the odd fate of being conferred by the good-natured Charles II. upon
the English comic poet," an episode in the
history of the colonies which is recounted
with much interest.

In addition to these articles, and many
more on kindred subjects, for six or eight
years, Mr. Diman wrote the annual holiday
articles, which were full of his own charm and
grace.

For the Fourth of July he wrote short historical essays, usually ending in a plea that the
day should not be degraded into a common
carnival.

" The profoundest conditions of national
development are spiritual rather than physical.
. . . This is the day in which the inspirations
of nationality are centered.

. . . . "In spite of the noisy demonstrations
which have rendered it well-nigh intolerable,
the Fourth of July is an anniversary full of
proud and sacred recollections, a day in the
calendar which no intelligent American will
ever willingly see forgotten or disregarded.

One of the purest patriots of the Revolution predicted that its annual return would never cease to be the occasion of patriotic rejoicing, and for half a century the elder Adams was spared to see his words verified in the gathering of his fellow-citizens to the temples of religion, where with solemn ceremonial, with the voice of thanksgiving, and with words of eloquence, the fires were kindled afresh on the public altars. We deeply regret that all this is changed, and that the Day which was once celebrated with fit decorum has been allowed to sink into an unmeaning carnival. We do not complain of the boys. We have no desire to see their fun restricted. But we would have grown-up men keep the festival after a different fashion. They are old enough to appreciate its lessons."

The Thanksgiving articles express the love of home and family so characteristic of their writer, and the Christmas celebrations are tender with his love of children. " In this over-worked and weary world little is left of Heaven save childhood with its innocent joys. Each new-born babe, had we but eyes to discern it, repeats the old miracle of divinity veiled in the flesh, and except we become as little children, Heaven hides itself from our searching ken."

For New Year's there are little sermons full of hope and courage, and constant looking for the things that are not seen : —

"As soldiers who with slow step and solemn dirge have followed a comrade to his grave, soon as the funeral service has been completed strike up a lively march, so we, who have just paid the last sad rites to Sixty-seven, hasten this morning to offer a cheery welcome to Sixty-eight. By such swift transition are we ever gliding from the Past to the Future ; so shadowy and evanescent is that ever-changing Present, which we seek in vain to stay in its restless course. In the pressure of new duties that crowd thick upon us, we have little time to bewail those that we have left undone. A wiser than any human teaching warns us to cast every weight aside, and run the race that is set before us. For our work lies in front, and not in the rear ; and the lessons of bygone experiences are only then useful when they lead us to act more wisely hereafter. Not from the things that have been, but from the things that shall be, does religion draw her most inspiring motives, and ever from the earthly Jerusalem does the eye of faith turn to the Jerusalem which is mother of us all."

This unknown work of newspaper writing sprang from sincere conviction.

"Of what value are letters, if they withdraw us from the duties of life?" he writes. "There is no room in this land for the cloistered seclusion of the old world. In a republic recognizing political equality as its corner-stone, every man, and especially every man of learning and culture, owes the commonwealth a debt. When public opinion shapes with resistless power the course of events, and the principles embraced by the masses are the inspiration of political action, those who are qualified to mould opinion, and enforce principles, should be the very last to retire from the arena."

It was in this spirit Mr. Diman's editorials were written. They were written with a rapid pen as he says, but it is amazing, in looking over the large volume that contains them, to find such finished and careful work. As his sentences fell from his lips perfectly balanced and rounded, or crisp and epigrammatic, according to his theme, so with his pen. He had no reserves of learning. It was all at command, ready to draw upon at the instant, and at the service of all. It illuminated his simplest paragraph, and weighted his strongest argument.

But few outside the Journal office knew the extent of his work, or conceived of the variety of subjects he treated. He held no public positions, but who shall say that "the earnest responsibilities of the citizen" were not worthily fulfilled?

The psalm in prose for Christmas, 1868, touches the chord which vibrated throughout his life, to which all else was tuned. The hearing of this "heavenly strain," amid the din of busy daily life, gave him his power and influence. It was this that opened his ears to the "music of humanity."

"It was while standing at sunrise on the ramparts of Quebec, as Mr. Webster tells us, and listening to the morning drum-beat as it reverberated across the plains of Abraham, that the fine thought was first suggested to him, which was afterwards elaborated into one of his most effective sentences, of the martial airs of England keeping company with the hours and encircling the earth with a continuous strain of music. But a thought more sublime than this may suggest itself, this morning, to any who have an ear for the ' music of humanity ; ' the thought of a heavenly strain that sounds from age to age, as well as from land to land, a strain that through eighteen weary and toiling centuries has made itself heard above the tumult of the nations, proclaiming peace on earth and good will to men, and which this morning, first greeting the early dawn in what is probably the most ancient monument of Christian architecture in the world, the church of the Nativity at Bethlehem, next circling amid the Isles of Greece, then filling with the grandest harmonies of modern music the matchless dome of Michael Angelo, and so onward and onward through sunny regions, where the Almighty is still worshiped in the ritual of Gregory and Ambrose, or where, beneath a more northern sky, the disciples of Calvin and of Luther join in joyous observance of the one great event to which Catholic and Protestant alike look back, crossing ocean and continent, making the waves clap their hands and the mountains break forth into singing, telling in every tongue the same marvelous story, how Christ was born, the Saviour of the world ! So let

it go, for in that strain are the hopes of men.
With it go the holiest influences, the purest
joys, that sweeten the life of man! Healing
is in its wings, and wherever its divine melody
is heard amid earth's unquiet strife, the wilder-
ness and the solitary place are glad, and the
desert rejoices and blossoms as the rose.

> ' Ring in the day, sweet chiming bells,
>   Earth's strangest tale your music tells,
>   How Christ, a little infant, came,
>   Born 'mid the beasts of Bethlehem.
>   Ring on, sweet bells,
>   Till mingling swells,
>   That tell his birth, chime round the earth.' "

CHAPTER X.

1868.   AET. 37.

THE letters to President James B. Angell, who in 1868 was still in Burlington, Vermont, have naturally a full account of Mr. Diman's college work. His own words, in relation to another, describe himself. " A true professor, like a poet, must be born, not made. He must have original aptitudes, and be swayed by enthusiasm for some particular study. There is no more ambiguous compliment than to say that a man could excel in any branch ; such general and indeterminate excellence is never the highest sort. True, Fontinelle declared of Leibnitz that he ' drove the sciences abreast ; ' but universal geniuses are century plants. The highest style of academic teaching can never be attained, save when each professor is called to his specific work by a diviner election than that of the college corporation." [1]

TO PRESIDENT ANGELL.

PROVIDENCE, *July* 8, 1868.

My prodigious devotion to academic duties is the only excuse I can urge for allowing your letter to remain so long unanswered. The term has been a very busy, as well as pleasant, one with me. In the first part I wrote a wholly new course of lectures on the Reformation, the most perplexing and difficult of all periods. How unlike the simple problems and easily analyzed phenomena of the mediæval era! The fundamental question raised, that of the limits of authority, remains to-day about where the Council of Trent left it. In the latter part of the term I went pretty fully into Colonial History, which I endeavored to present in its chief lines of development as a continuation of the great European movement, closing with new lectures on the Constitution of the United States, studied, not so much with regard to specific details, as with regard to fundamental political ideas, which were reviewed historically, as, *e. g.*, the theory of sov-

---

[1] *In Memoriam :* Robinson Potter Dunn, p. 64.

ereignty compared with the feudal; the federal idea compared with the ancient and European; the theory of representation compared with the English, not in form but in principle.

In this last I became very much interested. Many suggestions I derived from Brownson, J. C. Hurd, and the recent works of Farrar. It does not seem to me that either Kent or Story ever studied the Constitution profoundly in its relation to the whole course of modern political development. The former is particularly inexact in some of his statements. One part of the study in which I took great delight was in tracing the influence of Roman ideas on our political maxims. In this, Maine's "Ancient Law" was a help.

I have also had a capital class in Political Economy, in point of numbers by far the largest I ever had. It is, you remember, an elective study. I enjoy teaching it, as it admits of such clear analysis and precise statement.

Besides a good many books needed for my special work, I have recently been reading the concluding volumes of Motley, and am just finishing Kirk's "Charles the Bold." The sin of all American historians is diffuseness. Why do they not imitate the ancients?

Have you looked into the new " History of England " by Pearson ? He makes no claims to original research, but condenses all the latest results, which in the Saxon and Norman periods is a great convenience. There is also a new " History of the Norman Conquest" by Freeman, whose " History of Federal Governments " I have found very useful. I keep the run of English and foreign publications, and get for the library all that is valuable. For my religion I have been reading the "Life of Lacordaire," and "Unspoken Sermons," by George Macdonald, a book which you would enjoy.

Accept this letter as only a brief part of what I might say, were we face to face.

The lectures on Political Economy were a Junior " elective " for the last half year. There were usually about thirty lectures, two being delivered each week of the term. Mr. Diman divided the subject broadly into two parts, Production and Exchange. To the lectures strictly belonging to his subject he added a lecture on the history of Socialism in the United States, describing the growth of the various communities which have flourished here. At the end of the course he usually gave a lecture on taxation, and one on the National debt.

TO PRESIDENT ANGELL.

PROVIDENCE, *November* 11, 1868.

We are getting on very quietly at college. I have been hard at work studying French institutions at the time of Charlemagne. I find that from natural taste my lectures more and more resolve themselves into a study of political institutions. I derive much help from the capital works of Lehuerou.

To the young men of the Senior class, assembled in his lecture-room in University Hall, in the first week of the college term, Mr. Diman was accustomed to deliver a lecture upon the value and uses of the study of History. He usually read the lecture here given, which was written in 1865. If, in the latter part of his life, Mr. Diman dispensed almost entirely with notes, the substance was still essentially the same, as is shown by the lecture-book of Mr. F. R. Hazard, of the last class Mr. Diman instructed (1881).

One modification in the lecture may be specially noted, as marking the growth of Mr. Diman's own conceptions : the spiritualizing of his views. As written, a sentence reads, " Religion first taught the unity of the race." A pencil has crossed out the first word, and the sentence stands, " Revelation first taught the unity of the race." There are no means of telling how long an interval of time elapsed between the original writing and the correction. But the pencil makes marked modification, cutting out a few paragraphs and adding fresh illustrations, and is the guide which has been followed in the version of the lecture here given : —

INTRODUCTORY LECTURE.

Before entering upon a course so conspicuous in academic discipline as History, the scope and method of the study deserve to be considered.

" A Professor of History, if I understand his duties rightly," said Dr. Arnold (in his Inaugural Lecture at Oxford), " has two principal objects : he must try to acquaint his hearers with the nature and value of the treasure for which they are searching ; and secondly, he must try to show them the best and speediest method of discovering and extracting it. The first of these two things may be done once for all ; but the second must be his habitual employment, the business of his professorial life." [1]

At the present time, then, I shall discuss the nature and value of historical studies; and I shall fail of my purpose if I do not satisfy you, not simply that the study deserves the important place assigned it in academic course, but that for the American student it has certain distinct and peculiar claims, not alone as completing the culture of a scholar, but even more as providing an essential part of the education of the citizen. It is a study that yields to no other in its practical bearings.

Goldwin Smith informs us that when the chair of Modern History was founded at Oxford in the reign of George I., the primary object was to train students for the public service. But the spirit of our institutions does not contemplate the training of a distinct class for any specific public duty. It is our glory that all positions of public influence and honor are thrown open to all classes of the people ; but with this opportunity is imposed at the same time the responsibility — a responsibility that rests with peculiar weight on such as claim to be educated — of being qualified for the performance of these duties.

[1] *Arnold's Modern History,* p. 26.

The value of History has been very vari-
ously estimated by different men and at different times.   Dr. Johnson, it is well known,
despised it; and the saying of Sir Robert
Walpole, that it was a tissue of untruths, has
been often quoted.   Montaigne, in his inimitable essays, does not scruple to confess that
he loved to read History for the reason simply
that it was pleasant and easy.   But Johnson's
vigorous understanding was yet too narrow
in its range to comprehend the broad aspects
and majestic sweeps of History; Walpole
knew it only as the gossip of courts; while
Montaigne, though living in the midst of the
most momentous of modern centuries, seems
never to have felt its pulsations, but in his
secluded tower thought of History, not as the
living drama unfolding about him every hour,
but as the story preserved in the unimpas-
sioned pages of Plutarch.   And if History be
regarded as no more than the chronicle of
past events, if it teaches no lessons of truth
and duty, if its successive evolutions have no
vital and necessary relation to the living present, then was Montaigne right in regarding it
as simply " pleasant and easy."

It is, however, the more surprising that
Bacon, in his famous division of the parts of

human learning in accordance with the parts
of man's understanding, assigning History to
the memory, Poetry to the imagination, and
Philosophy to the reason, should still have
failed to conceive of History as anything
more than chronicle. "History," says he,
" which may be called past and present History, is of three kinds, according to the object
which it propoundeth or pretendeth to represent; for it either represents a time, or a person, or an action. The first we call Chronicles,
the second, Lives, and the third, Narratives or
Relations." [1]

As a matter of fact, it was not until three-
quarters of a century after the publication of
the " Advancement of Learning " that the
first adequate conception of the study was set
forth by Bossuet in his celebrated discourse
on Universal History. It is a fact to be remembered that Christianity alone, teaching, as
it did, that God had made of one blood all
nations of the earth, could supply that idea of
the organic unity of the human race, which
forms the basis of the Philosophy of History.
The religious idea of the unity and universality of Providence suggested the philosophic
idea of the unity and universality of human
history.

<hr>

[1] *Bacon's Works,* vol. vi., p. 189.

This grand conception, presented by Bossuet from a point of view too exclusively religious, was in the next century extended by the Italian Vico, in his "New Science," published in 1725, to political affairs, while it was reserved for the German Herder, before that century had closed, in 1784, to trace in his "Ideas relating to the Philosophy of History," the connection between physical phenomena and the progress of society. To these three illustrious thinkers the Philosophy of History owes its origin. Representing three different nations, they represent at the same time the three different elements to which History in its last analysis must be reduced. Bossuet, a theologian, lays greatest emphasis on the divine element, Vico, jurisconsult, on the human, and Herder, a man of universal culture, on the natural. But these three elements, God, man, and nature, are the three essential constituents of History. In the present century the philosophic study of History has been simply an attempt to follow out these three directions. A disposition to lay exclusive stress upon some single one of these elements is the fault of most modern works.[1]

This sketch of the progress of Historical

[1] *E. g.*, Guizot, Buckle.

study has already in part exhibited to us its nature, and only by comprehending its nature can we appreciate its true value.

We have seen, that, as conceived by the most penetrating minds, History is not a dead and disconnected chronicle, but is instinct with order and life, that its phenomena must be made in every case to illustrate principles, and that its truths, certified by actual and long experience, are truths which wake

"To perish never."

To quote a saying not less true for being threadbare, "History is Philosophy teaching by example," and its teachings are all the more impressive and pointed because drawn from the experience of successive generations of men like ourselves; setting forth truths, not cold and abstract, like those of natural science, but burning with the passions, burdened by the sufferings, and gilded with the hopes of our common humanity; its pages tragic at times, as those which picture the weakness of Lear, and the remorse of Macbeth; at times melodious and splendid, as the seraphic chorus of Milton's angels.

The question here naturally arises, how far History is to be regarded as a science; and how far its facts, arranged and classified, are capable of yielding by established rules of induction any fixed laws of historical development; a question which marks the limit to which the study has thus far been carried, and which at present is the foremost problem presented to the historical student.

The Science of History and the Philosophy of History are, however, not the same. Without announcing that History is a science, we may claim that it has a Philosophy; in other words, without asserting that the actions of men, like the events in the physical world, are governed by fixed and inevitable laws, and that these laws can be deduced with the certainty with which we deduce the law of gravitation, we may assume that there exists a divine order in History, and that the great lessons set forth in the successive evolutions of this order may be interpreted. Without holding, with Buckle, that the history of civilization is like the growth of a tree, we may, with Guizot, analyze its successive phases.

This distinction between the Science of History and the Philosophy of History is still more clearly seen if we consider the two fundamental truths on which the Philosophy of History is built. These are: 1st, Unity; 2d, Progress. These are truths which no in-

ductive science of society ever reached, and
which may well be doubted whether it ever
could reach.   Science has indeed had much to
say of late years of development, but it is development proceeding from no recognized beginning and tending to no recognized end,
the ceaseless transformation of material substance.

For these two controlling ideas we are in-
debted not to inductive science, but to Revelation.   Revelation first taught the unity of the
race, and in its doctrine of a superintending
Providence first taught that, beneath the apparent confusion of human affairs, a divine
eternal plan was running smoothly on towards
final accomplishment.   In the nature of things
an inductive science could never unfold this
plan while the course of development was still
in progress.   Thus the Philosophy of History,
inspired by religion, is made wholly independent of the Science of History.

With this distinction recognized, it may be
further said that the study of History, pursued
philosophically, is the study of society; not
the mere loading of the memory with dates
and names, but the enlargement of the understanding in the recognition of general principles; not the investigation of isolated facts,

but the perception of connected movement. In this view institutions are obviously much more deserving of study than ever, and aspects of society are to be taken into account rather than details of battles and sieges.

And further, when the nature of History is thus understood, the objections to the study fall at once to the ground. Those objections may all at last be reduced to two.

1st. That the statements of History, for the most part, are not true.

2d. That if true, they are not worth learning. In support of the first, the many and acknowledged contradictions of History are alleged; and in support of the second it is asked, of what possible importance is it at the present day to know what was cut on the Rosetta Stone, or whether Rome was governed in the beginning by kings?

It might be said, indeed, in reply, that the same questions may with equal propriety be asked respecting a large portion of the knowledge that awakens human curiosity and stimulates human inquiry. It might, for example, as well be asked what use there is in knowing what fishes inhabit the Amazon, or the distances of the fixed stars ; but History may appeal to other, and sounder arguments to attest the value of her results. These results have a practical bearing on human duty and welfare that no natural science, however far-reaching and sublime, can claim.

We may grant that the statements of History are, in many cases, shrouded in uncertainty ; but this becomes a matter of comparatively slight consequence, when we remember that the great value of History is in its broader aspects and in its general truths. Uncertainty in specific details does not in the least affect the stability of these conclusions. We may doubt whether there ever existed such a man as Romulus, but we can have no doubt as to the growth and structure of the Roman constitution. The account of Catiline by Sallust we may put aside as a party pamphlet, but we cannot question that terrible political profligacy which worked at last the ruin of the republic. We may charitably suspect some details preserved respecting the private life of Charlemagne, but we cannot mistake the influence of the feudal system. The study of long-established and widespread institutions or of the grand results of historic progress are as independent of any questions respecting specific facts, as the study of the successive phases of Gothic architecture is independent of the question who was the designer of the Cologne Cathedral.

Again, we may grant that many facts of History are of little or no consequence, and deserve as little to be investigated as the questions by Tiberius to the grammarians, what song the sirens sang, or what dress Achilles assumed when he hid himself among the women; but this does not at all lessen the value of other facts, — facts which, like the facts of the natural world, derive their value from their relation to principles. A circumstance recorded by Thucydides or Tacitus may, in itself, be merely a curious incident; but it at once becomes far more than this when seen in its bearing upon some truth of universal and lasting import, or upon some question that society is now seeking anxiously to answer. No one can read the writings of the founders of our own federal government without perceiving how carefully they studied the structure of the ancient republics; and though the problems now given us as a nation to solve are in some respects unlike those given to any former age, yet who would say that the terrible convulsion that grew from the refusal of the Roman senate to extend the franchise, may not have a lesson which we cannot afford to neglect.

If now the question be asked, what is the special use and benefit of Historical study? I answer, that as History is the record of man's career, not as an individual, but as a social being, so the study of History is his best discipline for the performance of his social duties. " Histories," says Bacon, " make men wise." It cannot be doubted that the study of History forms the best preparation for the judicious performance of those duties which belong to men as members of society, and which, says Algernon Sidney, " seem so far to concern all mankind, that besides the influence on our future life, they may be said to comprehend all that in this world deserves to be cared for."

This relation of the study of History to sound political training gives to the study an unprecedented worth in a country like our own, where all are called to exercise the functions of the citizen, and where any may aspire to the highest spheres of public service. No young man can be considered educated who is not educated for these duties. Whatever may be the special calling he has in view, whatever profession he means to enter, or whatever business to engage in, he should never neglect to fit himself to those larger duties which will devolve upon him as a citizen of the Republic.

But when we further consider the vast influence which educated young men have always exerted, and always must exert, in a community like ours; when we call to mind the remark of one of the most sagacious thinkers that ever lived, "that the knowledge of the speculative principles adopted by young men is the surest guide to political prophecy," then the immense practical bearings of this study become still more obvious. A broad Historical training is the best possible safeguard against rank political theory. While, on the one hand, the teachings of History inculcate a lofty faith in human progress and in human destiny, still, on the other hand, they warn us that this progress is slow and often interrupted; that it is purchased with great sacrifices and with bitter suffering, and that while it cannot be delayed, so it cannot be hastened, by rash counsel or by ruinous extremes. " Thus," to quote the excellent advice of the Earl of Worcester, commending the study of History to Charles II., then Prince of Wales, " you shall see the excellences and the errors both of kings and subjects, and though you are young in years, yet living by your reading in all these times, be older in wisdom and judgment than nature can afford any man to be without this help."

It only remains to say that the study of History, while in some respects the most fascinating of studies, is in some respects the most difficult. As it is the study of man, it requires the knowledge which is the rarest of all, — the knowledge of human nature. We greatly mistake when we regard History as a study that tasks only the memory. To be pursued with success, it demands a ripe development of the judgment and the reasoning faculties. The imagination also enters into it as an essential part. There is scarcely a department of human science from which it does not levy its contributions.[1]

[1] Then follows a list of authorities : —
Bossuet, Vico, Herder.
Cousin, *Introduction à l'Histoire de la Philosophie.*
Abbé de Mably, *De l'Étude de l'Histoire.*
Bolingbroke, *Letters on the Study and Use of History.*
Arnold, *Lectures on Modern History.*
Goldwin Smith, *Lecture on Study of History.*
Comte, *Positive Philosophy.*
Westminster Review, Oct., 1842, Vol. 38.
J. S. Mill, *Logic*, Book VI.
Wm. Adam, *Theories of History.*
Buckle, *History of Civilization.*
Kant, *Idea of Universal History in a Cosmopolitan Point of View.* Works, vii. 317.
Stephens, *Lecture on History of France.*

The course of study thus introduced was divided into two parts: lectures on Mediaeval Institutions, and lectures on Modern History. A whole week was given to each lecture, dividing it into five sections, to each of which an hour was given, and on Saturday came the summing up of the whole, and questions in review. A written analysis of a chapter of Guizot was also required each week. Beside the regular dictation, which occupied a few pages each day, many of the students took full notes, which give the feeling of the class-room, and explain the enjoyment they had in the lectures. From the lecture-book of Mr. Rowland G. Hazard 2d, which received Mr. Diman's commendation at the end of the year as being unusually full and accurate, these characteristic remarks are taken : —

" One would suppose from reading Hegel's lectures that the course of History ended when he stopped lecturing in 1820. Now it is possible that History may go on." The course

After these comes a page to be dictated to the students.

The branches of knowledge which are especially connected with History, and on which it depends, are : 1. *Chronology;* 2. *Geography,* (a) *Physical,* (b) *Historical.*

And then we proceed to its higher problems : 3. *Political Economy ;* 4. *Jurisprudence ;* 5. *Moral Philosophy.*

Books recommended : *Student's Gibbon, White's Eighteen Christian Centuries.*

is thus defined: " By Mediæval History is
meant in general the period from the fall of
the Western to the fall of the Eastern empire,
from 476 to 1453. But all chronological
divisions are imperfect, since the distinction
between one period and another is not chronological, but must be sought in the underlying
ideas which shape institutions and events.
Dates are merely like pegs to hang our hats
on, — not essential."

The lectures were on the Roman element,
the Christian element, the Germanic element;
and so on to the rise of Feudalism, the Crusades, — the great achievement of Feudalism,
— the rise of the Franks, the Church and the
Empire, to the dawn of the Renaissance and
the fall of Constantinople. The Saturday
questions, for which written answers were required, were always constructed to bring out
the student's conception of the whole subject,
never specific questions, to be answered by a
date or a fact. Early in the course occur
these, which are good examples of the kind
of comprehension required: —

1. Define the limits of the empire under
the Antonines.

2. Explain civil administration under Con-
stantine.

3. State the successive steps of the division of the empire into Eastern and Western.

In the lecture on Feudalism we find, " The duel was a restraint upon indiscriminate slashing, and was really the first step in civilization. Slavery was also a step in advance, since it took the place of butchery."

In the period of the Renaissance Mr. Diman always took special interest, and some of his most attractive lectures were delivered upon it. " All true architecture," he says, " is the expression of feeling, or the embodiment of thought. The oppressive gloom of the Egyptian sanctuary, the graceful symmetry of the Grecian temple, the endless variety of the Mediæval Münster, expressed in material forms the despair, the contentment, the aspiration of different races. Regarded in this light, Mediæval architecture is the most trustworthy record of the spiritual life of the Middle Age." The Renaissance in Italy is dwelt upon, with lectures full of apt characterization of the great artists. Michael Angelo is called the " water-shed of architecture." " Leonardo marks the highest pitch of art. He has the greatest depth of expression, and the most technical training. If we look back, training runs out, and ideals run up."

Thomas à Kempis, Reuchlin, Erasmus, and Ximenes were considered as preparing the way for the Reformation, and the half-year ended with the examinations which Mr. Diman says were "regarded as severe." Severe they were, because no "cramming" was of avail; the student had to have some real comprehension of the subject.[1]

After the mid-winter recess, lectures on Modern History were begun.

"In passing from Mediæval to Modern History, we pass not simply to a new period, but to new phenomena, to more complex interests, to more varied religious and political antagonisms. The revival of letters marked a revolution in thought from the religious to the secular spirit. The economic revolution came along with this, and the geographical discoveries followed, which changed the moral notions of Europe."

[1] The following half-year examination has been selected from several examination papers as a fair example : —

1. What essential service has been rendered History by the scientific method ?

2. What were the immediate sources of Feudalism ?

3. What was the real service rendered European civilization by Charlemagne ?

4. How did the Crusades affect the servile classes ?

5. How did the Renaissance contrast with Mediæval culture ?

The lectures on the Reformation, the Wars of Religion, Absolute Monarchy in France, the European Colonial System, the Balance of Power, and Modern Political Theory, it is not the place to follow here. Their very titles give an idea of the wide and comprehensive survey of European affairs to which Mr. Diman led his students. The "struggle after unity" in his religious convictions was also a forming force in his intellectual life ; and his philosophic grasp of the subjects he treated made them clear to his students.

The lectures were relieved with constant bright descriptive touches. Of Alexander Borgia he says : " Making a liberal allowance in his favor, he would still hold an eminent position among the sinners of any age." And of Philip of Spain : " Mr. Motley, though a very sprightly and brilliant writer, is not always to be implicitly accepted. As, for example, he would have us believe Philip II. to be almost an idiot who did nothing but correct the spelling of despatches. Philip was, however, a very remarkable man, with great powers of detail." Again we find : " The real founder of Prussia was Frederick William I., who was short, thick-set, and dumpy. He had veracity, chastity, and honesty, which are enough to distinguish any man in the eighteenth century."

After the spring recess about a fortnight was usually given to daily lectures on the Constitution of the United States, tracing the growth of the colonies, and their stages of development, and final separation from the Mother-country. The Constitution was fully expounded, and Mr. Diman's last word was like his first, — one of exhortation to the students before him. " The stability of our government depends on the correspondence of the Constitution with the convictions of the people. Hence the peculiar responsibility resting on the class of educated men, in a country like ours, by whom public opinion is shaped."

Being prepared by the study of History, the students devoted their last month in college under Mr. Diman to International Law. On this he delivered lectures founded upon President Woolsey's book. To these lectures reference will be found in several of the letters. For clear analysis and beauty of arrangement, they equal any he ever delivered, while wanting, in the nature of the case, in the picturesque description of the more purely historical lectures.

Of Mr. Diman's manner in the class-room, Mr. Rowland G. Hazard, 2d, writes : —

"To the average student who followed Professor Diman out of chapel into that low square room in University Hall, where the history lectures were given, there came a sinking of the heart, as he reflected that he *might* be the first man up.

" 'The Professor' was evident in the very manner of the man, as he swung into the room with that one-sided walk, laid aside coat and hat with an air of abstraction, and with nothing but his class-book in his hand, took his chair upon the little platform. He used eye-glasses, perhaps more as an occupation for his left hand than an aid to vision. As he adjusted them to read the roll-call, his manner was precise and formal, perhaps even a little stiff, and he read the names of the men rapidly, and with but one repetition of the name if a man were absent. Then very deliberately scanning the list, he selected a name and called upon the owner of it to give the points of the previous day's lecture. Professor Diman seemed to put all his intelligence at work to understand the foggiest recitation from the dullest one of us, provided it gave him the idea of any real effort on the student's part. He was sometimes impatient at bungling attempts, but rarely showed it by any prompting. No one on the Faculty, we all felt, was so quick to detect the man who, not having studied the subject, was talking against time ; and his quiet 'that will do, sir, — next,' on such occasions generally made such an impression as to effectually stir up that man for a while. But we used to think that he was sometimes deceived by our 'parrots,' — men who would reel off page after page verbatim as the Professor himself had said it. He used to tell us that he did not wish us to use his words, and preferred us to take our own, so that when a 'parrot' was well received we used to wonder a little. But it had to be a bright parrot, for the cross-fire of questions which always followed the recitation would have made it impossible for men without knowledge to have answered. The explanation of the high favor in which some of our 'rote' men stood lay, perhaps, in Professor Diman's not knowing exactly his own phrases. This might easily have been so ; for he never, so far as I can remember, dictated from fully written notes, but always used small sheets of note paper, which he had in his pocket, until he wished to use them, and which he put away again the moment he was done. I never remember to have caught more than a glimpse of these note-sheets, but always supposed they contained merely the analysis of the subject in hand. He was always extremely familiar with his subject. I have known him to go through a very complicated division of a topic into A, B, and C, with 1, 2, 3, 4, and 5 under each letter, without so much as taking the analysis from his pocket; and this with such perfect ease and fluency, that it was an inspiration to do the same thing. How often have I been disgusted with myself for failing to accomplish such a feat after once re-reading my notes! He did it so easily, so gracefully, why could not I?

"As to the manner of his lecture upon which we were expected to take either verbatim notes or such as should enable us to remember every point made, it was almost too rapid to allow of writing out fully, and a common complaint used to be that we had all missed some point of minor interest, which each one had relied on his neighbor taking down. The language used was always racy and delightful, full of life, and sometimes tinged with sarcasm. His fund of illustrative anecdote was apparently inexhaustible, and, as we learned by comparing notes with our predecessors, varied from year to year, as indeed the lectures did.

I never thought his appreciation of the humorous very keen, but he certainly enjoyed the ludicrous intensely. I have heard him tell of an examination in the Constitutional History of the United States, on which he always lectured at the close of Senior year. It was early in the subject, and a few recitations had been made on the condition of the States, and their readiness for the movement which culminated in the Declaration of Independence, when a man was called up who had been a blunderer always, but for whose zeal and willingness to work Professor Diman had a real respect. After a number of questions, all of which remained unanswered, had been put, willing to favor the poor fellow as much as possible, and intending to ask at least one question which the man must be able to answer, Professor Diman asked, 'Under what were the colonies living previous to the adoption of the Constitution?' the obvious answer being, 'Under King George.' But when the answer came, 'Before the Constitution? Why, I suppose they were living under the *Preamble*, sir,' even the gravity of the Professor was upset.

"Always fair, and ready to admit an error, if he had made one, which happened almost never, he yet had the reputation amongst many of his students of being very severe; they said he was a ' *hard man*,' and by some he was even disliked. His abhórrence of anything vulgar in a man was so strong as to in great measure account for this. As I think over the men who did not like him, I find they must all have offended him in this way. But even those who did not like him, who never got over the first impression of coldness and relentlessness which his impartiality sometimes produced, came to admit his power, and to feel the stimulating effects of his enthusiasm. It was under his inspiring guidance that the boys became men, and awakened to a sense of the wideness of study, and the necessity of concentrating every energy upon the work in hand, in order to make any worthy progress. This awakening faculty, the power to create in the immature nature a real desire for mental gain, an actual thirst for knowledge, Professor Diman certainly possessed to a remarkable degree. We all felt his influence strongly; many of us still feel it, and must be influenced by it as long as life lasts."

CHAPTER XI.

1869–1871. aet. 38–40.

THE year 1869 was the first that Mr. Diman delivered an oration at another college than Brown. The Amherst oration referred to in the following letter was on "The Method of Academic Culture," before the Phi Beta Kappa Society of Amherst College, at its meeting July 6, 1869.[1]

TO PRESIDENT ANGELL.

PROVIDENCE, *May* 15, 1869.

Our college term has gone through pleasantly, with an unusual amount of good, honest work. I am just now teaching Colonial History, which I endeavor to reduce to its con-

---

[1] *Orations and Essays.*

stituent principles, *à la* Guizot. It is wonderful how readily the bright minds take to the study, when they come to see that it concerns something more than mere memory. I have been busy about various matters, and so have not begun my oration for Amherst yet. I will hold myself in readiness for Burlington, but fear that I shall not be able to prepare fresh matter. This I very much regret, not less on my own account than yours.

I have been preaching a good deal this spring ; in fact, have not passed a Sunday in Providence since Easter. Most of the time I have supplied Dr. Bushnell's church, in Hartford, but to-morrow go to Boston. So you see the " Orthodox " continue to " get good," as you say, out of me.

At this time Dr. Bushnell had long ceased to preach, and the pulpit of the North Church in Hartford was vacant. For eight Sundays, during April, May, and June, Mr. Diman supplied it. " The committee always thought," writes Dr. Burton, the present pastor, " they had done one of the most acceptable things to the congregation when they had secured Mr. Diman. I frequently heard it remarked upon, that when he stood in the desk the place was thoroughly filled."

TO MISS TIRZAH EMERSON.

PROVIDENCE, *July* 28, 1869.

How delighted I was to get your letter, and such a charming account, too, it gave me of your travels. Much of it I had passed over, and I followed you in fancy through the Tyrol, the Salz-Kammergut, to Linz and Vienna. It makes me long for the time you will be with us again, and when, some winter evening, by a bright wood-fire, we may make the journey together. Then, too, we will discuss the deeper questions of the soul, to which you advert, as I passed through much the same experience during the two years I spent in Europe. I imagine it is an experience through which all young persons pass, whose spiritual nature is roused to much activity.

You ask what we have been doing this long time. We have been greatly blessed with health, and you would hardly know the children, they have grown so. M. came in from the garden just as I began to write, and sends her love to you. She has now been to school long enough to become quite proficient, and takes great delight in reading her little magazine. Master J., who has thus far pursued his studies with his mamma, displays as yet no particular love of letters, but we hope for better things by and by. Their lives have been very happy, and it really makes one better to hear every hour their merry laughter, and watch them trudging about the garden. They have a favorite visitor in an enormous dog, belonging to a neighbor, who comes regularly to see them every day.

When your letter came, I was just beginning to write a Phi Beta Kappa oration, which I had engaged to deliver at Amherst College. . . . Last week I went to Andover and repeated my address, and next week do the same at Burlington; so you see my time this summer is much taken up with " orating." My taste does not, however, incline strongly that way. To me it is far pleasanter to sit by my own fireside and chat with a dear friend.

I have been preaching constantly this spring and summer, most of the time in Hartford, and in the new Central Church in Boston. The latter is very splendid, much the most so of any church that has been built in New England; but unfortunately it leaves the Society burdened with a huge debt. Not the least charm of those glorious old cathedrals, which you tell me you enjoy so much, is the fact that they stand open to rich and poor alike. They were, in fact, the most democratic institutions of the Middle Age. I love to see handsome churches; the temples in which we worship God should not be inferior to our own dwellings, but they should be built as free-will offerings, and not paid for by the sale of pews. How much I enjoyed those old cathedrals, especially that of Vienna, and some of the quaint, irregular ones on the Rhine!

This charming picture of Mr. Diman's home life is completed by his Thanksgiving reflections for the same year, in the "Providence Journal" : —

"Next to that Faith without which all earthly blessings are but curses in disguise, there is nothing for which any of us should be so grateful as a happy home. In the pure affections that centre here is the spring of whatever is most ennobling in life. Whatever disasters and disappointments may have overtaken us, if they have not invaded this charmed circle, we may gather with cheerful hearts about our tables. For all burdens in life may be bravely borne, if no sorrow or shame has crossed the threshold. When the All-merciful and loving Father ordained that his children should dwell in families, he placed within their reach sources of happiness and strength that from age to age have been as springs of water in a dry and thirsty land. For all this let us devoutly bless His holy name to-day.

" Perhaps as time goes on we are getting to be a little old-fashioned in our notions, and do not keep pace with the social and political improvements that are so rife ; but sometimes in our moods of sober reflection we are led to ask ourselves the question, whether the aggregate of human happiness about us is increased at all in the ratio of all this bustle and stir that goes under the name of modern progress. Are the essential sources of our highest welfare multiplied with the multiplied inventions and discoveries of this anxious and unquiet age? In one important particular, at least, it may be doubted whether we have advanced upon the fathers. When we consider some of the more salient tendencies of modern society in relation to domestic life, and, for example, the lessened regard for the sanctity of the marriage tie, the lack of interest in the quiet enjoyments of home, the increasing love of excitement and of social dissipations that tend to render domestic cares a drudge, we may seriously ask ourselves the question, whether in one important respect, at least, we are improving upon the methods of those who kept their Thanksgivings before the age of the steam-engine and the telegraph.

" We have no desire to make ourselves obnoxious to the charge of unreasonably lauding the things of the past. We are fully alive to the failings of our forefathers, and our columns bear abundant witness to the fact that we are never indisposed to subject them to reasonable criticism : but when we recall some of the pictures that have been preserved of the home-life of the Puritans, these well-ordered households, a little austere and prim, perhaps, in their outward aspect, but so pervaded with lofty sense of duty, where was so much of reverence for age, such blending of strict parental authority with returns of filial affection ; when, above all, the precepts of religion were imbibed with the mother's milk, and the round of daily cares was perfumed with the fragrance of the morning and evening sacrifice, — we are tempted to think that we have, after all, but a poor substitute furnished in much for which we pay a high price, under the guise of modern accomplishments and modern improvements." . . .

Mr. Diman was offered the presidency of the College of the City of New York, this year (1869), and the first efforts were made to induce him to go to Cambridge. The letters to President Angell give a full account of the various offers that were made him.

TO PRESIDENT ANGELL.

PROVIDENCE, *September* 8, 1869.

I received this week, somewhat to my surprise, a formal offer of the Hollis Professorship at Cambridge. The plan is, that I hold my present place, going to Cambridge one day in the week, to lecture; the lectures being given in the Divinity School.

It is not, as I understand, in the least designed that I become in any way identified with Unitarians, the object of the corporation being to convert the Divinity School into something like the Theological Faculty of a German University, having no connection with any sect.

Now, let me know what you think of the plan. Is it possible thus to be connected with two institutions, for I should become a regular professor at Harvard holding the oldest foundation, and would my position in any way be compromised?

ions'   *September* 11.

I go to Cambridge on Friday to confer with President Eliot.

PROVIDENCE, *December* 7, 1869.

You were quite right in your conjecture that the Cambridge matter would not rest. Soon after the first arrangement fell through, I received another offer, which I have now under consideration, to go to Cambridge as full resident professor, with a salary of $4,000. My title would be Hollis Professor, but my duties about what I chose to make them. Eliot urges me very strongly to come, on grounds of public duty, "to aid in building up a veritable University." I was in Cambridge last week to look into things, and received a very cordial greeting. There are many things to be considered beside the mere academic question, and my mind as yet is far from made up. Let me hear what you think about it.

and

with nuary 9, 1870, Mr. Diman wrote to ing silent Eliot: "The scruples that I have we h?especting my own fitness to perform the nished in :~ned the Hollis Professorship are under the guise 'L++ I pledge myself to accept and modern improveth he corporation see fit to elect me to it." This was written on Sunday, the ninth. Before any action could be taken in regard to the matter Mr. Diman sought an interview with President Eliot, and withdrew his acceptance. Of this interview he writes : —

TO PRESIDENT ANGELL.

PROVIDENCE, *January* 14, 1870.

I went to Cambridge on Tuesday, failed to see Eliot, so went again yesterday. He received me with the utmost kindness, and was disposed to enter into a full discussion of the affair. I assured him that my feeling of doubt was so strong that I should not feel justified in allowing the matter to proceed. He seemed disappointed, but was exceedingly kind about it, evidently thinking that I was suffering from temporary reaction. I urged him to drop the thing altogether, but this he would not consent to do. He, however, ṣtion that he should proceed no further at preṣ otherwise I should have been elected tọf the He said I ought to look at it simply iṇected light of duty, and that I assumed a graṿṃe a sponsibility if I declined. So the ฅ฿ง the old- but I feel immense relief. ʼ my position in any

TO PRESIDENT ELIOT.

Providence, *January* 31, 1870.

I have been very deeply impressed with the earnestness with which you urge my coming to Cambridge, and have given the proposition in your last letter a most serious consideration. It is necessary for me to say that I fully appreciate the honor of the position, and that I feel the liveliest interest in the attempt to elevate education, in which Harvard College is taking the lead. But I am nevertheless far from being satisfied that my own usefulness would be enough increased by the change to justify relinquishing my present position. I am obliged, therefore, to decline the offer which you have made me.

TO PRESIDENT ANGELL.

Providence, *March* 28, 1870.

I have been very long in writing, but have had many trials. First, all my children have had the whooping-cough, the two eldest very severely, so that for a fortnight I got no good sleep, and, second, in the brief intervals of their terrific noise, I have had a lecture[1] to prepare for the course on " Christianity and

---

[1] *The Historical Basis of Belief.*

Skepticism," given in Boston. As I undertook to prove to a church full of Congregational ministers that the only true basis of belief
was that of the Roman Catholic Church, a little
more care than usual was needed in the preparation of the paper. However, I got through
without bodily harm. The lecture will be
published at once, and I will send you a copy.

Have you heard how Cambridge stands?
Soon after giving up the Hollis Professorship,
I received from Mr. Eliot a wholly new offer
of a historical professorship in the college.
I had trifled so long with the first, that I declined this with hardly any consideration.
Soon after I received a very kind note, asking
for a personal interview; so I went to Cambridge, and we talked it over together. But
after returning home, I wrote again that there
was no prospect of a change in my feeling.
I have been treated with so much kindness
that my conscience smites me for not going,
but somehow the change from here to Cambridge does not on the whole allure me.
Perhaps we shall both feel that we have made
mistakes — who can tell ? [1]

We are lame at college, as Mr. Chace has

[1] " Five or six years later I made another effort to get Mr.
Diman to Cambridge as Professor of History," President

broken his arm. My class has been doing finely. Have you seen Blunt's "History of the English Reformation"? He gives a view the reverse of Froude, making very much of Wolsey, and little of Henry. Bunsen's last volume, "God in History," I have also found suggestive.

At Commencement, 1870, the degree of Doctor of Divinity was conferred upon Mr. Diman by his own college. In a speech at the dinner following the academic services of the morning, Mr. Diman said : —

Mr. President : I feel that the very best acknowledgment that I can make for the honor which your too partial kindness has conferred upon me to-day, is to endeavor myself, so long as I shall have the honor to hold official position here, to come as near as I can to the high standard that has already been set. My own experience induces me more and more to respect the system of training and the general method of culture which has prevailed here for years which has, as you are well aware, some distinctive features. And I believe that with all

Eliot writes. "That time the health of his mother-in-law, and his own age, seemed to be his reasons for not entertaining the suggestion. He said, I remember, that a man of fifty was too old to transplant."

that we propose to do for the general exten-
sion of the University, still the true work, and
the best work for this college, and for any similar institution, is to work within, and to improve the courses that we already have. I believe that in a high standard of instruction, in
raising constantly the requirements of admission and of graduation, in carrying up from
year to year our own interior standard, we
are doing the truest work. And I need not
say that that work, in the main, devolves
upon yourself and upon your colleagues of the
Faculty. I believe that the question as to the
number of students is a subordinate question.
The true question is as to the quality of instruction we are giving. Here is the field
open, with the materials already at hand, with
the apparatus and endowments that we already
possess. Here is indefinite opportunity for
improvement; and I pledge myself, in return
for the favor which you have conferred upon
me, to do what lies in my power to carry out
and realize this ideal.

In 1871 Mr. Diman was sounded as to his
willingness to accept the Presidency of the
University of Vermont, and that of the University of Wisconsin was offered to him. To both
of these proposals the following letter refers.

TO PRESIDENT ANGELL.

PROVIDENCE, *April* 19, 1871.

I am greatly obliged to my Burlington friends for their good opinion, but I can conceive of no circumstances that would lead me to relinquish my present position. So far as I have ambition, it is much more for scholarship than for position. If I gave up my present place from convictions of duty, I should most likely be drawn back to the ministry.

The Wisconsin people have written again, urging me not to persist in declining till I have made them a visit; but I can see no good reason for going out there, and shall so write them.

Did you see I was chosen by the School board to look after music?

Mr. Diman was elected to the School board in April, 1869, and at the expiration of the three years' term of office accepted another election, ending his service in 1875. His one tune on the flageolet, which he played for the entertainment of his children, hardly entitled him to be considered a musician. Hence his amusement at the office assigned him.

In the summer of this year, Mr. Diman, and

three of his dearest friends, President J. B. Angell, Rev. J. O. Murray, and Mr. Rowland Hazard, spent a few weeks together in the Adirondacks. The eldest sons of two of the gentlemen, the "Little Rest" and "*Parvus Iulus*" of the company, were with them, and the happy days in the woods, where they lived on the "fat of the land," — namely, salt pork, — Mr. Diman used to say, were often referred to, and remained a cherished memory.

Shortly before the return of the party, the "Providence Journal" published from Mr. Diman's pen the following account of

A DEER HUNT ON THE RAQUETTE.

RAQUETTE RIVER, *August* 12, 1871.

Do you remember that charming passage at the beginning of "Walton's Angler," in which the lover of each sport so ingeniously commends his own chosen recreation ? I was ever inclined to the opinion which Venator there expresses, that hunting is a game for princes and noble persons. My own earliest impressions of the chase were derived from that renowned ballad, which, Sir Philip Sidney tells us, always stirred his soul like the sound of a trumpet. Once in my life this romantic ideal was nearly realized, when I chanced to meet the king of Bavaria on the Königsee, returning with a gay party from a chamois hunt. So when the word went forth, as we rose from our luscious breakfast of fried pork and maple sugar, that ere the day died we should dine royally from the haunch of the red deer, my bosom began to glow with strange emotion, and visions of mighty hunters, from Nimrod down, seemed to beckon me to " spheres of new activity." The fresh track of a deer lay along the river bank, where we had pitched our camp the night before; and our two dogs, Turk and Dandy, already snuffing the scent, were eager for the start. We had five boats along, and it was quickly settled that we should watch the ground from Little Wolf Pond to the rapids of the Raquette, a mile below our camp. At the outset I could but remark how notable the difference between hunting on the Cheviot Hills and along the Adirondack lakes. The stout Earl of Northumberland drove the deer with hound and horn, and woke merrily the woodland echoes as he swept through the forest. We, on the contrary, were to wait in silence till the deer, seeking a refuge in the water from the dogs, should become an easy prey. Our only promise of music was from the loons, which, from a safe distance, surveyed the impending havoc, much like the grim prophets of Israel in Kaulbach's cartoon of the Destruction of Jerusalem. But sport, thought I, is sport, however pursued, and one must not make ado because it is not carried on nowadays as when the gallant Fitz-James urged his panting courser over the Brigg of Turk. The post of observation assigned me was a low-lying island, on the west side of Raquette Pond. It was less than a mile away, and before many minutes our swift boat, gliding

> " Through files of flags that gleamed like bayonets,
> Through gold moth-haunted beds of pickerel flower,
> Through scented banks of lilies white and gold,"

noiselessly buried its bow in the soft bank.

Landing from a Saranac skiff is, like matrimony, a work not to be lightly nor unadvisedly attempted, more especially if one carries in his hand a loaded Ballard rifle. Proceeding with the circumspection which the situation seemed to demand, I had scarce tasted the " sober certainty" of landing bliss when I missed my guide. The next moment, raising my eyes, I spied him near the top of a young birch, almost the only growth of the little island, except a dense thicket of tall underbrush. " Is that your place for watching ? " I inquired, with ingenuous simplicity. "A man could see a thunderin' lot o' deer down there," was the prompt and encouraging response. A single glance at the smooth bark of the tree satisfied me that my part in the first "swelling act" of the day's "imperial theme" would be somewhat subordinate. Consoling myself, however, with the reflection that at all events I should be in at the death, I set about making the best of circumstances. The boat's bow furnished a convenient seat, and if I could not get the first sight of the flying deer, I could watch the blue light on the distant hills, or trace the windings of the opposite shore, where the dark green of the fir, the spruce, and the hemlock was drawn out in a long reflection over the glassy water. After all, I thought, I have the advantage over him who chased the stag, that

> "Deep his midnight lair had made
> In lone Glenartney's hazel shade."

That hapless huntsman, after a desperately hard ride over a rough mountain road, lost his quarry and his good steed both; while I, after gliding through lily-pads as serenely as a Venetian senator along the Grand Canal, have only to wait till the deer comes to me. I could but reflect with enthusiasm on the progress of the age. What did it matter that the age of chivalry was gone, so long as the age of breech-loading rifles had come? Why look mournfully upon the past?

The wide scope for reflection thus opened to an active mind had a natural tendency to make the hours go barefoot, till a burning sensation, as of one of the early martyrs roasting before a slow fire, called my attention to the fact that the morning breeze, which when we first landed had gently rippled the lake and rustled the tall rushes, had died wholly away, and the pitiless August sun was emptying his blazing urn upon my unprotected back. After whistling vainly for a breeze, I became convinced that a new departure was no less expedient for me than for the Democratic party; so, imitating the famous example of McClellan before Richmond, I discreetly changed my base, which by this time had got to be uncomfortably hot. The only covert was the thicket in the middle of the island, and thither, to borrow the language of the illustrious founder of Rhode Island, "I steered my course." But, as ill luck would have it, the refuge thus opportunely furnished had been preëmpted by earlier settlers, who, apparently not relishing my rash invasion of their

" Ancient, solitary reign,"

swarmed about me in countless numbers, presenting such an array of bills as almost drove me to the conclusion that, like another Rip Van Winkle, I had overslept six months, and stumbled unwittingly upon the first day of January. Nothing daunted, however, I drew on my buckskin gauntlets, and resolved that the stump on which I sat

" Should fly
From its firm base as soon as I."

Saul slew his thousands, David his tens of thousands; far be it from a modest man to boast achievements surpassing the leaders of Israel. The historic muse shall never, with my consent, record the slaughter of that day. But even as a concert of the Philharmonic Society becomes wearisome at last, so does slaying mosquitoes. And, however exciting, it was sport I could have in abundance nearer home. So having been in action precisely the same length of time as my uncle Toby at the siege of Namur, where he received his famous wound, I relaxed my active hostilities, and sought peace of mind in the pages of Harper's Monthly, a number of which, by advice of a more experienced sportsman, I had brought along. The article that first attracted my at-

tention was one giving an interesting account
of the system of meteorological observations
by which we are daily warned of the approach
of storms, and the mariner on the Atlantic
bidden to beware of an enemy creeping up the
slopes of the Rocky Mountains. I was soon
absorbed in a graphic account of the great
storm which wrecked the " Royal Charter,"
the course of which was so admirably traced
by Admiral Fitzroy. I forgot mosquitoes
and deer alike. Here, I thought with rapture,
is something to be proud of. What are the
victories of Worth and Sedan, compared with
those of science ? My imagination gratefully
disported in this new field. What benefactors
of the race were these tireless witnesses of the
phenomena of the air, whose observations,
winged to Washington by the " viewless
coursers " of lightning, were there condensed
and again sent forth by the same fleet messen-
gers for the benefit of mankind ! Thought-
less man that I was, that I did not bring with
me to these woods a Nigretti and Zambra
thermometer, a Wild's self-registering barome-
ter, a Hough's meteorograph, a barograph and
thermograph by Beck, of London, an anemo-
scope, an anemometer, and a copy of " Bu-
chan's Handbook of Meteorology" ! Kindling

with emotion at the thought of being thus permitted to add my humble mite to the great sum of human knowledge, I involuntarily lifted my eyes to see what grand atmospheric disturbances might be at that moment preparing, when, to my amazement, I saw that the birch-tree no longer had a tenant. The sun was seeking his western bed, and, not relishing the notion of being left alone on an island while my companions were perhaps gathering for high festival, I made at once for the shore. Then in a moment I descried the boat coming across the lake. In it was one of the dogs, lame and panting from his fruitless chase. All hope of seeing any deer, so far as we were concerned, was up, and there was nothing left but to row back to camp and see what luck had befallen the rest. One after another came in with the same story. Not one had so much as got sight of a deer except Little Rest, and whether indeed it was a young doe he saw or only a huge mosquito that boldly bestrode the patent sight of his Lewis rifle, I will not undertake to say. Charity believeth all things.

As we gathered once more that night about our festive board, and studied our somewhat familiar bill of fare, we were unanimous on all points save one, whether the scalding beverage presented to us by our attendant Ganymedes was distilled from the cheering herb of the Flowery Kingdom, or from the more aromatic berry of Java. By general consent the supreme honors of the day were accorded to the *Parvus Iulus* of the company, whose resonant smiles were echoed from Peter's Rock, as he came back to camp, bearing a magnificent specimen of the *Pilmelodus cattus*, a rare fresh-water fish of the family Siluridæ, found only in the rivers of America, and not by any means to be confounded with its salt-water cousin, a malacopterygious fish, so common on the English coast. The American variety is known to boys under the vulgar name of the bull-pout.

Angling has been commended by Walton as the contemplative man's recreation, but for contemplation commend me to deer-hunting in the Adirondacks. A penitent soul, who craved a calm season to review the sins of his youth, could find no such ample opportunity as in the exhilarating exercise of sitting in silence for six or eight hours on the banks of Raquette River, or the shore of Big Wolf Pond, in humble expectation of getting sight of a deer "there, or thereabouts." The mel-

ancholy Jaques, who was wont so much to
mark the poor sequestered stag,

> " That from the hunter's aim had ta'en a hurt,"

would scarce have found occasion here for his
" thousand similes."   Indeed, had I in hand
some literary venture, demanding for its perfect finish a little leisure, say some such trifle
as Gibbon's Decline and Fall, or Grote's History of Greece, I know not where I could dis-
pose myself with such advantage as in this
meditative work of hunting deer after the
manner practiced in the Adirondack solitudes.
In a letter to the historian Tacitus, that accomplished country gentleman, the younger
Pliny declares that Minerva coursed with
Diana on the hills; but for all that it fell to
my lot to see, the Goddess of Wisdom might
have the Saranac lakes wholly to herself. The
exercise is strictly of an intellectual sort.

Yet were it ungrateful to leave the woods
without confessing their quiet benediction.
The cherished friendships of early youth were
strengthened with new ties, and the burden
of the unknown future was lightened with
sympathy of hearts long tried and closely
linked.   Though we got no deer, we felt that
we had not environed ourselves with the sweet

surprises of nature in vain. In the midst of rollicking mirth, her deeper spiritual lessons were not wholly missed.

> "For who can tell what sudden privacies
>   Were sought and found, amid the hue and cry
>   Of scholars furloughed from their tasks, and let
>   Into this Oreads' fended paradise."

CHAPTER XII.

1871–1875.   AET. 40–44.

REFRESHED by the summer's rest, Mr. Diman returned to his work in the autumn with new ardor. As early as October he records two articles written, and new lectures.

TO PRESIDENT ANGELL.

PROVIDENCE, *October* 25, 1871.

I have a fine Senior class, and have much enjoyed my work. Besides rewriting my lectures, I have sent a long article to the " New Englander." [1] In the October number of the " Church Review " I have an article on English

[1] " The Roman Element in Modern Civilization," *New Englander*, January, 1872.

schools.[1] Much to my surprise, I received this fall a call to Princeton, but promptly declined it with thanks.

PROVIDENCE, *January* 20, 1872.

We have finished up our college work this week. On the whole, I have every reason to feel satisfied with what my class has done. The examination was both written and oral for the whole class, which was a new thing. But somehow I have felt less interested than usual in college work.

One thing that has tended to divert my thoughts, perhaps, is the fact that I have been preaching a good deal this winter, and under circumstances a little peculiar. Without the least intention or desire on my own part, I have awakened a good deal of enthusiasm in two Unitarian parishes, and, *entre nous*, could, I presume, have a call from either, if I would consent to act with the Unitarian denomination. I have had to-day two long letters from Boston, one official. Of course, I can do no such thing, but the talk about it diverts my thoughts somewhat from college work.

[1] "English School Life," *American Quarterly Church Review*, October, 1871.

What makes the matter more serious is the fact that the pressure comes from an earnest class, who wish to set their faces against the radicalism of the denomination. I often think that if I am to devote myself to an academic career, I had better give up the ministry altogether. One cannot ride two horses with success. Yet I have never been able quite to bring myself to this resolve.

The official letter referred to was from the committee of the Arlington Street Church, Boston, very courteously asking Mr. Diman if he considered himself a Unitarian, and if he would consent to be a candidate for their pulpit, with the understanding that the society is Unitarian, and that the pastor is to work heartily for the spread of Unitarian Christianity. Mr. Diman sent the following reply : —

TO EDWARD WIGGLESWORTH AND BUCKMINSTER BROWN, COMMITTEE.

PROVIDENCE, *January* 21, 1872.

It gives me much pleasure to answer your inquiries. My denominational position is not easily defined in a few words, as I am not a stickler for any formal statement of faith. I regard Christianity as emphatically a Life.

But while I often preach, and with great satisfaction to myself, in Unitarian pulpits, and fully recognize the service which the denomination has rendered in emphasizing aspects of divine truth too much overlooked, yet I cannot call myself in any distinctive sense a Unitarian, nor could I work heartily for the spread of Unitarian Christianity.

TO PRESIDENT ANGELL.

PROVIDENCE, *January* 20, 1872.

The lectures at the Normal School are very simple affairs, though I have a large audience. As both my History classes are now under way, my time is pretty well occupied. I am going in great detail over the period of the Renaissance.

The State Normal School was opened in Providence, September 6, 1871. Mr. Diman was present, and took part in the opening exercises. During the following winter he gave a course of twelve lectures, on Saturday mornings, before the school, on Mediæval History. "This course was prepared with special reference to the needs of teachers," writes Mr. J. C. Greenough, then principal of the school. "The lectures were enthusiasti-

.cally received, both by the pupils and by the large number of teachers and others, who were in attendance. Every subject was so clearly analyzed, and so vividly presented, that the written exercises of the pupils, which were prepared after each lecture, were usually full and complete outlines."

Each year, to the end of Mr. Diman's life, with only two exceptions, he prepared a course of lectures for the school. In 1874 he gave lectures on the Renaissance, followed the next year by lectures on Art. A course on the Reformation, in 1876, was succeeded by one on Ancient, Mediæval, and Modern Architecture, in 1877. The year following he gave no lectures, and in 1879 a course on American History, especially the growth and alienation of the Colonies. In 1880, the last course on the Constitutional History of the United States was given.

"Some have supposed that these lectures were simply repetitions of those given in Brown University," writes Mr. Greenough. "This is a mistake. However strongly I might urge him, he always declined, unless he had time to make the special preparation which he deemed necessary. The work which he here so admirably accomplished was ever the ripest results of his latest studies."

TO PRESIDENT ANGELL.

PROVIDENCE, *February* 26, 1872.

I have been busy this winter, but more in preparation for my private classes than for my college work. I have been quite thoroughly into the period of the Renaissance, and as some of the topics were new, I have been obliged to read up. Besides the old standard authorities, I have found two new books, the titles of which may be useful to you, if you have them not already in your library: "Die Cultur der Renaissance in Italien," by J. Burckhardt, a very thorough book; and "Italie et Renaissance," by J. Zeller, devoted especially to the political aspects of the period. I have been much interested in the subject.

The Friday Club met here a week ago, and President Caswell read a very interesting paper on the Mount Cenis Tunnel. Have you seen Whymper's "Scrambles in the Alps," a very fascinating book?

I have no local news, which, indeed, I seldom fill my ears with.

The private classes to which the last letters refer, and for which Mr. Diman did so much and such admirable work, began in the winter of 1870–71.

Mrs. Amasa M. Eaton, then Miss Dunnell, writes: " The idea of arranging a class in History was suggested to me during a visit that I made in Portsmouth, N. H., in the winter of 1869–70. Mr. James De Normandie, then minister of the Unitarian church at Portsmouth, was delivering a course of lectures to the young ladies of his parish. I was very much interested, and determined to see if we could not have a similar course for the girls who had been at Professor Lincoln's school with me.

" Upon my return I went to see Professor Lincoln, and asked him if he would like to lecture to a bevy of his old scholars. He replied, ' It would be pleasant for me to do so, but I don't think I am the right person.' He advised me to see Professor Diman ; I did so, and told him the whole story. The idea was new to him. I wish I could recall his words more vividly. Now I have only the impression of a very satisfactory visit, and the promise from him to think the matter over."

Just before Christmas the lectures began, and continued once a week, to the end of April. About twenty young ladies came to the pleasant Angell Street house, Tuesday mornings at eleven o'clock. The members of this class were almost all schoolmates, but lately out of school. In January, 1871, Mrs. William Goddard arranged the Friday morning class, which met in her parlors. It was to this class that Mr. Diman delivered the last lecture of his life. Still later, in 1873, a third class was formed by Mrs. Rowland Hazard, for her daughter and the girls of her age, just finishing their school studies. This was a Tuesday morning class, which met at Mr. Diman's house at one o'clock.

The lectures for these classes, each of which had about twenty members, were at first much the same as the college course. They began with the fall of Rome, and extended to the fall of Constantinople, for the first winter. But in a weekly lecture, and in some sense a more popular lecture, Mr. Diman dwelt more fully on picturesque details, and the essential facts were grouped together, and presented in the most simple statement possible.

In the first lecture he defined his plan : — " There are two ways of studying History : to take facts, as Guizot does, or to take individuals as types of the times, as Carlyle does. We shall try to combine these two methods in our winter's study. History is the only medium by which we can interpret the present.

It is alive ; we must make it personal, and use the imagination in studying it.

" The time has gone by for speaking with contempt or indifference of what used to be termed the Dark Ages. The researches of Guizot, of Eichhorn, of Lehuerou, of Von Raumer, have thrown a blaze of light upon a period that once only wearied and perplexed the student ; and it is now universally conceded that the only profound interpretation of the great social and religious movements of later centuries must be sought in an analysis of the institutions and tendencies of the Middle Age. There are the germs of the great problems that European society is still laboring to solve."

The lectures begun in such a philosophic spirit followed the college course until the Renaissance, when the ladies had the advantage of special lectures on Architecture, and on several of the great artists. " True art is a form of language, an expression of the higher workings of human consciousness." Leonardo, Raphael, and Dürer had each a full lecture given to them. For Leonardo, Mr. Diman had great admiration. " In him we see the culmination and perfection of art.

In an age pervaded by pagan tendencies, his art is still truthful and pure." Not only did he admire the Last Supper, but talked so eloquently of the Mona Lisa, " the suggestion of a woman," as he called her, as to inform that mysterious picture with new powers. Her haunting smile appealed to him more than all the beauties of Raphael. Even the Sistine Madonna, which in earlier life he had declared realized all his ideal in art, he did not grow enthusiastic over, but rather dwelt on the portrait of Julius II., the fighting Pope, as a wonderful masterpiece. From this it will be seen that his sympathies in art were all on the intellectual side ; that he cared not so much for beauty of color and form as for beauty and subtilty of expression. Hence he talked of Albrecht Dürer with great delight, dwelling especially on two plates, the Melancholia, and the Knight and Death.

This is the bare outline of the first winter's course; but who can describe the charm of Mr. Diman's manner, the wit of his sallies, and the convincing eloquence of his argument? It was in these informal lectures to the ladies he knew, many of them dear friends, that he was at his best. In Mrs. Goddard's parlor were beautiful pictures, which he enjoyed ; and in his own room, lined with the books he knew so well, he was even more thoroughly at ease. The high courtesy which distinguished him never let him forget that he was the host, and the ladies who came to him were not only to be instructed, but also entertained.

He used to come into the parlor, as the hour struck, generally with a couple of volumes under his arm, from which to read a few paragraphs in the course of the lecture. He bowed slightly and gravely to his near neighbors, and smiled, that smile in which the eyes had more part than the lips. Then, with a glance that took in the whole room, he seated himself in a large leather chair, and crossing his knees, began immediately. A few sentences gave a masterly *resumé* of the last lecture, and the new subject stood on a firm foundation. In his hand, or on the table beside him, Mr. Diman had a thin, green, covered blank book, of essay - paper size, containing the analysis of the lecture. Often he did not refer to it at all, so fully was the subject in mind, and so readily did the names and dates spring to his lips. When people wondered how he lectured so easily, they little knew the care and accuracy with which his notes were prepared.

Here is the analysis of the fifteenth lecture in the second year's course, dated February 27, 1872: —

Analogy between German Revival of Art and Revival of Letters.

   German art, serious and spiritual.

   How affected by life and architecture.

German Mediæval Art (Byzantine).

   Wilhelm and Stephan of Cologne, 1380.

Revival of German Art began with the 15th century, at Bruges.

   John, Hubert. and Margaret Van Eyck.

   John reported inventor of oil painting.

   The Giotto of the North.

      For Margaret, see "Arts of the Middle Ages," p. 300.

      For Characteristics of the Flemish School, see Taine, " Art in the Netherlands," p. 105.

Influence of the Flemish School on German Artists.

   At Augsburg, Holbein.

   At Nuremberg, Albrecht Dürer.

Albrecht Dürer, born 1471, died 1528.

   Characteristics of life at Nuremberg.

   His marriage.

   His journey to Venice.

   His connection with Raphael.

      See " Albrecht Dürer," by Mrs. Heaton, p. 98.

   His characteristics as an artist.

   a. The peculiarities of the Northern or Gothic mind.

   b. Tendency to the subtle and the supersensuous.

   c. Love of the grotesque and fantastic.

   d. As compared with the Italians, deficient in grace.

>   *e.* Yet thought, as lying further from the surface,
>   requires more imaginative effort to grasp.
>   *f.* His freedom from tradition, and sympathy with
>   the Reformation.
>   Dürer and Melancthon.
>   His picture of the Twelve Apostles.
>   Called by Schlegel the "Shakespeare of Artists."

This analysis is shorter than many, and less full, but has been chosen as an illustration of Mr. Diman's method on account of its completeness in itself. As the lectures were in a course, though each one made an integral part, many derived much of their interest from what went before and came after. How this analysis was filled up in the delivery, those who heard the lecture will remember. How vividly the life in picturesque Nuremberg was described, what witty thrusts were made at Dürer's termagant wife, and with what enthusiasm his work was dwelt upon!

Mr. Diman had a fashion of stating things in a very startling way, occasionally, and would look up with a merry smile to those of the class of whose appreciation he was sure. How his eyes twinkled as he said: "When the Crusaders went to Palestine they went in a fury of religious zeal. The two most valuable things they brought back were playing-cards and sugar!" But then followed a long

and interesting explanation of the service of
playing-cards in developing the arts of en-
graving and printing, and of the revolution
in all culinary methods which the introduction
of sugar created.

The lectures on the Renaissance were followed, the next winter, by a course on A Century of French History, the period from Fran-
cis I. to Louis XIV. The development of absolute power, dating from Henry IV.'s time,
and the antagonistic development of a spirit
of free inquiry from Montaigne and Descart,
was expounded in lectures on Catherine de
Medicis, Montaigne, Bossuet, and Richelieu.
The ladies were shown how " absolutism
paved the way to democracy, and free inquiry,
at first not irreligious, was pushed by the an-
tagonism of the Church into infidelity."

The next year the French Revolution was
shown to be the logical outgrowth of this state
of affairs.

That Mr. Diman turned to his ladies' classes
with pleasure, as contrasting with his more
official duties, the following letters indicate.
Many of the ladies took notes, and not a few
submitted them to his inspection, but the
work was, of course, purely voluntary.

TO PRESIDENT ANGELL.

PROVIDENCE, *January* 10, 1874.

Our examina...., closed this week. I have done, on the whole, a satisfactory term's work, with a class diligent rather than brilliant. But it is a great comfort to feel that you have one or two men on whom you have made a living impression. Much college teaching becomes from necessity sadly mechanical.

My time is very much taken up with the reading required for my outside classes. We are going over the French Revolution, and I want to seize the opportunity to make as thorough a study of it as I can. I have just finished Morley's Rousseau, which gives a good outline of his political writings. There is also a good analysis of the Social Contract in Janet. But the subject is overwhelming.

PROVIDENCE, *January* 30, 1875.

I have been up to my eyes all winter in the Thirty Years' War, which I have been expounding to the ladies. I manage to kill two birds with one stone by selecting the subject which I know least about. It is a tempting theme for an historian, as we have in English absolutely nothing about it of any value, save the meagre outline in " Epochs of History."   There are books, but all second-rate.[1]

These lectures on the Thirty Years' War were afterwards elaborated into the course so successfully given in Baltimore, as will appear in a subsequent chapter. They were prepared with the greatest care, and listened to with delight.

Lecture V., delivered January 5, 1875, has the following complete analysis : —.

New phase of the war.
    Swedish army lands June 24, 1630.
Gustavus Adolphus, born December 19, 1594.
    His personal appearance.   Vehse, 1–363.
    His winning manners.
    His careful education.
    His marriage.   Early love.
    His administration.
    His three wars.
    His diplomacy.
His military genius.   (Napoleon.)
    Restores ancient discipline.
    Reforms art of war.
        1. Reduces size of regiments.
        2. Lengthens the musket.
        3. Shortens the pike.

[1] Written in 1875. Several Histories have been published since then.

4. Reduces the number of files from **ten to six.**

5. Changes the artillery charge.

6. Introduces light artillery.

His leather guns.

His humane theory of war.

Motives of his invasion of Germany.

His profound religious spirit.

His cause one with German Protestants.

His leave-taking.

Presentiment of death.

A unique character.

His position on landing.

Attitude of Saxony and Brandenburg.

Alliance with France, January, 1631.

Treaty of Bärwalde.

His military policy.

Convention of Leipzig. February, 1631.

Fall of Magdeburg. May, 1631.

All neutrality ended.

Battle of Breitenfeld, September 17, 1631.

" The Lord turned Lutheran."

Gustavus occupies South Germany.

His demands at Mayence.　Vehse, 1–170.

Suspected by the princes.

Supported by the cities.

Gustavus enters Bavaria, March, 1632.

Crosses the Lech, April 15.

Tilly killed.

Enters Augsburg, April 18, Munich, May 17.

Elector of Saxony enters Prague.

Retrospect of the campaign.

All Germany, except Austria, at his feet.

The first Tuesday class, and the Friday

class, followed the same course of lectures, but the second Tuesday class, having begun two years later, studied a different subject. Thus, while the first Tuesday class heard the Thirty Years' War lectures, the second class had lectures on the Renaissance. There was only an hour between the delivery of the two lectures, involving so complete a change of thought. Refreshed by a cup of coffee, Mr. Diman came to his class, and made them live for the hour in the times he dwelt upon. His facility in turning from one subject to another was not the least remarkable thing about him.

As the years went on, the two Tuesday classes were thinned by the marriage and removal of their members, and for the last year or two were united in one. The final course of lectures was the same to both Tuesday and Friday classes, and only ended with Mr. Diman's life. Thus for ten years a company of ladies sat under his teaching.[1] To many of them it was the best part of their education.

At the end of each lecture, Mr. Diman recommended books upon the subject under consideration, — Guizot, Carlyle, Dante, Froissart; the list fills pages. But his own careful habits

[1] See note at the end of the chapter.

of reading, dating from his college days, and fostered throughout his life, were made of service to his pupils. "Such a chapter of Carlyle, or such a canto of the Inferno, bears on the point we are studying," he would say.

Beside the classes of ladies, and the courses of lectures at the Normal School on Saturday mornings, for the last few years of his life, Mr. Diman had evening classes. One, which counted some eighty ladies and gentlemen as members, heard part of the course here outlined. In the winter of 1877–78, a course of ten lectures on Mediæval History was delivered to this class, followed the next season by ten lectures on the Renaissance. In the fall of 1879, a smaller class was formed, which included some of the younger college professors and their wives, and other ladies and gentlemen. To this class Mr. Diman gave a course of ten lectures on the Thirty Years' War, having the subject freshly in mind from his recent preparation for the Baltimore lectures. The following winter, a course on English History was interrupted by his death.

Beside these classes, Mr. Diman lectured at the "Friends' School." In 1868, and the two following winters, he gave occasional lectures on various subjects. "But in 1871," writes

Miss B. T. Wing, long a teacher in the school, "he began a course of historical lectures, which he continued every succeeding winter during his life. His habit was to select some period of history, and to give what he used to term 'familiar talks' upon the events, political and social, the prominent characters, the discoveries and inventions connected with it. The Rise of Christianity, Monastic Life, The Invasion of the Barbarians, The Fall of Rome, The Eastern Empire, The Renaissance, The Reformation, with wonderful character sketches of Luther, Loyola, Calvin, and the English reformers — these were some of his subjects. In one of the later courses Mr. Diman brought the history of England down to the time of George III., and connected with it the history of the American Revolution.

"The lectures were given on alternate Friday evenings from October to the first of May. He always appeared to take great pleasure in talking to the scholars, and often expressed his delight at the interest and attention shown by the *younger scholars*. He evidently enjoyed adapting his talks especially to them, in a way particularly charming to his older listeners. Never before, I believe, was the story of human progress so charmingly told."

"In his last lecture," writes Mr. Augustine Jones, the principal of the school, "he said with unusual tenderness, 'I visit no place where I receive so much pleasure as I do in coming here and looking into your young, bright faces.' How little we dreamed it was his last mortal look ! It seemed as though the very foundations of the institution tottered as he was taken out of our lives."

Subjects of lectures by Mr. Diman, delivered to a class of ladies at Mrs. William Goddard's house : —

1st Course. January, 1871, to April, 1871. The Middle Age. From the Fall of the Western Empire, 476, to the Fall of Constantinople, 1453.

2d Course. January, 1872, to May, 1872. The Renaissance, and the Reformation.

3d Course. December, 1872, to April, 1873. The Renaissance in France, and the Religious and Civil Wars.

4th Course. December, 1873, to April, 1874. Decline of Monarchy in France, and the French Revolution.

5th Course. December, 1874, to April, 1875. The Thirty Years' War.

6th Course. December, 1875, to April, 1876. English History. Illustrated by English literature.

7th Course. December, 1877, to April, 1878. English History after the Restoration.

8th Course. January, 1879, to May, 1879. English History in connection with the American Revolution, and the Administration of England under the younger Fox and Pitt.

9th Course. April 9, 1880, to May 14, 1880. Six lectures, — an Abridgment of the Lowell Institute Course, — delivered in February and March, 1880, on the Theistic Argument as affected by Recent Theories.

10th Course. December 17, 1880, to January 28, 1881. Modern Statesmen.

CHAPTER XIII.

1872–1876. AET. 41–45.

Letters to President Angell. — Preaching in Hartford. — "George Fox Digg'd out of his Burrowes." — Election to Massachusetts Historical Society. — Europe. — Letters to his Wife. — Letters to President Angell. — Offer of a Parish in Boston. — Letter to Dr. Rufus Ellis. — Friday Evening Club. — Recollections by Dr. S. L. Caldwell.

In order to secure a more comprehensive view of the work done for the History classes, and the other lectures outside regular college work, we have anticipated a little, and must now return to the letters.

The following letter shows Mr. Diman's interest in contemporary art, of which his study of the great masters made him an admirable critic.

TO PRESIDENT ANGELL.

Providence, May 7, 1872.

I had a delightful visit with Murray last week, and while I am still full of it, will write to you. He told me he was soon to make you a visit. It almost made me sigh to be a

Presbyterian, that I also might be a delegate to the General Assembly.

In New York I saw the first pictures I have seen for many a day, — among them the "Parthenon," by Church, the "Slave Ship," by Turner, which you remember Ruskin pronounces the finest rendering of water ever made, and the "Good Sister" of Bougereau, worth, in my opinion, a dozen of the best Madonnas ever painted. I had long been familiar with it through photographs, and was delighted beyond measure to see the original.

As to the question you put me, how to prevent our Universities from being overrun with half-educated men, I can propose no remedy, save to do everything possible to elevate the proper academic department. If you can succeed in turning out every year a few really educated young men, by degrees the rest will come, perhaps, to note their own deficiencies.

I am quite busy just now, as I have the Seniors twice a day, the labors of Professor Chace being ended. I am teaching at the same time the Constitution, and International law. What a clumsily written book is that of ——! What is the benefit of studying Greek, if one writes in such a loosely jointed style?

If Murray had been willing to go with me, I should be looking towards Europe; as it is, I put it off a while.

In the summer Mr. Diman preached several successive Sundays at the Park Congregational church in Hartford, during the vacation of the pastor. He stayed on these occasions with Mr. William H. Post. "He never seemed like a stranger in my house," writes Mr. Post, "but rather as a member of the family, and the children anticipated his coming, and were delighted with the stories he would tell them, while they gathered at his side, or sat on his knee."

President Angell was now in Ann Arbor, Michigan, just beginning his successful administration of the University.

TO PRESIDENT ANGELL.

Providence, *September* 11, 1872.

Several of the more important points touched upon in your Report, we have discussed together, especially the connection between the University and the high schools. This is a wholly unique feature in your system, and is, it seems to me, a great step in the right direction. But what I like most of all in your

Report is its constant looking forward "to the things that are before." No school of learning can flourish that is content to rest on its oars. I hope we shall follow your example in requiring French for admission.

A little later, Mr. Diman writes : —

"So far as the diminution of Freshmen is due to more rigorous requirements, it is a matter that will soon right itself. I wish ours might be reduced the same way."

This autumn the fifth volume of the "Publications of the Narragansett Club" appeared, edited by Mr. Diman. "George Fox Digg'd out of his Burrowes" is a much longer work than "John Cotton's Answer to Roger Williams," filling a volume of over five hundred pages. Instead of arranging his comments on the text in notes, as before, Mr. Diman prepared a careful introduction of over fifty pages, citing all his authorities, arraying opposing arguments, and disentangling conflicting testimony. For clearness and grace of style, this essay equals any Mr. Diman ever wrote.

This critical study of the " fourteen *Proposalls,* made this last summer, 1672 (so call'd), unto *G. Fox*," and " Of Some scores of *G. F.* his Simple lame Answers," left Mr. Diman a warm defender of the Quakers. Six years later he wrote : —

" Let us never forget the inestimable service rendered, in an age of dry dogmatic controversy, by the religious body which revived, in modern times, the almost forgotten doctrine of the Holy Ghost. It is said that the Society of Friends is gradually passing away. They can ill be spared from the household of faith. But, should they become extinct as a sect, it will be only because their mission is accomplished. The great cardinal truth of the Christian system to which they called attention, which kindled the enthusiasm of Fox, and moved the eloquence of Barclay, must appeal to human souls with increased power, as the years roll on, or Christianity itself will become as sounding brass and tinkling cymbal." [1]

At the February meeting of the Massachusetts Historical Society, Mr. Diman was elected a corresponding member of that body. In acknowledging the election, under date of

[1] *Orations and Essays*, p. 387 : "The Baptism of the Holy Ghost."

February 20, Mr. Diman says he is deeply
sensible of the honor conferred upon him, and
always spoke with pleasure of his connection
with the Society. The date of this election
is one of the very few which he gave himself,
when asked for such data for a biographical
dictionary.

TO PRESIDENT ANGELL.

PROVIDENCE, *February* 5, 1873

As to my own work, the most useful book
I have recently gotten hold of is Studd's
"Select Charters," illustrative of English history. You will find it essential for the study
of the English Constitution. Freeman's lectures on the "Growth of the English Constitution" are worth looking at. I have also
been studying the new edition of "Gaius,"
by Poste, in connection with Sander's "Jus-
tinian."

PROVIDENCE, *April* 27, 1873.

As everything in my household seems pros-
pering, I shall sail for Europe on Wednesday
by the Cunard steamer "Cuba," to be gone
three or four months. I hope to meet Henry
in Paris, and take a run with him to Italy,
and then return with him to Portugal.

To get away at this time, I have been
doubling up my work at college.

Mr. Diman's household at this time included the son and daughter born in Brookline, and two other little girls, the youngest of whom was only a few weeks old. The following extracts from letters to his wife give some account of this trip.

TO MRS. DIMAN.

At Sea, *May* 8, 1873. I have nothing special to tell of the voyage. Most of the time the weather has been clear, and my only amusement has been pacing the deck and conversing with my fellow-passengers, among whom I have found some pleasant companions.

London, *May* 12. Our ride to London took us through Rugby and Harrow, two towns in which I felt an especial interest. Attended service in Westminster Abbey. I fear that my thoughts wandered more than once from the sermon to the surrounding scenes. The fine statues of Canning and Palmerston were just behind me, and my foot was on Palmerston's grave.

Turin, *May* 15. I write you my first letter from Italy, about which you have heard me talk so much. The country going through England and France was beautiful, and the ride through Burgundy interested me very much. At 2.20 we entered the famous Mont Cenis Tunnel, and in twenty-five minutes were through the mountain, descending the valley of Susa into Lombardy. The scenery was grand beyond description. The engineering work on the Italian side is, perhaps, more wonderful than the tunnel itself. The ride was one never to be forgotten.

Rome, *May* 20. The ride across the Apennines was of wonderful beauty, especially in descending the southern slopes. Indeed, I came to Italy to see art and antiquities, and was not prepared for the extraordinary charm of the natural scenery. The ride from Florence to Rome was an endless succession of delights, an alternation of richly cultivated fields, in which men and women were gathering hay, quaint old battlemented towers, hills crowned with ruined castles, and distant mountains lifting their snowy peaks in the sunlight. I was entirely alone all the way, and had almost forgotten to mark the hours, when suddenly the great dome of St. Peter's came in full sight. I am fairly astounded by the remains of imperial Rome. I was not prepared for anything so vast.

Naples, *May* 25. This my fourth Sunday since leaving home, I spend in this lovely spot. I sit by an open window, through which a delicious air blows from the bay, which is hardly more than a stone's throw off. Directly in front rises Capri, where Tiberius used to celebrate his orgies; on the right is Baiæ, and on the left Sorrento, each stretching away into the distance; and standing on the balcony I have a complete view of Vesuvius, the white steam pouring from the summit. Though it is warm in the sun, the air is delicious. One can realize the meaning of the old saying, "See Naples and die."

Yesterday was given to Vesuvius. We did not reach the cone till noon; the blazing sun made it very hot, and about half way up I gave out, and had to be carried. But we were abundantly rewarded for every fatigue. The view into the crater far exceeded my expectations. It was awful beyond description, and seemed like looking into hell itself. The sulphurous steam poured up in dense masses, and when the wind blew it toward us we had to run to escape suffocation.

Wednesday morning the rain had ceased, and by laying the dust had made the day a delightful one for Pompeii, where I passed several hours. Herculaneum in some respects impressed me more than Pompeii, since it is still a buried city. Pompeii has been so uncovered that it seems like other ruins; but here was a great city, with its treasures still hidden.

ROME, *June* 1. The afternoon was spent among the wonderful ruins of the Palaces of the Cæsars, and at the magnificent basilica of Saint Paul, without the walls. Saw also the Temple of Vesta, and the Moses of Michael Angelo.

FLORENCE, *June* 8. I left Rome last Tuesday. Although I had enjoyed my visit so much, yet I left with rather a feeling of relief, there seemed so much to do every day. My visit was very successful for the end that I had in view, and I could not but feel that my ten days have been well bestowed.

— The return to Florence was made by way of Leghorn and Pisa, and the sights in Florence were seen. — The statue of the Venus de Medicis more than met my expectation. The pictures here are finer than in Rome.

VENICE, *June* 15. We climbed the Campanile, and had a fine view of the city and islands. Toward the north the snowy summits of the Austrian Alps towered above the clouds. We strolled for a while in Saint

Marks, and then attended service at the Greek church.　I was anxious to witness this service, but found it stupid beyond measure.　The prettiest thing I saw in the church was a little girl holding her brother's hand, her shoes out at the toes, who reminded me of L.

Venice is not a place to be seen in a day, but one where there should be time to dream and muse.

MARSEILLES, *June* 21.　Friday morning I left Genoa, and came to this city by the superb road along the coast.

So ended my long meditated tour through Italy, in just six weeks and two days after entering it, — weeks full of ever-changing interest, and passed without sickness or mischief of any kind.　The way by which I went out was as striking as that by which I came in, but wholly different; one over the mountains, the other by the sea.

BARCELONA, *June* 25.　The contrast is very striking between Italy and Spain.　In Rome and Florence, life was quiet, and the very atmosphere was impregnated with art and culture.　Here all is stir, and the whole talk is of war.

MADRID, *June* 30.　We left Barcelona for Valencia.　The road was most of the way by the sea, so we did not suffer from heat, but the scenery was singularly uninteresting. Valencia is a semi-Moorish city, with narrow crooked streets. We have visited the Gallery and the Arsenal, both unrivalled of their kind. We go to-morrow to the Escurial, and hope to start by Wednesday for Toledo and Granada.

GRANADA, *July* 6. Yesterday morning we started with an excellent guide for the Alhambra, spending the entire morning there. Aside from its beautiful situation and romantic history, the place is a little disappointing, and the exteriors of all the buildings are mean and the interiors small. The stucco work, however delicate, seems a little cheap, after the costly marbles of Italy. In the afternoon we visited the famous gardens of the Alhambra.

LISBON, *July* 13. We left Granada at midnight Sunday, the only time when any conveyance started, to return to Cordova. Part of the journey was a wild diligence ride through the hills, each carriage being drawn by eight mules, driven up and down hill at the top of their speed by two drivers and a postilion, all three making the most unearthly howls.

We passed a day at Cordova, where the

great object of interest is the Cathedral, formerly a Moorish mosque, and the largest in the world. The roof is upheld by nearly a thousand columns of every style, and stolen from every Christian land on the Mediterranean.

Tuesday morning we kept on our way to Seville, once the most beautiful city in Spain, but now in great decay. The attractions were numerous. First we saw the Cathedral, a vast pile of mixed styles, the Gothic predominating.

Then we saw the Alcazar, the former palace of the Moorish kings, partly unimpaired, and the rest splendidly restored, so that it seemed to me more magnificent and impressive than the Alhambra.

LONDON, *July* 21. My wanderings are safely over, and I say to myself with delight that *next week* I shall sail for home. I shall stay here a few days, and then make a short run to Paris. In my letters I have done little more than give you the external history of my trip. It has had, too, an inner history, which I cannot write. It has had many moments of, I trust, not unprofitable reflection.

TO PRESIDENT ANGELL.

Providence, *February* 26, 1874.

As this is the day set apart for the annual College Fast, instead of being at this moment in my class-room expounding the Wars of the Reformation, I am in my easy-chair at home, exploring the recesses of my own heart to discover, if possible, a few shortcomings.

On the whole, the sin which moves me to most poignant repentance is having inadvertently omitted to thank you for your very graceful speech at Cornell last summer. . . . I have also to thank you for a copy of your University Calendar.

I will frankly confess that I am no more than ever a convert to the plan of educating both sexes together. Not that I dread any moral difficulties, but I believe the two sexes have a different work to do, and should receive a different training. But we won't go into the question here.

We have begun on our second term, and I am now teaching Political Economy. What a field you have before you to enlighten the West on this subject! It is inconceivable how such a flood of nonsense could be poured forth as the debates in Congress show. Alas!

what are we coming to, with such arrant fools to make our laws ?

Now that I have written this confession of sin, it is surprising how comfortable I feel. I can almost say with Rousseau, in his Confessions, " that a glance into my heart convinces me that I am the best of men." But I have still before me as a part of the day's duty listening to a sermon, and that, no doubt, will put an end to my complacency.

I kept quietly at home during the vacation, only going to Boston to give one of a course of sermons in King's Chapel. I had a fine congregation, and a very good time.

PROVIDENCE, *May* 21, 1874.

We are rapidly drawing near to the close of our year's work. This week I finish with the Seniors ; the last part of the time I have been on International Law. Public international law interests me, especially in its connection with natural rights, but the details of Private seem to me rather fitted for professional study than academic.

The summer vacation, with short trips away from home, followed. In August Mr. Diman was in Providence again. The foreign journal, containing the record of his student life abroad, has the following note added to it : —

PROVIDENCE, *August* 12, 1874.

My old and dear friend Tiffany dined with me to-day, to commemorate the twentieth anniversary of our sailing together for Europe. None with us but Professor B. and J. Had a most pleasant time recalling old scenes, and sat up late into the night talking over the days of the past.

Twenty years! *Eheu, fugaces annos!*

Mr. Diman continued to preach. What he wrote of Professor Dunn was equally true of himself : " He relinquished the ministry with profound regret, and often looked back upon it with longing eyes. To the end of his days, and amid the most engrossing academic duties, he could find time for the preparation of new discourses, and himself derived from preaching the satisfaction which he afforded others."

In speaking of a friend who had left the pulpit for a college chair, he writes : " I have sometimes thought he might exchange for a rural parish, but never dreamed of his becoming a fallen angel like myself." There is a world of pathos to those who knew him, in this half-playful yet wholly serious sentence.

TO PRESIDENT ANGELL.

Providence, *October* 21, 1874.

I was waited on last week by a committee from the Second Church in Boston, with an offer of the parish. They have a new edifice on the Back Bay, and the plan is to have an Independent church, that will draw from Unitarians and Orthodox alike. Dr. Peabody has written, warmly urging me to go, but I do not incline to it.

January 30, 1875.

I have been preaching a good deal, and go to Boston to-morrow, but have not changed my opinion with regard to a charge.

TO THE REV. RUFUS ELLIS, D.D.

Providence, *March* 11, 1875.

I thank you for your very kind letter of the 2d inst., which reflected almost precisely my own feeling. My own difficulties are, in the main, those which you express. For success in the ministry, a man needs to be the mouthpiece of a sect, or at least to be able to express himself with great distinctness on certain disputed points. On many of these points my own judgment is in suspense, and it would be hypocrisy for me to assume to speak with au-

thority; and in such a position as that which
the minister of the Second Church would almost of necessity hold, he would be continually
called on to define his position.

Aside from a general indisposition to resume
the responsibilities of the pastoral office, it
does not seem to me that such an independent
position as that which I am invited to assume
is, in itself, desirable; and I quite agree with
you in thinking that the Back Bay is not precisely the part of the world which stands most
in need of additional pulpit ministrations.

With regard to the Good Friday service, I
hold myself always ready to render you a help;
but I fear that your congregation will have
too much of me.

Dr. Roswell D. Hitchcock about this time
wrote, "Will you be kind enough to tell me
whether you have any wish, or willingness to
return to pastoral life?" and called Mr.
Diman's attention to the needs of a large
church in New York.

TO PRESDENT ANGELL.

PROVIDENCE, *May* 29, 1875.

I have done with the Seniors for some time,
and next week all the classes finish. Com-

mencement will come June 18, which winds us up rather earlier than when you used to heed the summons of the old bell. The term has gone through very smoothly, and the students have done good work. We have less variety in our courses than many colleges, but the work is as thoroughly done as anywhere.

TO PRESIDENT ANGELL.

PROVIDENCE, *January* 20, 1876.

My time has been a good deal taken up with my outside work. I am trying this winter to give the ladies some idea of English history. Our club meetings have been pleasant, as usual, and a good deal enlivened by Dominie Thayer, who is passing the winter here, and is amazingly cheerful for one in feeble health.

The English lectures began with the legendary period of English history before the invasion of Cæsar. How England came to exist; How England came to be Christian ; English Institutions, — these are the titles of the following lectures. The course was particularly rich in illustration, and gave the greater pleasure in that it showed the logical sequence and relative significance of events and facts, with which the classes were somewhat familiar.

TO PRESIDENT ANGELL.

PROVIDENCE, March 25, 1876.

Do you remember how seven years ago we climbed up Mt. Mansfield, to witness the total eclipse of the sun? Well, the Journal says there is to be an eclipse to-day, unfortunately hidden from our mortal gaze by a snow-storm; and how can I more appropriately commemorate such an interesting celestial phenomenon than by answering your most welcome letter. . . .

We had the last meeting of the club last evening, at Lincoln's. Caldwell read a finished paper on the Mendicant orders.

College has gone on very quietly. Work on the new library will recommence soon. For the money we shall have, on the whole, a very satisfactory building. This, with the new court-house and city hall, will change the architectural appearance of the city.

I have been busy with my outside classes, and with considerable preaching in Boston; but I have a depressing sense of labor frittered away by not being concentrated on one thing. But to whom is life wholly satisfactory? Certainly not to me.

The club-meetings spoken of in the previous letters were those of the Friday Evening Club, which was organized in the winter of 1867–8, Mr. Diman and .one other member drafting the rules and regulations. It had a dozen members, — professors in college, a bishop, a judge, several business men, clergymen, and a state officer. These gentlemen met fortnightly at each other's houses, to read and discuss an essay, and follow it with a supper. Of a hundred and forty-nine meetings during Mr. Diman's lifetime, he was absent at only seven. "I think we all felt," writes Professor Lincoln, "that from first to last he was the life of it more than any one else. I will not say that we all thought him *facile princeps* in the club, but certainly he was a conspicuous chief, not only in his papers, always marked by ripe learning and scholarship both in conception and in style, but also in the discussions, where he spoke readily, and from a full mind, and to the point, no matter what the subject; and then, too, in conversation at the table, where always the 'largest liberty' was allowed, and everybody was in an atmosphere of good-humor and gladness, there his wit and wisdom rang out rich and free and melodious in its gladness, even as the clear, fresh singing of a bird (Shelley's Skylark, for instance), that must and will sing for very joy. With every one of us, I am sure that the memory of him in those evenings will abide as an inspiration forever."

To this club of personal friends most of Mr. Diman's essays and addresses were read before their public delivery. The "Historical Basis of Belief," of which he wrote to President Angell, was read here. The winter following his Spanish trip a delightful paper on Saracenic Architecture in Spain was read, succeeded the next winter by an essay on Spanish Artists. In November, 1875, the article on "Religion in America," published as a centennial article in the North American Review, in January, 1876, was read to the club.[1] Throughout Mr. Diman's life, some of his best work was read here, much of which still remains unpublished.

As a young man Mr. Diman felt the need of companionship, and emphatically declared that man is a social animal. This he continued to believe. He enjoyed society, he enjoyed conversation, and was in every way fitted to shine in social life. His tall and well-made figure, his fine head and noble bearing,

[1] *Orations and Essays.*

made him noticeable; and his conversation,
full of graceful turns, of witty allusions, or
of clever paradox, was delightful. How often
have the ladies of the house, at the club-
meetings, heard his clear and resonant voice,
followed by a shout of laughter from his companions! He had always a story to cap the
climax, and told it in his inimitable way,
with a perfectly grave face, and perfect command of voice, but with such laughing eyes!
"Diman is well, and as dry as ever," a college
class-mate wrote of him in the days of early
manhood; and this peculiarly mirth-provoking
quality of humor he always retained.

Dr. Samuel L. Caldwell writes of these
club evenings : —

"It is difficult to analyze, at all events to
describe, the charm of Mr. Diman's conversation. A part of it belonged to the pose of the
head, and indeed of the whole body, — the
perfect control of every muscle, the firm chin,
the fixed yet pleased, the piercing yet kindly
look of the eye, the sharp cut which the
teeth gave every vocable, even with the deeper
tones which came from the other vocal organs,
the composure, the assurance rarely broken by
any passion into confusion or demonstrative

force, the smile, the laugh, which never got beyond what he had to say to spoil its effect, and yet which kindled a beautiful light on all he was saying, and sent its contagion through a company of listeners, and whatever a very striking and impressive person imparts to a man's talk. He had all the physical gifts of a good talker. His voice, never loud, rarely lapsing into softness, had a clear, intellectual ring, a fixed, decisive quality, not aggressive and yet not hesitating, which shot his words to their mark. And yet his conversation was as far as possible from that impressive and elegant manner of saying nothing which makes some persons, apparently eloquent, really wearisome.

" His conversations come back to me now chiefly as we had our long walks together, when they took the form of dialogue, or, if I inclined, of monologue, and at the Friday Evening Club, *noctes, coenaeque deûm,* where, in ' the combat of wits,' he was kindled into his best. And yet I do not think there was any great difference in quality. With only another, or with company, there was the same aptness of words to the thought, the same freshness or fullness of knowledge, the same mixture of sobriety and fun, the same dis-

position to banter, the same originality with
what seemed a fondness for paradox, the same
courage of his convictions and boldness in their
assertion, which made his talk so stimulating
and so provocative of discussion. Strangers,
people with whom he was on no confidential
footing, often were startled by his fearless
way of talking about things which seemed to
them sacred, or about which they were very
sensitive. He was not one of the over-careful
sort, so afraid of being misunderstood that
they are really unappreciated. He had enough
to say, and he was never afraid to say it,
even when it seemed singular and not according to accepted opinions. And in the
club, where for years a dozen of us spent
an evening together once a fortnight, with a
recognized parity, and on terms of entire confidence, it was delightful and refreshing to
have him started, not only in criticism of the
paper of the evening, — in that never ram-
bling into discursive platitudes, but sticking
to the subject in hand, while always adding
something to our knowledge or breadth of
view, — but in the unfettered table-talk afterwards, with bright wits at his heels to spur
him on. Nobody could trip him ; he held
his own, even in the drollest paradoxes. The

gravity with which he would maintain them might puzzle persons unused to his conversation, and leave them uncertain how far he was in earnest. We came to learn how much deep conviction often lay under his enigmas and raillery. And often he would straighten himself to a strain of subdued eloquence, in which his deepest thought and best feeling came out. He was not given to much story-telling, and I think would hardly pass for a brilliant *raconteur*.

" Senator Anthony once gave me an instance of the ludicrous perplexity into which a stranger could fall over some of his bold, and what seemed paradoxical, utterances, in the case of the Turkish Minister at Washington, who once met him at a dinner-table in Providence. He was of the Greek obedience, and was so puzzled by the talk of the brilliant Professor, that he asked the Senator what his religion might be, for he talked as if he might belong to the Orthodox Apostolic Church. Probably he had shown an acquaintance with the doctrines of the Minister's own church, which he mistook for acceptance of them, and very likely talked in the large catholic way which was natural to his mental temper, with just enough of that mixture of fun which charmed those who understood it, and perplexed those who did not.

"I may as well give up here trying to translate that subtle charm of his talk, which is so easy and sweet to remember, and so hard to put into any fit description. The silver resonance of that voice still dwells in our ears, though it is silent forever. That fine sarcasm which I see now going down that speaking face, and into his nose and lip and tones; that incisive wit and wisdom which penetrated his very voice and manner; that swift passage of his mind and his talk from grave to gay, from lively to severe; that rich culture which made his words, his very manner of saying anything, music; that calm power which held listeners like a magnet, — it is all like water spilt upon the ground, which cannot be gathered up again. Hardly a drop of it, in its fresh beauty, have I been able to recover; for how great, and yet how indescribable, the charm of our friend's conversation was."

CHAPTER XIV.

1877–1879. AET. 46-48.

UNDER date of June 26, 1876, Mr. Diman wrote to President Angell: " At such intervals of time as I could command, I have been working on a Phi Beta Kappa oration,[1] which I am to give at Cambridge this week." This is his only allusion to what was the most noticeable event of his academic life. The brilliant assembly in Sanders Theatre were won by his calm and forcible delivery, no less than

---

[1] "The Alienation of the Educated Class from Politics." *Orations and Essays.*

by the depth and richness of his thought, as he set forth his conviction "that a seat of liberal discipline fulfills its noblest functions in the rearing of wise, magnanimous, public-spirited men, — of men not merely equipped for scientific pursuits, but accustomed to the most generous recognition of the responsibilities resting upon man as man."

TO PRESIDENT ANGELL.

January 2, 1877.

What better beginning can I make for the New Year, after paying my small bills, than by writing you?   How long ago already seems our day's fishing at Gay Head, yet how swiftly the weeks have fled. . . . My work at college has gone on as usual, and since Thanksgiving I have had the additional occupation of my History classes.   On the whole I do not know that I have suffered in mind or body, save in the attempt to read "Daniel Deronda" aloud to my wife.   I think I told you last summer of Gilman's offer.[1]   He came

[1] May 29, 1876, Mr. Diman wrote to President Gilman : "The substance of my letter to you was, that while I feel a deep interest in the undertaking in which you are engaged, and under ordinary circumstances should regard it as a privilege to coöperate with you, yet considerations of a purely domestic nature would render any change of residence at the

on to see me this fall, but with no other result. There is much in the position that would be tempting, were there no other claims upon me. Last week I went to Boston by invitation to see the new editors of the North American, who want to enlist my zealous coöperation. Their plan is to make the venerable quarterly a sort of Contemporary Review. I confess I am not without doubts as to the success of the plan.

The year was a full one, as all Mr. Diman's years were. The History classes, of which there were still three, the Friends' School Friday lectures, the Normal School Saturday lectures, made four or five lectures a week, besides college work, which required a daily lecture to the Seniors, and in the last half-year two lectures a week on Political Economy. The revision of examination papers and weekly analyses, or written answers to questions, also required time.

Most men would have considered this a sufficient amount of work; but to this Mr. Diman added frequent preaching, and the duties on the School Board, which, however,

time so difficult that it would be unjust to you to allow you to urge your flattering proposal any further."

were given up in 1875; and he was also a trustee of the Rhode Island Hospital, and of the Reform School. To the latter office he was elected in 1871, continuing in office till June, 1880, when the duties of the Board of Trustees ended with the transfer of the institution to the State. For two months in each year Mr. Diman conducted the religious services of the Institution. "No one," wrote Superintendent Eldridge, shortly after Mr. Diman's death, "can estimate the influence of his instructive addresses to the children, and of his noble presence and exalted character. The learned and great all over the land will pay fitting tribute to his memory; but to my mind the tearful, sad faces of a hundred and eighty friendless children, each feeling a personal loss in the removal of one they knew cared for them and sympathized with them, is no slight testimony to his worth and nobility of character."

That the boys of the school really trusted him was shown by an incident which occurred one Sunday afternoon, by which Mr. Diman was touched and pleased, and also a little troubled. Two boys had escaped from the Reform School, and a reward was offered by the State for their capture. As Mr. Diman was walking in his garden, one of these boys came to him, told him who he was, his reasons for making the escape, and what he considered the injustice of his treatment. As they were talking together, a policeman came by and slowly walked the whole length of the garden. Mr. Diman said he was puzzled. As an officer of the school it was his duty to have the boy returned, but the boy had confided in him, and come to him as a man as well as an officer. As the policeman passed, Mr. Diman said : "I could have called that man and had you arrested." "I know you could," said the boy, "and I was ready to run, but I saw you were not going to."

Mr. Diman was elected a trustee of the Rhode Island Hospital in November, 1874. The trustees appoint the surgical and medical staff, and have the entire control of the affairs of the hospital. Each trustee has a term of service, which requires a weekly visit of inspection during its continuance. These visits Mr. Diman punctually made, often making more than the stated number. In addition he was often placed upon special committees, and entered heartily into all the interests of the institution.

His love of all children made him particularly tender to the little ones in the hospital, and interested him strongly in the establishment of a children's ward, which he did not live to see. One poor little girl, who was suffering from a most repulsive disease, particularly attracted his sympathy, and she became ardently devoted to him. She would come running to meet him, and with her little hand in his make the tour of the wards with him. On one occasion he promised her a doll, and found her at his next visit sitting on the stairs eagerly awaiting his arrival.

At Portsmouth, on the island of Rhode Island, July 10, 1877, Mr. Diman delivered the oration on the capture of Prescott, by Barton, in 1777. This was soon after published by Mr. S. S. Rider, and is the first number of the "Rhode Island Historical Tracts."

The address at the unveiling of the Roger Williams monument followed on October 16 of the same year.[1] This address was most rapidly written. The sheets were sent to the printer as they were finished, so that Mr. Diman never saw the whole of the manuscript together. The proof came back to him, which he read over a few times, and with it in his pocket as a safeguard in case of any

---

[1] *Orations and Essays.*

embarrassment, delivered the whole oration
with splendid effect, without a pause or hesitation. Mr. S. S. Rider asked Mr. Diman if
he would give him the manuscript to preserve.
Mr. Diman told him, certainly he could have
it if he could find it, and Mr. Rider secured
it from the printer's waste-basket! He found
it without a single erasure or correction. " I
remember his telling me," writes Mr. Vose,
" when I expressed surprise at the orations he
delivered without notes, that it was scarcely
any effort, but after a few readings the words
and phrases came to him, without care, in their
perfect order."

Of this oration Mr. Diman writes : —

TO PRESIDENT ANGELL.

PROVIDENCE, *November* 1, 1877.

The Roger Williams affair turned out far
beyond my expectations. An enormous crowd
was assembled, and everybody seemed very
enthusiastic.

This year Mr. Diman made his first contri-
bution to the " Nation," which published, July
16, an article on " Baptists and Quakers," —
a theme which grew naturally out of the preparation of the Roger Williams address.

TO PRESIDENT GILMAN.

PROVIDENCE, *January* 14, 1878.

It will give me great pleasure to accept the invitation conveyed in your note of the 4th instant, to give one of the afternoon courses of lectures at the Johns Hopkins University, during the session of 1878–79.

TO PRESIDENT ANGELL.

PROVIDENCE, *January* 27, 1878.

Will it be laid to my charge by the recording angel, if I turn from the task of reading examination papers to write you a few lines ? . . .

I read with much pleasure the account of your success at Cincinnati. I am anxious to hear more about it, especially your method of treatment, as I expect to have a similar task next winter at Baltimore. How much do you. write, and how much prepare merely by notes ?

I have been very busy this winter, as I have had a good deal of outside work. Next week I have a Sunday address[1] to give at Boston. But it is a sort of work that does not satisfy, it is so much scattered.

---

[1] Sermon on Future Punishment. Preached at King's Chapel February 10th.

Part of the "outside work" this winter was an address at the opening of the Rogers Free Library in Bristol,[1] delivered January 12, 1878. For Bristol Mr. Diman always retained his early love, and there also he was greatly beloved.

TO PRESIDENT ANGELL.

PROVIDENCE, *June* 20, 1878.

While the impression of Commencement is still fresh, I will give you some account of it. . . . To me personally the day is always a little sober, for I miss the old circle that used to meet at your house. I fear the "tender grace" of that day will never come back.

The "tender grace" of the days that return no more has cast its charm over the reflections with which Commencement day was greeted by the Journal of that morning.

Among the great festivals which break the rapid and unending rounds of the seasons, there is none that brings with it the peculiar associations which belong to that which we celebrate to-day. There are others more

[1] Dedication of the Rogers Free Library, Bristol, Rhode Island. Providence: Sidney S. Rider, 1878.

closely connected with household memories, or with the great events of ecclesiastical or civil life ; but Commencement calls back the buoyant feelings of the early days when hope was bright and aspiration was high ; and the long procession with which it fills our streets, led by the alert and eager step of youth, and closed with the tottering steps of age, is a solemn panorama of human history. There are other processions which have more to attract the attention of a crowd, but there is none more impressive to a thoughtful observer. Year by year, for more than a century, it has pursued its accustomed route ; each year some familiar form is missing from it ; yet each year the vacant places are filled, and it grows larger and larger with the sturdy growth of the ancient University, each season bringing its new accession, one day in turn to become gray-haired and pass away. We cannot but think that some wholesome lessons are conveyed by such a spectacle, and that few can walk to-day in this long line, in which successive generations are thus represented, without having reflection tinged with a more sober coloring. It must be a benefit, once a year, to turn aside from the accustomed associations which so often are centered in selfish and limited aims, and which, when eagerly pursued, so often withdraw us from a wide sympathy with our fellows, and revive the generous aspirations of youth, and renew the cordial fellowship which is the distinctive note of a liberal culture. It is easy to understand the feeling which restrains many, especially of the older graduates, from taking part in this annual academic festivity. The thinned ranks of the classes that close the procession mingle a bitter drop in the joy with which the survivors greet each other. Yet we cannot but think that they act more wisely who keep green in old age the recollections of youth, and who once a year make themselves young again among their old college mates.

The following note is the first of Mr. Diman's in the correspondence regarding the course of Lowell Institute lectures : —

TO AUGUSTUS LOWELL, ESQ.

PROVIDENCE, *August* 17, 1878.

It would give me great pleasure to accept your invitation to deliver a course of lectures before the Lowell Institute, but for the fact that I have agreed to give a course before the Johns Hopkins University of Baltimore before the close of next winter, and I fear that, with my other duties, it would be impossible for me to do justice to both engagements.

TO PRESIDENT GILMAN.

PROVIDENCE, *October* 2, 1878.

I find that the month of April will suit me better than any other time, as our Spring recess comes then.

I propose to take the subject which I mentioned to you, "The Thirty Years' War," but shall treat it very broadly in its relation to general European history, as preparing the way for the state system. If you have any suggestions to make with regard to the subject, or the manner of treatment, I beg you will make them.

A busy autumn and winter followed. If in 1875 Mr. Diman had been "up to his eyes" in work on the Thirty Years' War, this winter he made even a fuller study of the subject. All the French and German authorities were consulted, as is shown in the announcement of his lectures, giving a list of the books to be used in connection with them. The private classes went on as usual, having lectures on English history. At the end of the winter Mr. Augustus Lowell wrote again, proposing a course of Lowell lectures upon some theme connected with religion and modern speculation. In reply, Mr. Diman writes:

TO AUGUSTUS LOWELL, ESQ.

PROVIDENCE, *March* 3, 1879.

It gives me great pleasure to accept the invitation, which you have kindly renewed, to lecture before the Lowell Institute during the coming season.

With regard, however, to a theme, will you allow me to say that for many years past my attention has been exclusively directed to historical studies, and that I feel much better prepared to deal with an historical subject.

Will this modification of your suggestion meet with your approval?

PROVIDENCE, *March* 10, 1879.

With every possible disposition to yield to your preference, I still cannot resist the conviction that any lectures which I might prepare would derive their chief value from the fact that I was dealing with a familiar subject. For some time past I have been giving my attention to the history of Europe during the Thirty Years' War, a period which the late Mr. Motley meant to handle. A course upon this period would supplement the lectures upon the Reformation given a few years ago by Professor Fisher. I have collected a considerable amount of material which has never been presented in English, and if I took this subject I could rewrite and improve what I have prepared to give in Baltimore.

Should you, however, deem it essential that some theme should be selected bearing more directly upon religion, I would suggest "The Relation of Christianity to Civil Society; or, the Spiritual and Temporal Powers in their Historical Development."

But I fear that were I to attempt a specific course upon either Natural or Revealed Religion, I should simply repeat what has been better said by others.

TO PRESIDENT ANGELL.

PROVIDENCE, March 24, 1879.

I have had a very busy winter getting ready for Baltimore, and preaching a good deal at King's Chapel in Boston. I leave for Baltimore at the close of this week, not without some solicitude as to my success; for I have not written my lectures out, but shall deliver them from my full briefs. Of course, the success will depend much on the mode of delivery.

The briefs were prepared in the same manner as those for the History classes, examples of which have been given, but were fuller and longer. The notes for each lecture cover from ten to fifteen foolscap pages. A few sentences at the beginning and end are written out in the way they were delivered, but the rest of the lecture is only suggested by heads of subjects and disconnected phrases. No written report of these lectures exists; and as it would require a scholar of Mr. Diman's own research and attainment to write them from his notes, they will probably remain unwritten.

"The subject will be treated throughout in its general relation to European history, and as marking the transition from ecclesiastical to secular politics," the announcement reads. The topics treated are : " The general causes of the struggle as connected with the state of Europe ; the House of Austria after the Reformation ; the religious parties in Germany ; the Evangelical Union ; the revolt of Bohemia ; the foreign policy of James I. ; the conversion of a Bohemian into a German question ; the military system of Mansfield ; the

Danish war; the rise of Wallenstein; the connection of Sweden with German politics; the designs of Ferdinand; the career of Gustavus Adolphus; the relations of Spain with the Empire; the fall of Wallenstein; the policy of Richelieu; the social condition of Germany during the late years of the war; the peace of Westphalia, in its relation to the Empire and the state system of Europe; the general results of the struggle in their bearing upon German unity and nationality." Twenty lectures there were in all.

President Gilman, writing after Mr. Diman's death, says: "Among the many visitors brought here by the Johns Hopkins University during the last few years, I do not think there is one who so thoroughly gained the affectionate respect of our community as he did. His catholicity of spirit, his nobility of character, his wide and accurate knowledge, made a strong impression on all who heard his lectures, and those who knew him privately loved as well as they esteemed him." . . . Of the lectures, President Gilman says: " He seemed to be talking to a company of friends on a subject of great importance, which he perfectly understood, with an unhesitating command not only of names and dates, but of

exact epithets and discriminating sentences.
The ease with which he lectured under circumstances of very considerable difficulty, was
only equalled by the instruction and pleasure
he gave the auditors."

Mr. Diman's years of training in lecturing
to his students, to his private classes, and on
public occasions, of course stood him in good
stead at this time; but of his special preparation for these lectures, and of the method of
delivering them, the following extracts from
letters to his wife give some account.

TO MRS. DIMAN.

BALTIMORE, *April* 2, 1879.

My first lecture was given at five o'clock
yesterday. The room will hold comfortably
two hundred and fifty, and there had been
four hundred applications for tickets. All
the seats were taken six weeks ago. I was
not in first-rate condition, and am sure I can
do better than I did. But I spoke wholly
without notes, though I had them on the
desk. The audience filled the room, and was
very attentive.

April 5.

As I have got a little used to the room
and audience, I feel more at ease, and find no

difficulty in getting through an entire lecture with no reference to my notes. I am now reaping the advantage of my hard work during the winter, as I have my work for each day already marked out. But the method I pursue imposes on me some hard study each day, in order to fill my mind with the subject; and as the lecture does not come till five o'clock, the day is fatiguing. I take a very light dinner at one, which is the hour at this house, and then a cup of tea at half-past four. So I manage very well.

April 9.

It does not seem to me that I do as well as at home, for the room is now crowded to over-flowing and often very warm, and the lecture comes at a time of the day when I feel less bright than at any other; but everybody expresses great satisfaction, so I ought to feel content. Yet it is not pleasant not to be doing one's best.

April 17.

I have to give much of the day to preparation for my lecture. First, I go carefully over what I have written, and compare it with the French history of the war which I brought with me for the purpose, and which is based upon the same authorities that I used.

In this way I see whether I have omitted anything of consequence. Then I write out a
condensed analysis of the lecture on the first
and last pages of my manuscript, which I left
for the purpose. This I carefully commit to
memory, studying the lecture in connection
with each point. By doing this I have been
able to give every lecture thus far without
once opening my manuscript. When people
ask me how it is that I do it so easily, they do
not know how much study I have given to it.
But as my work is not over till six o'clock, I
feel very tired, and prefer generally to stay in,
rather than go out of an evening.

My lectures have been resumed this week
(after the Good Friday recess), with no sign
of any abatement of interest. Although each
day thus far has been rainy, the room has
always been completely filled.

April 23.

My lectures have been going on as usual
this week, with no lessening of the attendance.
It must be confessed it is a pretty hard pull
on the patience of an audience to give them
twenty lectures on the same subject.

April 27.

Yesterday was devoted to an excursion to
Annapolis, a place I was very glad to see.

The town itself is old and curious, with a few
stately mansions, memorials of colonial days.
The only drawback was the heat, which during our stay at Annapolis was very oppressive.

April 29.

I am rapidly closing my work, and hope
very soon to set my face homewards. This
week I have been busy making farewell calls ;
to-morrow I shall give my last lecture, and
Thursday morning I hope to start for home.

The letters are also filled with accounts of
the many delightful social gatherings, which
Mr. Diman enjoyed, and to which he often
referred with pleasure. A dinner given by
Mr. Reverdy Johnson, a visit to the Archbishop, and the meetings with many interesting people, are fully dwelt upon.

The official report of attendance on these
lectures gives an average of one hundred and
ninety-two, and the whole number of over
thirty-eight hundred persons present. Even
on the very rainy days a hundred and thirty
people gathered, and on two days of rain a
hundred and ninety.

CHAPTER XV.

No sooner had Mr. Diman returned from Baltimore, than with his inexhaustible energy he plunged into fresh work. The course of five Saturday morning lectures at the Normal School, beginning May 17, he would doubtless still have spoken of as "simple affairs." The subject was American History, especially the growth and alienation of the Colonies, and the lectures were among the most admirable he ever delivered, embodying his latest studies, and being presented with all his accustomed fullness and aptness of illustration.[1]

[1] See Library Journal, Vol. V. p. 329.   Reference List on Special Topics, by W. E. Foster.

" I know that to some the history of other lands seems more attractive," Mr. Diman wrote in 1878. " In the picturesque incidents of the Feudal period, in the splendid epochs of Monarchical rule, there is more at first sight to arrest the attention and stir the imagination. Compared with these, our own annals may seem tame and homely. But when we have outgrown the romantic longings of youth, we come by degrees to realize that no portion of history better deserves our attention than the chapters which recite this great experiment of self-government in the New World. Rightly comprehended, there has been nothing grander in the past, and there is nothing with which the hopes of the future are more closely linked. Nor is it really lacking in picturesque incident, and in the highest examples of virtue and public spirit. To become thoroughly imbued with the temper of that experiment, to realize intelligently its scope, is itself an education for any man.[1] "

The summer vacation passed quietly, with short trips away from home. The autumn opened with unusual pressure of work. At an interview in Boston with Mr. Augustus

---

[1] Address at the Dedication of the Rogers Free Library in Bristol.

Lowell, some time after the date of the letters in the previous chapter, Mr. Diman "yielded to my urgent request," writes Mr. Lowell, " and agreed to deliver the course of lectures upon the 'Theistic Argument as affected by Recent Theories.'" Though the subject was not that pursued during his life as college professor, yet it was one in which he was profoundly interested, and to which he came with ample preparation. Twenty years before he had written : " I have often thought that of all things I should prefer to write some little work connected with man's highest interests." These " highest interests " he had ever before him in all his teaching. The touch-stone of moral worth was applied to the lessons of History, and to the lives of men, however brilliantly they were described. His study of philosophy, and constant interest in philosophical topics, prepared him to deal with the questions raised ; and the special preparation needed was only a careful review. Though his knowledge of modern scientific research and speculation was accurate, yet for these lectures he made a thorough examination of all recent works on the subject. " In particular," writes Professor George P. Fisher, under whose supervision the lectures were published, " the most recent writers, such as Mill, Spencer, Huxley, Darwin, Tyndall, who have dealt directly or indirectly with these topics from points of view more or less at variance with prevalent opinion, he examined afresh. At the same time he did not pass by the ablest writers in defense of theism. I perceive that he had profited especially by the perusal of Janet's thorough treatise on 'Final Causes,' and Professor Flint's excellent volumes on Theism, and Anti-Theistic Theories."

For the first time Mr. Diman began to feel the pressure of his work. His usually buoyant spirit was oppressed by the weight of the arguments brought against him. Not that he ever doubted his own position, or failed to see the goal at which he should arrive. But the fairness of his mind allowed him to pass by no obstacle ; each must be fully met, and honestly conquered. And it was to some degree a new line of thought to which he bent his energies. The difficulties of the problems, he said, he had not fully appreciated when he undertook the subject, and at times they almost overwhelmed him. There were no morning History classes this winter, and but one evening class, which heard ten lectures on the Thirty Years' War. All Mr. Diman's time

was taken up with the engrossing theme. His
habit of mind was so elastic that he did not
dread interruption, as many scholars do. In
the less busy days of his early professorship
the morning's work was usually broken by a
visit to the nursery and a frolic with the children. Even now, in this pressure of work,
his intimate friends were admitted to his study
in the busy morning hours. The door would
open into the pleasant sunshiny south room,
with its smouldering wood fire, and he would
rise a little wearily from the study-table covered with books and manuscript. "It goes
slowly," he would say, with a smile and a
sigh. Then the big cat would be ousted from
the easy-chair, where she dosed. "Here,
puss," he would say, reprovingly, and put
her gently down, or sometimes keep her on
his arm a moment. His visitor seated in the
chair thus vacated, all work was pushed aside
— or only talked of for that visitor's pleasure.
Those who loved him naturally claimed but a
few moments in such a morning, and left the
sunny room in perfect confidence of his ulti-
mately conquering all difficulties.

How fully Mr. Diman did so is expressed in
Professor Fisher's preface to the book. "It
is marked by the elevation and grace which,

as they were part and parcel of the author's mind, could not fail to enter into all the productions of his pen. The discussion is conducted throughout with absolute candor. Nowhere is there an attempt to forestall the judgment of the reader by raising a prejudice against an opinion that it is to be controverted. The doctrines and the reasonings of adversaries are fully and even forcibly stated. Vituperation is never substituted for evidence. Nothing in the way of objection that deserves consideration is passed by. The entire field suggested by the theme is traversed. Whatever dissent may arise in the reader's mind in reference to any of the positions which are taken by Professor Diman, or the reasons by which they are maintained, there can be, as I believe, among competent judges but one opinion as to the acuteness and vigor, as well as the learning and fairness with which the argument is pursued."

Professor George Ide Chace, Mr. Diman's early instructor in metaphysics and philosophy, among the very last acts of his life wrote : —

" His grasp of the great theme is as comprehensive as it is vigorous. His thought flows with a breadth of current attesting the amplitude and fullness of its source. As the stream moves onward, affluents are continually swelling its volume. Everywhere along its course evidences of a fertile and abundantly watered land present themselves. With him theology has no barren deserts. Wherever his foot presses, flowers spring up, and a beautiful landscape spreads around. His way lies through a continual succession of oases. His large stores of knowledge, his rare command of language, and his unequalled power of drawing from the most varied sources illustrations of singular aptness and beauty, enable him to invest every step of his great argument with a marvelous interest, and to carry the reader along with him a willing captive to the end.

"Some of the positions assumed by Mr. Diman in the progress of the discussion will scarcely bear a rigid examination. It is probable that his own maturer judgment would have led him to modify them. The marvel, however, is that an extended course of lectures, on a subject outside of his special department of instruction in the University, and involving some of the most difficult questions in philosophy, should have been prepared on so brief notice, with so little in them open to just and fair criticism. Even where there is error, it is graced by so much beauty, and is so instinct with right feeling, that we are ready to adopt the sentiment of the great Roman orator, and exclaim, ' Errare, mehercule, malo cum Platone, quam comistes, vera sentire.' "

Professor Chace, it will be noticed, has a slightly different estimate of some of the conclusions of the volume from that of Professor Fisher, or of Mr. Rowland Hazard, who prepared a careful review of the work for the Friday Evening Club.

" I read the proofs," writes Mr. Hazard, " as it was passing through the press, and as I read I seemed to hear his voice in the cadence of the sentences. I have read the book again ; I have studied it ; and I am more and more impressed with the strong logic, the great ability with which the argument is presented, and the flow, the rhythm, the eloquence of the style. The personality of the author has impressed itself upon the printed page, and I lay down the book with regret, unwilling to quit his presence. . . .

" Within the present century a great change has taken place in the method of dealing with the questions here discussed. What was formerly approached from the metaphysical side is now regarded from the physical or material. Problems which the older philosophy grappled with the aid of pure reason are now sought to be solved in the laboratory of the chemist. So great has been the change in the current of philosophic thought that the old land-marks of belief have appeared to be in danger of being swept entirely away. The alarm has been general and widespread. The position of the advocates of the new philosophy has been too frequently misunderstood, and the unauthorized utterances of a few unbalanced ultraists have been taken for the teachings of a school. As a consequence, the impression has become general that the tendency of modern science is toward infidelity, toward the unsettling of the most venerated beliefs which have come down to us through the ages. The holders of these beliefs, thus suddenly attacked with strange weapons, have been thrown into confusion, and in their eagerness to repel the assault they have frequently wounded their friends.

" From time to time some cooler spirit has examined with care the armory of this new school of philosophy, and has pointed out the harmlessness of the weapons which have created the greatest consternation. But the books containing the results of such examinations have been for the most part adapted to the use of scholars. They have been too abstract for the general reader. Without any disparagement to such valuable works as Janet's 'Final Causes,' Flint's 'Theism' and 'Anti-Theistic Theories,' and Herbert's 'Realism Examined,' I think it safe to say that a book was needed which should bring the subject within the reach of any reader of common intelligence. This need has been supplied by the work of Professor Diman. It has been supplied in a most admirable manner. It is not too much to say that there is no book in the English language which contains in so small a compass, and so agreeable a style, such an accurate and candid statement of the course of human thought on the great question of the existence of God. This alone would be high praise; but when it must be added that the book also contains a most forcible and logical presentation of the Theistic argument, unfolded, as it were, from this history of human thought, in eloquent and delightful diction, it seems to me that we have a book of no common order."

The lectures were twelve in number, and were finished by the end of February. The fourth of the course, on " The Argument from Order," was read before the Friday Evening Club in November. They were delivered in Huntington Hall, Boston, beginning on Tuesday evening, February 24, 1880, and continuing Tuesday and Friday evenings until the conclusion of the course. As they began at half-past seven o'clock, Mr. Diman went to Boston in the afternoon, returning to Providence after the lecture, and gave his usual college lecture at half-past nine the next morning.

He did his work with such ease, and made so light of it himself, that the accomplishment of all this did not at the time seem remarkable to his friends. But the strain was beginning to tell upon him. In reply to an invitation to deliver an oration before the University of Michigan, he wrote : —

TO PRESIDENT ANGELL.

PROVIDENCE, *March* 10, 1880.

I have delayed longer than I should have done to answer your letter, hoping to see my way clear to accept an invitation which would give me so pleasant an opportunity both of visiting you and of seeing your great University; but there are some indications which seem to render it advisable to give up extra work for the present, and as I have an engagement already on my hands, I had come to the conclusion to write you, and decline the invitation.

How fully Mr. Diman gave his sympathy to his friends is shown from the fact, that, although the night before this letter was written he had delivered the fifth in his course of lectures, there is not a word of his own work, but the rest of the letter is filled with congratulations and inquiries concerning the appointment as Minister to China his friend had just received.

The Lowell lectures ended March 30, and in April and May a course of six lectures was given on the same subject to the Friday morning History class, in Mrs. Goddard's parlors. In these six lectures Mr. Diman put the substance of the whole course, freeing the theme from all possible technicalities, and presenting the subject in the simplest and yet most comprehensive manner.

In May and June Mr. Diman delivered to the Normal School a course of five lectures on

the Constitutional History of the United States,
— a continuation of the subject of the previous
year. These lectures are considered by competent judges the most remarkable Mr. Diman
ever delivered.

His practice of using only the briefest notes,
which made his lectures so effective, and made
each listener feel he was directly spoken to,
is now our loss, for it is impossible to repro-
duce them. Some idea of their wide scope,
and the general treatment of the theme, may
be gained from Mr. W. E. Foster's admirable
list of references, prepared to accompany the
lectures.[1]

TO PRESIDENT GILMAN.

Providence, April 29, 1880.

It will give me great pleasure to accept
the invitation which you have extended to me,
to repeat my recent Lowell lectures at the
Johns Hopkins University. I think, consider-
ing the subject, it would be advisable to reduce the course to ten lectures, and I should
prefer, if possible, to come as before, at the
time of our spring recess.

---

[1] Economic Tracts No. II., series of 1880–81 : *Political
Economy and Political Science ; The United States Constitution*, p. 24.

Warned by symptoms of fatigue that a complete change was necessary during the vacation, after one or two short visits, Mr. Diman joined his friends, Rev. J. O. Murray and Mr. Rowland Hazard, in a stay in the Maine woods. From there they wrote to the fourth friend, who usually completed their party.

TO HONORABLE JAMES B. ANGELL, PEKING, CHINA.

Rangeley Lakes, Camp Kennebago, *August* 15, 1880.

May it please your Excellency: Here we are, the old party, saving yourself, and as we are debarred by the laws of God from fishing to-day, we could think of nothing better than writing to you. I might add, that as the laws of Maine forbid our fishing on all other days in any place where trout are likely to be found, we might just as well spend the remaining days of the week in literary employment. Yesterday we were coming across the lake, when we fell in with Dr. M——, the one who was so eminent as a surgeon. We asked what luck he had found, and he replied with considerable emphasis: " Two days, and not a darned bite." This is a pretty fair description of sport in these famous fishing grounds dur-

ing the month of August. R—— and F——
fished two days with no success. After Murray and I came, the luck began. I have taken
the largest fish thus far. We had no scales
to weigh him, but fortunately R—— sat in
the stern, so the boat was not dragged under.
Yesterday we caught fifteen fish, and also a
good drenching. The latter was more equally
distributed through the party than the former,
as I took no fish, but considerable water. . . .
We are having a capital time, and as we gather
at night about our blazing fire of logs, we
think much of you and of the pleasant days
of old. If good wishes would assure success,
you will not fail.

REV. J. O. MURRAY TO PRESIDENT ANGELL.

Camp Kennebago, *August* 15, 1880.

Diman, by some hocus-pocus, managed to
hook a trout on Friday. I saw him the moment before he did it. He was much more
surprised than the trout. But since then he
has been talking often of the Apostles. He
seems to think he is lineally descended from
one of them. He has put on airs. Hazard has
done his best to tone him down. So have I.
All in vain. If you were out here, I should
have some hopes; as it is, all we could do was

to eat his trout and take him yesterday on a wet expedition. But we must give him up.

The trout here disdain flies. As Lewis phrases it, vermicular fishing is what succeeds. So if you can get any hints on that subject from the Chinese fishermen, send them on to us. I read aloud to Hazard and Diman to-day Renan's lecture on Marcus Aurelius. I thought the old Roman's splendid patience and submission to the inevitable would prepare them for fishermen's luck to-morrow.

Refreshed by the summer's rest, Mr. Diman returned to his work with all his accustomed vigor. The engagement on his hands to which he referred was the oration at the Bi-Centennial Celebration of the Settlement of Mount Hope. This was delivered September 24th, and was one of his most successful addresses. It was given entirely without notes, with an eloquence and dignity that delighted his hearers.[1]

Four days after this oration, Mr. Diman addressed a ward meeting in Providence. It was in the days of the Garfield and Hancock campaign. His speech was reported in full, and excited universal attention throughout

---

[1] *Orations and Essays.*

the State. The "Scholar in Politics" he was
called. The opening of the address is of
more than transient interest, marking, as it
does, Mr. Diman's convictions of political duty.

"I am not here to-night simply in response
to a courteous invitation, but I am here in
obedience to my own sincere and deep conviction of duty. Those of you who have
known me in other relations — some of you
as a teacher — will no doubt remember that I
have always insisted on the paramount duty
of every citizen in a free State to take a personal share in political affairs. I hold that
no man, no matter how high his position, no
matter what his official or personal relations,
can count himself released from this sacred
responsibility. We are here as members of a
great and common country. We are all of us
charged with duties, as citizens of a free
State, than which no duties in this life can
be more responsible and more sacred. I hold
that no man has a right to lay these duties
aside. Let us remember that this government
under which we live, which we have vowed to
support, and of which we are so justly proud,
is a government of public opinion. The governing power here is the public sentiment of

the nation.   There is no power behind this, and there can be none.   The seat of our government is not that majestic building whose dome rises above the Capitol of our country, an object of admiration from afar.   *There* is simply carried out the administrative business of the nation.   The real governing power is not *there*, but *here*.   It is in assemblages just like this,—assemblages of intelligent freemen, met for free discussion, met to influence each other by rational argument.   Here we found the foundation and the safeguard of our whole national system.   I say we are a government of public opinion, and in public opinion the only power that ought to prevail is the power of reason and of argument; and I am proud to-night to stand before an assembly which acknowledges no other control and no other influence than these.   And I hold, that in a crisis like this, and with regard to questions like those that bring us here to-night, every one of us is bound to have an opinion."

Then followed a strong denunciation of " that wicked, pernicious, and damnable doctrine introduced by Andrew Jackson, that ' to the victors belong the spoils,' " and a clear discussion of the issues of the campaign.

TO PRESIDENT GILMAN.

PROVIDENCE, *October* 23, 1880.

. . . Our recess next spring will begin on Saturday, March 26th. Can you let me begin on Monday the 28th, and occupy the two following weeks? There will be, you remember, but ten lectures.

TO PRESIDENT GILMAN.

PROVIDENCE, *December* 3, 1880.

I inclose a list of the topics included in my lectures. It is a source of sincere regret to me that I cannot arrange to give them earlier in the season, but my engagements here are of such a nature that I feel compelled to reduce my period of absence to the least possible limit.

The list of lectures sent with this note omits the second and eleventh of the Lowell lectures, on the Relativity of Knowledge, and The Alternative Theories.

The lectures to the ladies' classes, of which two were formed, began on the seventh of December. The course was to be on the Nineteenth Century. The reasons for studying it Mr. Diman's notes give: — " It is the completion of our course from the outset, — a ten years' course, which began with the dawn of Modern History. We have traced its great phases, and now come to its last results. What does it teach? The knowledge of our own age is the most important. We must study the past to comprehend the present. This is its highest use. The present can only be understood by showing its whole growth, for the present is the product of the past.

" We shall not make a detailed study of the nineteenth century, but select its salient points in its chief aspects, politically and intellectually. We shall also study its leading men, — the statesmen who have played a creative part, and the thinkers. There are two difficulties in studying our own age: its complexity and the lack of perspective. Three questions must be asked: What is evolution in History? Is there progress in History? Is this progress moral? Man's whole nature is involved. Human Destiny is the great lesson of History. The nineteenth century gives the last answer to this problem."

The lecture continued with a survey of Europe at the time of Napoleon's appearance. His career was traced in subsequent lectures, his overthrow, and the regeneration of Prussia through the agency of Stein. Metternich, and the Congress of Vienna; Talleyrand, and the Restoration; Alexander I., and the Holy Alliance, had each a lecture devoted to them. The notes for these lectures are unusually full. The complexity of the subject seemed only to stimulate Mr. Diman's powers. The reaction and interdependence of the various political movements were shown, so that his hearers received a clear idea of the whole progress of Europe.

In spite of the summer's rest, and the apparent renewal of perfect health, those who knew Mr. Diman best thought him looking not quite well, and his work dragged a little upon him. But so great was his buoyancy of spirit, he proceeded to new duties, as the following letter shows. The two Lowell lectures delivered in Manning Hall many will remember.

TO PRESIDENT ANGELL, PEKING, CHINA.

PROVIDENCE, *January* 19, 1881.

It is hard to think of you so far away in Peking, especially when I recall the years, that now seem so far back, of our college life, when you and Murray, and R. and I, were all dreaming of the future together in University Hall. Whatever high hopes we may have had, I do not think it entered the thoughts of any one of us that you would one day negotiate a treaty with the Emperor of China.

The season has passed thus far very quietly with us. . . . I have had nothing to break my own routine save the celebration at Bristol, which was conceived and carried out in admirable style. I think I have now done quite enough of local celebrating, and propose to leave it alone for the future. In my college work I have had a little change in an elective class in Roman law. I gave the subject a broader treatment than Woolsey, and became much interested in the study. A new departure at college has been a course of evening lectures by the professors, which have been well attended by ladies and gentlemen, and have been very well received. I gave two of my Lowell lectures. I am to repeat the whole course in Baltimore in April.

I have been busy with reading, but have come across no book of exceptional interest. I have my ladies' classes as usual, and am busy with the history of the nineteenth century.

January 28th Mr. Diman gave a lecture to the ladies on the attitude of England, which

had acted with Austria and Russia, but now
through the influence of one statesman inau-
gurated a more liberal policy. How the class
were made to sympathize in the wide views of
Canning, with his generous aid to Portugal,
and cordial recognition of the South American
States ! And how brilliantly did Mr. Diman
describe Canning's wit, the amiability of his
private life, his devotion to his mother, and
with what feeling dwell on his premature
death, in the midst of his brilliant career !
Who among his listeners could imagine that
so kindred a fate awaited Mr. Diman himself ?
At the time of delivering the lecture he was
suffering severe pain, and returned home immediately after, never to leave his house again.
That same evening the Friday Evening Club
met with him. With his accustomed self-for-
getfulness he ignored his own suffering, so
that all, except the few members who knew
him best, thought him as well and brilliant as
ever. The next day he was not able to leave
the house, though no alarm was felt till the
following Tuesday, when what was at first
considered trifling developed alarming symptoms. Anxious inquiries were constantly
made for him. On Thursday afternoon, February 3d, his Senior class sent him flowers,

which he was able to receive with pleasure, though they learned he was very ill. A couple of hours after, while the dusky red of the winter sunset was still in the sky, word came that he was dead.

Friends gathered from far and near early in the following week, to pay a last tribute of affection. The best and wisest in the city and State, and from other cities and States, came to honor him.

In the House of Representatives, on Monday, February 7th, Mr. Sheffield of Newport made mention of the great loss the city and State had sustained, and moved the adjournment of the House to attend his funeral. Other gentlemen followed, bearing testimony to his worth. The speaker, Mr. Henry J. Spooner, said : " His life and his labors were largely devoted to the advancement of many of our most important public interests, and nearly allied to the public weal. The motion before the House seems an appropriate recognition of our appreciation of the loss to the State." The House then adjourned, — a most unusual, if not unprecedented, occurrence in the case of a private citizen.

The beautiful service of the Episcopal Church was the only one used, and the pallbearers were selected from the Senior class which so lately had heard him lecture. Under a peaceful sky and the pure snows of winter, all that was mortal was laid to rest in Swan Point Cemetery.

Few have been so deeply loved, or so heartily and widely mourned. How true are his own words, written of one who was dear to him: " Our only consolation is in the thought that the life which to our blinded vision seems so suddenly blasted, in the sight of God was ripened and complete."

A stately ship sailed brave and free
Upon the sparkling summer sea,
The light winds blew caressingly.

The same winds blew a summer cloud,
Soft, white, and warm, a lovely shroud
Enfolding waves that were too proud.

On came the ship, the cloud she cleft,
It parted ; then like one bereft,
Closed over all, no sea was left.

A moment still the spotless sails
Are bright with sunshine ; naught avails,
She hastens on, till all sight fails.

Gone, gone ! we say, and draw a sigh.
What, gone ? my spirit makes reply,
Because we see not, you and I ?

Who knows her new and vast expanse
Of sunlit sea, where wavelets dance,
And stars are aiding her advance.

If we but see with eyes of faith,
If we could hear, the Spirit saith —
The sea is Life, the cloud is Death.

LIST OF PUBLICATIONS.

The Theistic Argument as affected by Recent Theories. A course of lectures delivered at the Lowell Institute in Boston. Houghton, Mifflin & Co. 1881.

Orations and Essays, with selected Parish Sermons. Houghton, Mifflin & Co. 1882.

> Orations and Essays: The Alienation of the Educated Class from Politics. The Method of Academic Culture. Address at the Unveiling of the Monument to Roger Williams. The Settlement of Mount Hope. Sir Harry Vane. Religion in America, North American Review, January, 1876. University Corporations, Baptist Quarterly, October, 1869.

> Sermons: The Son of Man. Christ, the Way, the Truth, and the Life. Christ the Bread of Life. Christ in the Power of His Resurrection. The Holy Spirit the Guide to Truth. The Baptism of the Holy Ghost. The Kingdom of Heaven, and the Kingdom of Nature.

Dr. Grant and the Mountain Nestorians. New Englander, August, 1853. Early Christianity in China. New Englander, November, 1853.

Review of "The Signs of the Times," by Baron Bunsen. Bibliotheca Sacra. April, 1856.

Life through Death. A Sermon. Monthly Religious Magazine. January, 1861.

Father, Son, and Holy Ghost. Doctrine unto Life.

A Sermon, in the Monthly Religious Magazine. September, 1863.

Follow Me. A Sermon. Monthly Religious Magazine. March, 1864.

The Nation and the Constitution. An Oration before the City Authorities of Providence. July 4, 1866.

Master John Cotton's Answer to Master Roger Williams. Edited by J. L. Diman. March, 1867. Publications of the Narragansett Club. Vol. II.

The Christian Scholar. A Discourse in Commemoration of the Rev. Robinson Potter Dunn, Professor of Rhetoric and English Literature. Delivered at the request of the Faculty, in the Chapel of Brown University, October 16, 1867.

The Late President Wayland. Atlantic Monthly. January, 1868.

The Method of Academic Culture. An Oration before the Phi Beta Kappa Society, at Amherst College, July 6, 1869. Published in the New Englander, October, 1869. (Orations and Essays.)

De Costa. Discovery of America. North American Review. Vol. 109. July, 1869.

University Corporations. Baptist Quarterly. October, 1869. (Orations and Essays.)

The Historical Basis of Belief. A lecture in the Boston Lectures on Christianity and Scepticism. Baptist Quarterly. April, 1870.

English School Life. American Quarterly Church Review. October, 1871.

The Roman Element in Modern Civilization. New Englander. January, 1872.

Meline's Mary Queen of Scots. North American Review. Vol. 114. January, 1872.

George Fox Digg'd out of his Burrowes. Edited

by J. L. Diman. 1872. Publications of the Narragansett Club. Vol. V.

Fisher's The Reformation. North American Review. Vol. 116. April, 1873.

Motley's John of Barneveld. North American Review. Vol. 119. October, 1874.

Bancroft's Native Races of the Pacific Coast. North American Review. Vol. 121. October, 1875.

Religion in America. North American Review. Vol. 122. January, 1876. (Orations and Essays.)

The Alienation of the Educated Class from Politics. An Oration before the Phi Beta Kappa Society, at Cambridge, June 29, 1876. (Orations and Essays.)

The Capture of General Prescott by Lieutenant-Colonel William Barton. An Address delivered at the Centennial Celebration of the Exploit at Portsmouth, Rhode Island, July 10, 1877. Published, with notes, as No. 1 of Rider's Rhode Island Historical Tracts.

Address at the Unveiling of the Monument to Roger Williams erected by the City of Providence, October 16, 1877. (Orations and Essays.)

Address at the Dedication of the Rogers Free Library in Bristol, Rhode Island, January 12, 1878. Providence: Sidney S. Rider.

Dr. Woolsey's Political Science. New Englander. May, 1878.

The Settlement of Mount Hope. An Address. September 24, 1880. (Orations and Essays.)

LIST OF ARTICLES PUBLISHED IN THE "NATION."

July 16, 1877. No. 633. Baptists and Quakers.

May 23, 1878. No. 673. Masson's Milton. Vols. IV. and V.

June 27, 1878. No. 678. Bauer's Einfluss des Englischen Quäkerthums auf die Deutsche Cultur.

March 6, 1879. No. 714. Mozley's Essays.

July 24. 1879. No. 734. Gladstone's Gleanings.

June 24, 1880. No. 782. Fisher's Historical Discussions.

Sept. 16, 1880. No. 794. Dexter's Congregationalism.

Nov. 11, 1880. No. 802. Crawfurd's Portugal.

Dec. 9, 1880. No. 806. Hillebrand's German Thought.

Feb. 3, 1881. No. 814. Note on the Wampanoags.

UNPUBLISHED "CLUB PAPERS."

April 24, 1868. The Representation of Minorities.

April 19, 1872. The Position of Albrecht Dürer as an Artist.

Nov. 7, 1873. Saracenic Architecture in Spain.

Nov. 6. 1874. Spanish Artists.

Nov. 3, 1876. The Relation of the Ottoman Power to European Politics.

Dec. 21, 1877. Phases of Political Thought in America.

INDEX.